The Seeing Eye Fish
R.B. BEANS

Moon Shot Books—West Bend, WI
ISBN: 978-0-578-32411-1
Library of Congress Control Number: 2021923919
Title: *The Seeing Eye Fish*
Author: R.B. Beans
Digital distribution | 2021
Paperback | 2021

Dedication

iii

This novel is dedicated to my wonderful husband Gavin who always supports me and listens for hours as I detail every outline of every idea that ever crosses my head. Thank you, Gav, for your never-ending patience.

Lorrinda Cannon, Karl Dilkington, and The Milwaukee Brewers, are pretty great, too, and I love them all.

Dedication

Chapter 1
The Office, The Birthday, and The Bad Boss

Today she is 30.

If any age indicates adulthood, 30 is it.

But adulthood is overrated.

Moira Lovegood is awakened by the same blaring alarm as she has the past 12 years, lifting her head of unruly chestnut curls from her flattened pillow, aggrieved by the morning's arrival. Outside, in the near distance, a police siren wails, a car alarm screams, and a dog barks. It's the same dog every morning and every morning Moira, the girl who won't kill a spider, thinks about his untimely death.

Just like any other Wednesday, Moira gets up, gets dressed, and gets working. She'll punch, kick, and squat along with Jillian Michaels, work-out Nazi extraordinaire. She'll shower and dry; she'll cross the narrow hall of her tiny—no, *cozy*—apartment to her single bedroom and stare into her bursting closet. Despite being packed with names like Calvin Klein and Prada and Versace, she will pull out some unbranded skirt, unbranded camisole, unbranded blazer. She'll cross that narrow hallway once again, dress, and then stare at her reflection. It's the same mirror, same speckled Formica vanity with the same chrome faucet and white porcelain basin as the last 12 years.

It's the same reflection but a year older, a year more jaded. No grey in her dark hair, no crow's feet around her emerald eyes— why would there be, what's there to smile about? —her freckles still small and light over her nose and across her cheeks.

A year older. A year more jaded.

Just like every other year since the day she turned 18.

Birthdays are meant to be celebrated but there are no party hats today, no champagne or balloons, no shower of gifts. There will only be the same route to work with the same red light that doesn't grant her the green turn arrow even on her birthday! Why should it, anyway? Today is the same as every other day, the same as all its predecessors.

Eventually, Moira makes that deadly left turn after using much caution—as she does with every other aspect of her quiet life—and continues on her way to Skylit Marketing, where she pulls her purple BMW into her reserved parking spot at the front of the building and sighs. First into the office as always.

In the back of the building, the rear parking lot will be full of cars from the factory and warehouse staff who will have been punched in and sweating well before sunrise. They are kept out of sight and out of mind, but Moira never forgets. Ten years ago, that's where she was working 14-hour days in 100-degree heat counting t-shirts coming off the conveyor of an industrial dryer. Count the shirts, box them, keep counting in an endless cycle of tortuous heat and a string of obscenities from the plant manager behind her. After two years of this same routine, which she grew to cherish, Moira was spotted by Arthur, the owner of Skylit and promoted to the receptionist position and then up and up and up until she got the reserved parking spot, the office with the bay window, oak desk, and $800 ergonomic executive chair.

So here she is, Executive Manager—just a fancy name for Office Babysitter—where she tackles the menial tasks of office work, ever boring, ever meaningless in the grand scheme of the universe (whatever that maybe).

Staple the invoices, staple the purchase orders, staple the bills. So many staples.

If Moira understood the stock market, she would buy stock in staples then she'd become so rich, she could buy Skylit and knock it down. The reality is that she doesn't understand the stock market, so she'll unlock the front door as usual and head inside to start her day of the never ending, never fulfilling office work that awaits her. It must be done—those invoices aren't going to staple themselves—so she heads to her office situated near the receptionist's desk in a small lobby and switches on the light with the same expectation that an intruder will jump out and bludgeon her to death.

There is no intruder, there never is, but when the florescent lights above come to life on this day, they reveal a wonderland of streamers and bouncing helium balloons hovering like a forest of shiny jack pines all around the perimeter of her office. Happy

Birthday hangs as a sequined valance over the bay window in front of her desk. There are presents and cards and she doesn't know half of her coworkers' names despite working with most of them for more than a decade.

They know her, though. The goody-two shoes who lamented getting two bags of chips from the vending machine when she only paid for one. The girl who rescues the crickets that wander into the office, who will trip and fall flat on her face if it means avoiding stepping on an ant. She speaks more often to the half dead plant in her window or the solar powered Flying Pig than she does to any one human being.

More importantly, they know she is their protector.

Arthur is a small man, both in stature and morals—he'd abandon his children in a burning building to save himself or to save a buck—but when he flies into a rage, no one is willing to stand up to him. Suddenly, the office employs only bus drivers looking to protect themselves and their jobs. Except for Moira, though. In the same tone that she speaks to the crickets as she ushers them out the front door, she will talk him down. Their jobs will be saved, their lives will continue.

Half the staff would have been fired by now if not for Moira's unyielding determination to defend them, though she is not invincible and sometimes she loses the battle for someone's job. It's never Arthur who does the act of firing an employee, of course—you would need a spine to do such a task—this is left to Moira, who will do as she is told.

And then hide in the bathroom and throw up...her spine isn't particularly well developed either.

It's why she can never tell him to not stand so close to her or to please, *please* stop smelling her hair. He thinks she doesn't notice but when he nears and inhales, she freezes, grimacing until he passes. She tried switching from her Orange Blossom and Vanilla shampoo to unscented, but he was undeterred, so she switched back.

Why should she suffer for no reward?

For all that she does around the office, and for being the unofficial spokesperson for the staff, you would think that someone could offer to staple all the invoices and file them for her. Especially since they now somehow know it's her birthday. How did someone find out this date that she has skillfully kept hidden for the last 12 years? What spy is lurking within her colleagues?

Moira knows she should be happy, flattered even, but instead she gazes around her office with a sense of trepidation for the unwanted attention this may drive her way. She hasn't celebrated her birthday in 12 years and has no reason to start inviting people back into her life now.

Watching the colorful balloons bob in the ambient air, she chews her thumb nail hypnotized by their motion. Twelve years ago, balloons so sickeningly similar to these floated along the spiral staircase, were entwined in floral bouquets in the foyer, they were tied to the wrought iron gate that surrounded her parents' million-dollar property on the scenic shoreline of Lake Michigan.

Their home was filled with people, all her parents' rich friends and clients; every room was filled with laughter and joy, food and champagne. It was her 18th birthday, after all, so of course the daughter of a powerful lawyer, her father, and affluent socialite, her mother, would demand the attention of the all the Wisconsin prestigious. They came in droves; they came with money in the thousands, gifts of jewelry and gift certificates to Milwaukee's best spas and fanciest boutiques.

There was a toast in her honor, and she blushed as her mom pulled her close and talked about the day she was born, talked about the midnight cravings, talked about the 16-hour labor. She laughed and begged her to stop before managing to escape her mother's drunken, though delighted, embrace and slip away to her bedroom, to her en suite bathroom.

But she was followed up those balloon lined stairs.

She knew him her whole life, he was like a grandfather to her, but...she cannot think about this. She cannot let these memories haunt her any further, not here, not now. There are emails to answer and papers to staple. With legs of jelly, she pushes forward through the forest of balloons and streamers to her desk. She locks her purse in the bottom drawer, just like normal, and goes about her morning with determination for the impossible...that this day should pass like every other day.

It's not like there's a kidney in a cooler waiting to be delivered to a patient in mortal danger and yet the office is in a state of panic with women in pencil skirts and men in ties frantically moving from one office to another, shouting and whining.

Panicking as though a kidney in a cooler is somewhere in the office.

There isn't, though. This is, in fact, a marketing and decorating firm. They print promotional t-shirts, embroider logos onto hats, and pad print pencils, pens, coffee cups all destined for Goodwill in the near future. If those embroidered towels aren't shipped on time, or the hats, or the printed t-shirts, no one is going to die or go to jail. Someone might have a temper tantrum…or a stroke…

Still, not a kidney in a cooler, not a liver where the heart goes. Life will go on and today life goes on with the phone ringing off the hook and for every email answered, three more come in, two workers—a warehouse clerk and an accounting clerk—both sobbed in Moira's office, and the main dryer has broken down.

Is this success? Moira wonders, head in her hands, staples spilled at her feet, a stack of invoices toppled down the side of her desk and still Arthur hasn't come into work. Not that this is surprising as he's often last in, first out but it would be nice to have someone else in charge who isn't her, who isn't Moira on her 30th birthday trying to ignore the swaying balloons that swish in her peripheral vision. Every time they catch her attention, she thinks of him coming into her bathroom behind her, calling her a Goddess when she was just turned 18.

She thinks of the night she screamed at her parents, but they refused to understand, to protect her. They wouldn't risk standing up to the man who made her father one of the rich and powerful. Not even for their baby girl. Later that week, on a Thursday afternoon when she was supposed to be in her final physics class before graduation, she met with her new landlord to pick up the keys to her new home. It wasn't anywhere near the designer topiary, marble fountains and circular drives of where she grew up, but she could afford it and that was all the mattered.

After graduation she found Skylit where the hiring criteria was to be a living, breathing human being. Twelve years later…

No matter how loud the office is, people are arguing in the hall outside her office, the phone is still ringing, Leah, their young, flighty receptionist is either hiding in the bathroom or one of the people in the hall bickering, Moira can't get out of her own head, escape her own thoughts. All because of these stupid balloons! How can she escape this day for the last 12 years and suddenly now it comes crashing around her, crushing her like a python? Such a beautiful, tormenting gesture, such lovely gifts waiting for the chaos to die so they can be opened and enjoyed. But she just doesn't want them.

No doubt there is a gift outside her apartment eagerly awaiting her arrival with immaculate gift wrap and a card tucked securely under the shiny foil ribbon addressed to her in her mother's perfectly pristine penmanship. Every year there's a gift waiting for her and every year the card is tossed along with every other piece of trash; the present is tucked away in her closest never to see the light of day. There must be thousands of dollars' worth of names in there, bags and shoes, blouses and dresses and cardigans all unworn and unwanted. Often times she'll think about selling them all but that certainly seems like a lot of effort when she is perfectly content with her salary from Skylit, perfectly content to sit around doing crossword puzzles all day long.

If there was an Olympic sport of crossword puzzle solving, Moira Lovegood would win gold every time.

Every year she thinks about reading the card but can never get herself to tear open the envelope even though she is a professional mail opener as is evident by the garbage can under her desk filled with ripped envelopes…that once contained invoices that got spilled down the side of her desk as she tried to stop the staples from falling.

Both tasks were unsuccessful so, after wallowing in her memories, she rises and prepares to exit her office to rein in the entropy that has engulfed Skylit, to be the righter of wrongs, once again. As she stands, Leah stomps in, her jet-black hair frizzed from where she incessantly keeps running her hands through the thick dyed locks, panting with tears threatening to spill over. From her ears dangle her gold leaf earring with the long brown feathers. Not a day goes by that Leah isn't wearing these earrings, no matter what clothes she has on.

"Moira!" she cries, her arms flailing around, her feet pacing, dragging her from the doorway to Moira's desk and back. "I called the…I don't know, the dryer people. They can't get anyone out here. What am I supposed to do? And Megan keeps shouting at me 'cause I sent the wrong invoices to the wrong people. I don't know." The girl sticks out her lower lip and tugs on one of the helium balloons. "Happy birthday, by the way." She tries to smile, and Moira tries to smile back. "You like your office? A bunch of us stayed late last night. Not that I want credit or anything, but it was my idea. You're always so nice to me."

"It's nice to be nice." Moira replies, grimacing through the gut-wrenching guilt that bubbles into her throat. She hates her office like this, the balloons and the presents, the sequin valance, too. She hates that they remind her of that night. She hates that the phone is ringing and the receptionist is standing in her office crying. How many more people are going to come to her with tears in their eyes?

And there's staples all over the floor.

This is not what success looks like.

For a moment there is an irresistible urge to walk away, grab her purse and go but this urge is quickly replaced by a strict foreboding. Pure fear that she could lose her precious routine. This might not be success, but it is a paycheck; it might not be a kidney in a cooler ready to save someone's life, but it is security. Isn't that all she really wants?

Happiness is overrated anyway.

"I'll call the dryer company and get them in this morning," Moira tells Leah, her voice motherly but exhausted. "And you tell Megan to take any issues up with me."

"Thanks, Moira. Sure is a shit day for your birthday…" Leah's eyes wander to the window behind Moira, growing wide as Arthur's truck pulls into the spot beside Moira's in the parking lot. "Shit." Spinning, she bolts, scurrying to return to her proper place lest Arthur see her once again not manning the phones.

Leah is one of the many Moira has saved from Arthur's fury, multiple times. With the attention span of a flea and her attention to detail nonexistent, reception isn't her strong suit, but she wore a low-cut top during her interview so how could Arthur turn her down?

Moira slumps back down in her chair, mentally preparing herself for Arthur to step into her office per his usual morning habit. He'll check with her that his business is running as it should, that her hair smells delicious as usual, that she has everything under control as always. Once confirmed, he can return to his office to stare at the security cameras and watch the warehouse staff to make sure no one ever stops counting boxes then he can close his door and browse the internet.

Not for deals on new equipment for the screen printers or the embroidery machines, not for office supplies. After his second wife left him last year, he rekindled an old habit of gawking at certain images that when Moira once stumbled upon the viewing, she spun so fast she smashed into a doorframe so hard her nose bled all over her white blouse on a day she was meeting with one of Skylit's biggest clients.

The images are still burned into her eyes even a year later.

She hears his voice, nasal but booming, as he greets Leah; she will be the next stop. His footsteps near and soon he will be behind her placing a hand on her shoulder, leaning down (only slightly since he is almost as tall as Moira is when seated) and inhaling deeply but as quietly as possible. He'll tell her good morning, ask her how she is, maybe ask about her evening before asking if there are any messages. It's the same routine every morning and it is only for routine that she stays somewhere so depressing.

Footsteps, footsteps.

They stop and she braces for his entrance, but he is rooted in the door.

Silence.

She turns to meet his eyes, offering a bright, albeit fake, smile and a 'good morning', which is returned briskly before he slips away as suddenly as he appeared. Taken aback, startled by the sudden disruption in the routine, she stares, blinking slowly.

And then it sinks in.

Chapter 2
The Psycho, The Whore, and The End of Days

Only last month it was Arthur's birthday—50 years old! —and she forgot! When his second wife was still in his life and helping run Skylit, she would decorate the office with balloons and encourage every client to send him an email or a gift; she would go to each employee and shake them down for cash to put in a card. Those who could not or would not contribute would find themselves unemployed within a week.

She's gone now and Moira forgot. Her plan was to take the money from Petty Cash to put in a card since she was never going to ask the employees for money.

But she forgot, everyone forgot.

Shaking head in hands, Moira rests her elbows on her knees and sighs; she needs to call the dryer company. And pick up these staples and the invoices and why is the phone ringing *again*?

Leah pops into her office, beaming, a purple vase of red roses in her hands. "Someone sent you flowers!" Moira looks up, tearing her eyes from the staples on the floor and stares, a serious expression bordering on anger draped over her visage. "What's wrong?" Leah's cheerful smile fades into concern.

"This is going to be trouble."

What trouble? There's no trouble, just a regular day at Skylit. 56 emails in Moira's inbox, staples and invoices on the floor, and Arthur stomping around the office raging at anything in his path. The office has gone silent except the sounds of fingers on keyboards and Leah's voice as she answers the phone with the most professional voice she can muster.

There's no trouble.

Arthur slips into Moira's office unnoticed only getting her attention by slamming the door closed; she jumps and a box of paperclips spill to the floor from her hands, joining the staples in a rogue mission to escape their sole duty.

Moira lets out an audible yelp, spinning to face this intruder, placing a hand on her racing heart. "Arthur, you scared me!"

"Look at all these gifts. Look. At all these gifts." His voice is slow and rough, his mouth dry.

"I sure have been spoiled this year, but I guess 30 is a pretty big birthday." She tries to sound casual, like this is nothing. No big deal. It shouldn't be a big deal, but her heart pulsates in her throat.

"Yes, you're 30 now. I got to watch you grow up from a shy little teenager to a beautiful young woman." He has yet to meet her eye instead watching the balloons sway in the wake of his movements; his eyes wander to the papers on her desk, settling briefly on her chest before becoming entranced by the flowers in the purple vase. "Look at all you got here. Look at all of this." He moves back to the filing cabinet where he picks up an alluring red package with a curly rainbow bow affixed. He shakes it but there is only silence, so he sets it back down with a sigh. "My birthday came and went and not one person even blinked." His voice is low and dangerous. He smacks his cotton lips and wipes at them with the back of his hand trying desperately to find moisture. "Not even you."

"Oh…" Moira sits back in her chair, "I'm sorry Arthur. It's been so chaotic lately." She knows this is a feeble excuse but it's the first thing that tumbles from her mouth. There will be no excuse good enough.

"Not even you." He repeats turning to her and smacking his lips again, pulling his mouth uncomfortably. "You're supposed to lead by example. You didn't even give me a hug." He scoffs and shakes his head. "Do these people realize that I'm the one that pays them? Don't they realize that it's me they should thank?"

"Oh, Arthur." Moira says in a calming voice, "You know people are uncomfortable talking to the real boss. You're too important for the trivial fires we start. That's why you have me so I can filter the real problems right to you."

Arthur begins to hum as he paces around her office again, his cheeks are twitching with rage, his protuberant brown eyes bulge further from their sockets than normal; dilated, they jerk from one end of his face to the other. Still, he smiles. The hum grows deeper and louder as he paces like a tiger in a cage, starved and beaten.

A Pit Bull on a chain, left in the heat.

The humming grows softer and then louder again before it stops all together along with his pacing and he turns to her. His jaw tightens, he pulls at his mouth again with a skeletal hand trying to make his cheeks stop twitching. Moira shifts uncomfortably in her chair and tries to keep eye contact with this speck of a man, his shirt sloppily tucked in, half coming out at the side, and manic.

"You are fucking shameless. The way you walk around here like you matter." He leans close to her, balancing with one hand on her desk, "Just shameless." He clicks his tongue sending a shower of spittle on her face. Slowly, he inhales as he backs away, his fingers running along the smooth edge of the oak desk. "You are nothing but a whore."

"Now hold on a minute!" Moira snaps, slamming her hand on the desk but he doesn't hear her.

"A shameless whore." He says, casually, almost dreamily, as though he were speaking to himself. His voice once frenzied now is heavy with sleep and the low hum emerges once again from his throat; he walks around the perimeter of the room, his eyes going in and out of focus at the various decorations, settling once again on the bouquet of flowers. "No one even blinked when it was my birthday." Like a child he puffs out his bottom lip and crosses his arms, his eyes blink slowly and heavily. "No one."

Certain he might fall asleep at any second, Moira takes a deep breath and bites her temper, fighting it with everything she can despite her hurt pride and bubbling anger. This is just one of his moods; she has been through this before and she has always been able to calm him down.

"I want you out of here." He says suddenly, his eyes snapping up to her face.

"Excuse me?" Moira cocks her head, sure that she has misheard.

"Get out. Pack up your shit and get out." Standing now, alert and focused solely on her face.

"Are you…are you firing me?"

Humming, he nods and sticks his bottom lip out even further. "Yes."

Blindsided, Moira remains seated as the words sink in, as reality reaches her brain. She opens and closes her mouth several times trying to iterate a response but no words, no sounds, emerge. Arthur continues to glare at her, his hands now shaking; he reminds her of a chihuahua.

"You're a psycho." She finally tells him meeting his glare with her own fiery one.

"I may be a fucking psycho but at least I'm not a whore."

"This is ridiculous." Moira says while getting to her feet. Arthur watches her as she moves, as she kneels to get her purse from the bottom drawer of her desk; watching her, his anger swells to a destructive level and in a fluid motion he knocks the vase from the table it was resting. As the glass shatters into dozens of purple shards, she jumps back from the shock and a startled scream escapes her lips. The flowers lie on the floor in a puddle of water looking like Moira feels, wounded and wilting.

"I'll send one of your little," here he sneers, "*friends* to bring your shit to you. Right now," he stomps over to the door and throws it open where it slams against the wall, the handle breaking into the drywall, "I want you out!" he shouts. "Get out! Don't you understand? Gone! Fired!" Now with the door open, the scene can spill into the hallway so the entire office can listen in. Everyone in the office will freeze and listen.

Who's getting fired? What's going on?

Moira will know!

Someone will whisper that it *is* Moira. No! Not Moira. That's impossible. Who will get rid of spiders and call the dryer company? What about her emails?

Who will protect them?

Moira, still in shock, stares down at the broken flowers at her feet.

"Are you deaf?" Arthur growls.

"What's wrong with you?" Moira asks quietly, shaking her head as she passes him. She is grateful that he doesn't follow her out but instead remains in her office probably drinking in the passing fragrance of her perfume.

"Are you okay?" Leah asks, through lowered lashes.

"Yes." Moira whispers harshly as she heads to the door. "Leah, do me a favor. Don't stay here. Find something better. You deserve so much better."

The girl chuckles, pulling on one of her feathered earrings. "Oh, don't worry. I'll be fired before you get to your car."

Chapter 3
The Ride Home, The Facts, and The Fish

In her car, she rests both hands on the wheel, but the keys are still in her purse. There are no tears and she isn't sure if there will be tears. Can there be tears for losing a job you hated? She shakes her head bitterly. She gave 12 years of her life to Skylit and to Arthur and even now, no longer employed, she thinks about the unfinished tasks in her office—her workload—who else can do it? No one. But certainly, that's a conceited thought. Skylit will go on without her.

Just like she will go on without Skylit.

She finally fishes her keys from her purse and jams the key into the ignition with shaking hands. Leaving the parking lot for what will be the last time, she doesn't look back in her rearview mirror once. She pulls out of her reserved parking spot at the front of the building and starts the journey home, which today feels tedious instead of welcome; the road shakes around her with trepidation…every red light giving her time to replay the final scene in her office over again. Green stops the thoughts; she focuses on the road, the potholes, the cars around her, pedestrians on the sidewalk. Red brings Arthur's wild eyes back to her, brings back thoughts of what she should have said instead, how she might still be employed if only…

Green and she drives away from all thoughts.

30 miles per hour turns to 40, 10 over the limit, but the light in front of her is green. It's green and when it's green she doesn't have to think about Arthur. It's green but still the black car waiting by the intersection is there. He's stopped, maybe it's a she. Why is she moving? She has a yield—she must yield to the people owning the green light. Moira has the green light, but the black SUV goes cutting in front of Moira as she comes flying through the intersection.

No sound from Moira as she slams on the brakes of her BMW, her rear end fishtails but the car comes to a stop, though it screams as is does so. The black SUV lurches to a stop also in front of Moira's car before reversing back behind the yield sign. Moira stares forward, stunned. Her hands shake on the wheel, but green means go, means leave your thoughts behind. Slowly, she moves forward; behind her, the golden Cadillac blares her horn so Moira for the second time in 30 seconds slams on her brakes again, making the Cadillac do the same.

"Don't you know I was almost killed?" Moira shouts, looking into her rearview mirror at the red-haired woman behind her. "Can't you see that?" No, she doesn't care about that. That woman in the gold Cadillac doesn't care that Moira almost died on her 30th birthday right in front of her. That woman doesn't care that Moira got fired on her 30th birthday!

She doesn't care. The world doesn't either.

Why should it? The world, the universe, is infinite and she is just a fleck of flesh and blood and emotion. The sun does not revolve around her; the moon does not rise in her honor. It should, she thinks angrily, it should. Today she is 30 and the world should celebrate for today she has been freed.

And just what is Leo going to say?

How can she face him and his understandable fury when she comes home and tells him that she was fired from the only job she's ever had in her life? And all because she got more presents on her birthday than Arthur did on his! It's laughable, pathetic, but now her tears fall as she parks in the parking lot of her apartment complex.

Outside her door, a present awaits just as predicted; inside the lights are out and Leo is still asleep. Quietly, she sits down on the couch, setting the flat box wrapped in purple foil paper on the floor and her purse beside her. Staring at the black screen of her television she thinks about all the things she left behind. Her calendar of fish wearing hats, her mug telling her she's the best that Leah randomly gave her a few months ago, and all her presents that she never got to open. Her plant, although nearing death, and her flying pig that flaps its wings when it gets enough sun.

"You're home early." Leo greets, sleepily lounging in his favorite spot; he doesn't move to welcome her home but lazily gazes at her with his usual gaumless expression.

"I got fired." She says without hesitation to the television.

Leo shakes his head, "What? For real?" Moira replies with silence, tears streaming down her freckled cheeks, tumbling from her long, black lashes. "Well, well, well. Get the champagne!"

She turns angry eyes to him, "Don't you understand?"

"I sure do."

"Oh, Leo!" Moira cries, throwing her hands in the air as she jumps from the sofa. "What am I going to do?" She throws herself to the floor before him, placing gentle hands on the glass that separates them. "I can't believe I got fired." He brings his shimmering pink body to where her fingers rest so she can pet him through the glass of his 20-gallon tank. He is her only friend, her sole companion for the last five years.

Leo has guided Moira through her darkest days at Skylit and her loneliest weekends spent alone in her apartment completing crossword puzzle after crossword puzzle. He has been her ignored voice of reason since the day she brought him home from the pet store and her patient listener. Even now as she recaps the events of this morning through her tears, he listens with kindness and sympathy. She is slumped against the wall in the dining room next to where his tank sits with her knees to her chest, hugging them. She tells him about Arthur's wild eyes and the flowers in the purple vase, she tells him how Arthur insulted her and how she left all her presents behind and how she almost got into an accident.

When she is done, her tears have stopped and she is breathless. "What am I going to do now?"

"First, we are going to pop some champagne and celebrate." Leo tells her. "I've been waiting for five years for this moment and it's finally come! You should be bouncing off the walls with ecstasy."

"This is not a joke." She snaps, getting to her feet.

"I'm being serious!"

"I'm unemployed, single, and talking to a fish!" She slumps onto the sofa and stretches her legs out in front of her, her hands twisting her Claddagh, then lifting her shirt to fiddle with her sunflower navel ring. What a dumb sixteen-year-old decision it was to let her friend pierce her tummy with a Do-It-Yourself kit, a sign of her independence and freedom.

"You have enough in your savings to live a whole year, easy. Besides, once we're done celebrating, you can go to the unemployment office. Actually," Leo floats to the surface of the water and drinks in a mouthful of air, "that sounds like a Monday problem."

"A Monday problem?" she mutters, pulling her shirt down over the flower piercing.

"Take the rest of this week and this weekend to just…do what you do. You know, nothing."

Around her is a rare moment of silence. There are no car horns or police sirens and the dog isn't barking; there is no bass music bumping and her upstairs neighbors were evicted last week so there is no shouting from above, no slamming doors or Clydesdale feet. Everything is quiet in Moira's crumbling world.

She thinks, as she lay on the sofa staring up at the ceiling, about looking for a new job. What a daunting task for any sane adult. Job hunting. Looking for the job, applying for the job, interviewing for the job. Not getting the job, starting over for another job. Eventually you'll find, apply, interview, and then get the job only to find that you hate it more than your last job for less pay and a longer commute.

Chapter 4
The Unemployed, The Slovenly, and The Turning of a New Leaf

The first couple of weeks, when May turns to June, depression settles over Moira. It started the moment she returned from the unemployment office. She sleeps until noon, showering becomes optional, and eating is no longer a necessity. The dust is thick on the surfaces, her mailbox is packed so the mailman now leaves it by her door. The present from her parents remains unopened beside the sofa and she has had no human contact since that last day at Skylit.

The loneliness is severe and it makes her wish for so much of her past, her family, her job, even her ex-boyfriends, though there's only been one since her promiscuous high school days. She met Jonathan as he was working on the landscaping at Skylit. She was timid, frightened as she always is with men, but he seemed so shy and sweet and his muscles rippled under his t-shirt, the sweat glistened off his arms like diamonds in the sun.

She gave him a chance, he won her over, and then he reminded her of why men can't be trusted. That was five years ago then Leo came into her life and she never needed another person since.

Until now.

One afternoon when reality sinks in, she begins to sob into her pillow that she holds to her face tight enough to turn her knuckles white. She wishes now, more than ever, that she had someone to wrap their arms around her and comfort her, even Jonathan who always knew the wrong thing to say, but at least his arms were strong, his embrace warm.

She cries for her lost security, the loneliness, and her shattered routine; she cries for her pitiful, lonely existence that she has fallen prey to and she the predator that put herself there.

How many tears can be in there, in her body, she wonders, wiping them away with the back of her hand; how long will she live unemployed, overwhelmed with self-pity, in a dusty, dirty apartment? It stops now! The first thing she is going to do is take a long, hot shower since she hasn't showered since her birthday.

The water leaves a warm trail down her back and legs, over her arms and chest. The scent of orange blossom and vanilla shampoo fills her nose and reminds her of springtime, it reminds her that her apartment should be condemned.

So many things need to be done and the list grows as she dresses in a pair of soft, wide-legged lounge pants that cover her feet and a tank top. She can feel the despair creeping over her when she walks down the hall, but she knows she must keep her feet moving.

She starts in the living room. Cleaning everything. Dusting, vacuuming, tidying up. The kitchen, her laundry. She strips her bedding and replaces it with fresh linens; she fluffs the pillows and turns down the comforter so it will be ready when she is.

Tomorrow, she decides, she will wash the floors, bake some cookies, she'll go grocery shopping and maybe find a new hobby, maybe a new job. All of that will come tomorrow, for now she will continue to clean.

"I wish I decided to be tidier earlier in my unemployment. Or develop new hobbies sooner." She announces to Leo, dropping her bedding into a pile by her door so she can carry it down to the laundry room. "I could be a French speaking artist by now."

"You know, even if you have a job, which you do have to get, you can still do other things. Work doesn't have to be your life."

"Skylit was all I had, though." She mumbles, sitting cross-legged in front of his tank and rubbing her tired eyes. She thinks for a while, about her job and how when she was 16, she had a job for a few weeks at a florist, how she loved that job but the schedule interfered with softball practice so she had to quit. She loved that. Being creative and making people smile, helping design bridal bouquets and corsages, sending getting well vases and birthday vases like the one Arthur smashed. "Maybe I could become a florist."

"You'd like that."

"Eh." She shrugs, "I don't think that'll pay the bills." The pair fall silent, Moira's mind racing with options all leading her from finding a job she loves back to a well-paying office job, something she knows she's good at.

After a moment, she stands and goes to her bedroom where she retrieves a book and returns to Leo. Lying on the floor in front of his tank, she begins to read aloud to him like she often used to do every night before she was fired. Today they start a book they've read a thousand times, a touching love story that always makes Moira smile but soon her eyes become heavy, her limbs, her head. All become weighted down like gravity is pulling her through the floor.

When she dreams, she dreams of Skylit, of Arthur and Leah. She sees her flowers smashed on the floor; she sees herself at work walking around them, ignoring the wilting petals. In the dream, she goes to the bathroom and looks in the mirror to find that she is old. Her smooth face is wrinkled, her bright greens eyes have become dull with exhaustion, and her hair is grey and frizzy. Behind her in the mirror is Charles Kent. He was like a grandpa to her, but he followed her to her bedroom and into her en suite bathroom.

She broke his nose that night but still when she dreams, he's there. He's always there.

Charles grabs her aged frame, his own the same as it was 12 years ago and Jonathan, standing in the background, just laughs.

She jolts upright, eyes darting around the dining and living room, frantic, through the darkness. The only light comes from the soft blue LED of Leo's tank and the pale golden glow sneaking in from the courtyard lights passing through the sheer white curtains. Outside, that stupid dog is barking and there are children running through the night, but inside, in her home, she is safe.

And alone.

Her body aches as she stands from the hard floor; she stretches her arms and back with a groan as her joints pop. Tomorrow will be better, she thinks, feeling unaccomplished because of her five-hour nap. She feels crippled, bleary eyed, but tomorrow. Tomorrow she will be happy so that when the morning comes and the sun pokes its shining face out from the early morning clouds, she will rise with it.

In the morning, she goes outside, purse clutched to her side, and breathes in the warm summer air, the freshness of lilies in bloom, the scent of sunshine and happiness. There are robins bounding around the apartment complex, grackles and starlings amongst them, the chickadees dance in the blooming tree branches above. Cheerful and carefree.

That's what she wants to be like: happy.

Happiness always seems to elude her but she won't let it today. Moira goes to buy everything she needs to bake brownies and cookies. She buys a shepherd's hook, a bird feeder and some black oil sunflower seeds from the hardware store and canvas board and paints, brushes and pencils from the hobby store. At the mall, she buys two new skirts, a black denim one and a flowing peasant maxi covered with a bright floral pattern.

From a second-hand shop, she buys a turntable that has a Learn French record in; it's Lesson 2: Food. She's never had a single lesson in her life but starting on lesson two should be fine. She thinks.

The most important purchase is from the pet store, fresh blood worms and a crocodile skull for Leo.

Today is going to be the start of her new life.

Maybe.

She returns home with her bags and unloads them in the kitchen, leaving her turntable in the trunk since her hands were full, while Leo watches her from the moss at the bottom of his tank. In the spotless kitchen, she lays out her things to bake; she places her new clothes on her bed. Back in the living room, she sits on the sofa and stares at her reflection in the blackness of her television screen.

It's been three weeks since Skylit, since the last time she had human conversation and it makes her realize that she enjoyed work simply for that human experience. She loves Leo and she hated every minute of being at Skylit but she needs to be amongst people. To know she isn't alone and that she's needed.

She loved hugging people either to comfort them or to congratulate them, she loved getting a random high five in the hall or a hip bump from Leah in passing. She was safe there, they were safe people, who liked her and now, in her loneliness, she regrets keeping her distance from them outside of work, for passing on every invitation to lunch or dinner or a party. She misses them and wonders if they miss her.

Maybe someone would call her, bring her things to her; maybe Jonathan wouldn't have left her if she could see past her wall of distrust. Leo is constantly telling her to open her heart and her eyes; to get her to see that not everyone wants to hurt her. This blindness has backed her into a corner of loneliness, leaving her alone with regrets and unfounded fears.

She stands from the sofa and shakes her head again to remove these dark thoughts from her mind. She will be happy and when she finds a new job, she will make friends and when she meets a nice guy, she won't fear him. He won't be Jonathan or Charles.

She'll find happiness but for now, the first step to happiness is washing the curtains and the windows! Happiness is rearranging the furniture.

Wrapping her hair up in a handkerchief like Rosie the Riveter, she moves her sofa and her credenza only to move it back. She relocates a bookshelf only to put that back, as well. There is only satisfaction with Leo's new home in front of the window instead of in the dining room. Hands on her hips, sweat beading down her forehead, she nods at Leo who fights the current of the filter as he watches her.

"This way, we can talk easier!" she tells him, "And you can watch the birds." She slides open the window as wide as it will open allowing the warm breeze to come in. Scurrying outside, she pulls the shepherd's hook, navigating it carefully from the back seat through the trunk. Hook and birdseed in hand, she goes through the building, past her apartment door, out the back door to the courtyard. In front of her living room window, she stabs the hook into the ground. Back inside, she fills the bird feeder to hurry back outside, giddy with excitement, to hang the bird feeder on the shepherd's hook.

"See." She cups her hands around her eyes to peer through the window at Leo, "We can feed the birds now." Going back inside she once again nods her approval with this new set up. "This'll be great. This is the start of happiness. Of the new me."

"I like it." Leo says, watching outside now, waiting for a bird to show up.

"I'm going to bake cookies!" she exclaims, "And while they bake, I'm going to paint a picture. Maybe I can paint a picture of a bird on my feeder. I took art classes in high school. Mr. Frost always said I had talent!"

"Is happiness hyperactivness?" Leo asks but she ignores him and shuffles to the kitchen.

The once clean kitchen is now covered in flour and cookie dough, Moira, too, is dusted with flour. More flour ended up on the floor than in the bowl but there's no time to fret over spilled powders.

She sets up an art station with an end table and a kitchen chair next to Leo. As the cookies bake, she paints a picture of Leo first then decides she should paint a picture of one of the many house finches that visit her feeder. She paints a male in a wash of color on a flowering branch.

"This'll be good for me. Painting, I mean. I like this." She tells Leo, stepping back to admire her handy work and wondering if she could make this a job.

"You got more paint on yourself than on the paper."

Moira looks down at her pink tank top covered in flour and now splashes of paint, her favorite wide-legged lounge pants have smears where she wiped her hands and the carpeting, too, has splotches of color. "Oh no! I'm such a child!" She hurries to get something to clean the carpeting when the oven beeps for the cookies. "Oh goodness." She sighs and detours to the kitchen.

Removing the paint from the carpet proves unsuccessful but it does lead her to scrubbing the rest of the floors and returning the kitchen to its shining cleanliness. The road to happiness, she decides, is exhausting but she knows she has to keep herself busy or her lonely thoughts will overwhelm her.

Head to toe in paint, flour, and Pine Sol, Moira flops onto the sofa with a grunt and wipes the sweat from her brow. "Being happy is frigging hard." She whines, swiping at the flour she inadvertently added to the sofa.

"You're a mess."

"Shut up, fish. I swear I will flush you." She moans and leans her head back on the back of the couch, "I'm so tired now."

"Why don't you open your present from your parents." Leo says, drifting with the gentle flow of the filter. "And maybe the card this year?" Moira shrugs and picks up the present from the side of the sofa. She removes the card from under the bow and holds it, her whole body is still, her eyes focused on her name written in cursive on the envelope.

What could they possibly say to her?

"You know what?" she throws the card onto the floor and shoves the wrapped box to the side, aggressive with tears suddenly threatening, "We are going to learn French today." She hops up from the sofa and runs her hands down her paint-stained pants and straightens her tank top. As she slips on her flip flops, she wonders if she should change. Leo told her she's a mess and it's true, she has paint and flour all over, her hair is chaos and her black bra is clearly noticeable through the thin pink fabric. She shakes her head; she'll be outside for two seconds.

"This'll be great." She tells Leo before disappearing into the hallway.

Moira pushes out the door leading outside hastily, pushing herself into the warm June evening, into the sunshine and breeze. These dreams are instantly quelled by an unfamiliar green Jeep parked next to her BMW. A man stands with John, her landlord, leaning against the back with his arms folded.

Her face goes flush with anxiety, her keys tremble in her hands.

"I swear to you, John. I'm not joking. I am not paying to do laundry." The man says and John laughs. "I will take my laundry to my mom's house like a real man."

John laughs harder and turns to Moira with a big smile. John's a large man, tall and muscular, with thick black hair and tattoos up his arms and over his neck. He played in the minor leagues but never got his call up to the Bigs so now he helps his wife run the apartment complex that was handed down to her from her father. He has always been kind to Moira since that day he handed over the keys, even though he knew he was taking a chance on a kid clearly running away from home. He never did regret the decision considering she is the best and the longest lasting tenant he's ever had. "What do you think, Miss L? Is the laundry too expensive?"

She pops the trunk and takes a deep breath to steady her racing heart, "Uh…"

"See." John interrupts before she can articulate an answer, turning his attention back to the man. "Be like Miss L, here, okay?" John says and the other man laughs, running his hands through his shaggy blonde curls, peeking at Moira from over the top of his sunglasses.

She's thankful to no longer be in the spotlight of this strange man or John, to no longer be part of the conversation. Placing her keys between her teeth, she pulls the turntable from the trunk as the two men talk; she will not let the presence of this man distract her from being happy and learning some French. No, this man with his stylishly unkempt hair and his Warby Parker sunglasses is not here to hurt her, to torture or murder her. He's just a guy living his life.

"I was thinking, Miss L." John turns back to her and she cringes, trying to adjust her grip on the record player. He laughs, "You take up painting?"

Nervous and insecure, her eyes flickering to the man by the Jeep, she tries to smile at her landlord and nods.

"Good for you. Anyway, I was thinking about replacing some of the fixtures in your apartment."

Stifling a sigh, she carefully drops her keys from dangling between her teeth onto the turntable so she can properly reply, too aware of the stranger's eyes watching the interaction with a smirk.

"That would be nice." She says, her eyes moving to the man's arm, covered with a colorful sleeve tattoo of a koi fish hidden amongst intricate tribal designs, leaves, and what looks like the sun's rays and lily pads with a stained-glass appearance. He notices her looking at it, he looks down at his arm, too, then back to her with raised eyebrows, a questioning glance; she quickly looks away, blushing, back to John who still talks about what he wants to do in her apartment, including gutting the whole bathroom.

John asks her a series of questions while she struggles to keep a grip on the turntable; her answers are perfunctory but nothing short of polite. All the time, the stranger watches with amusement as she nearly drops the player several times during the conversation. His presence makes her face burn with shame; her black bra, her paint stained, flour covered clothes, her messy hair. And his eyes are on her, every inch of her disheveled appearance.

"Oh, what am I thinking?" John exclaims, throwing his hands up in the air, "Son, this is your new downstairs neighbor." The man's attention is suddenly alert when addressed, as though he's been caught doing something he shouldn't be, his eyes snap over to John then back to Moira with a smile.

"Hey." He greets, straightening and extending a hand for her to shake, which she looks at and scowls. His lips purse, suppressing a smile. She knows that he knows that she cannot possibly or comfortably shake his hand.

She nods curtly, unamused by his amusement, and spins to go back to the safety of her apartment.

"She's always been shy." She can hear John say to the man. "Such a sweet girl, though." Her heart plummets, her face goes red with fury but the heavy glass door closes, cutting off the man's reply, cutting off the remainder of their conversation.

When she finds the sanctuary of her apartment once again, she growls angrily and tosses the record player violently onto the sofa. "Why did John say that?"

"What's the problem?" Leo asks in a tone indicative of his irascible temper, knowing that whatever she is about to say will be exasperating.

"Tell that guy where I live? Tell him I'm *shy*! I don't want some guy knowing where I live and that I'm shy!" she moans, slumping next to the record player. "Why'd he have to move in above me?"

"So, your *neighbor* knows where you live." If Leo had eyebrows, he would raise them.

"I don't want to be pointed out to strange men. I don't want people to look at me, period."

"He is not a rapist. He's not a murderer." Leo's tone is scolding and cantankerous. She knows she is being absurd. There was nothing about the guy standing with John that would incriminate him, no reason to accuse him of atrocities he has not committed, no reason to hate him but she does. She hates that he moved upstairs from her, she hates his pierced ear and his tousled hair and his tattoos, even if it has a fish on it. His smirk, leaning so confidently on his Jeep purposefully, *maliciously*, offering her a hand to shake!

"I hate him."

Chapter 5
The Unlovable, The Impolite, and The Hated

Days later, the record player sits untouched on the sofa, callously ignored and forgotten about. Moira sits on the sofa beside it chewing the top of a pencil as she mutters a cross puzzle clue repeatedly out loud trying to summon the answer.

"Flag talk…flag talk…"

"You're ridiculous." Leo grumbles, bobbing to the surface.

"Flag." She pauses, "Talk. Why? Flag talk…it starts with an S."

"I thought you were going to get yourself back on track but really you just cleaned the stupid apartment and went back to sitting on the sofa in sweatpants."

"So what? So what? I'm happy. I showered!" Moira throws the book to the side and rises to her feet, turning to meet Leo's black eyes.

"This is not happiness. Happiness is not 30 years old living alone in a one-bedroom apartment with no job, no friends, no boyfriend."

Leo's words echo her own thoughts; she knows he's right. She has to look for another job, she can't just stay holed up in her apartment doing crosswords because a strange man moved in upstairs from her.

She shakes her head, fighting back tears. "I'm so scared of being lonely for the rest of my life but I am more scared that I will be hurt again. What if Charles Kent moved upstairs? Or what if I open myself up to someone and he just hurts me the way Jonathan did? I'm sick of being hurt by people who are supposed to love me." Her voice is just above a whisper, barely holding back the tears, her hands shake. There is nothing left for Leo to say, no words of comfort. "I'm unlovable."

She stomps into her bedroom and looks around first at her bookshelf lined with books, to her dresser with the television sitting on top, mostly unwatched, then to her made bed. She promised Leo, although she never spoke the words, that she would change but she hasn't done that. She hasn't changed, she only keeps her apartment tidy. Her bed is always made. Nothing has been done for the quality of life, to find joy, to bring pleasure to her lonely existence. Painting, crossword puzzles, baking. These things fill a small void but they are not happiness.

In her room, she grabs the flouncy peasant skirt with a cheerful floral pattern she bought, still in the bag from the store she got it from; from her dresser, she pulls a hot pink scoop neck t-shirt, form fitting and flattering. She changes, deciding that she needs fresh air. Sunshine. She leaves her hair to tumble down her back in a carefree freefall, stylishly untamed and heads to her front door where she exits without a glance towards her fish, leaving with all the fluidity of a raging river.

She just needs some fresh air, she tells herself as she leans against her apartment door, panting. Unemployment has done her no favors as her fears have exploded since losing the safe routine she was used to. Leaving her apartment was never so frightening before as it is now, never so daunting.

Charles Kent is not waiting for her outside, neither is Arthur, or anyone else. Sweeping away from her apartment, she heads for the heavy glass door leading to the outside world trying to remember a time, not that long ago, when she would go out for walks in the summertime around the neighborhood when the weather was hot and the sun was shining without fear.

The popping green of summer is shining bright outside in sharp contrast to the dank hallway that has remained unchanged since Moira first moved in 12 years ago. The only light a fluorescent one buzzing on the wall and what comes in through the outside doors; the carpeting must be the same as what it was when the building was erected 30 or more years ago and even though it was cleaned two weeks ago, it clings to the specific smell of aged and unwashed carpet. Simply old.

At the door, she peers outside through the thick glass as she contemplates her next move, where will she go once she's outside? One last deep breath and she starts to move when a voice, a man, calls to her from the staircase directly behind her.

"Hey, since you're there..." His tone is lighthearted and friendly but it makes her freeze, "Would you mind holding the door for me."

Moira glances over her shoulder at the stranger, who she is sure will be Charles Kent. Her upstairs neighbor, the one with the shaggy blonde hair and sunglasses hops down the stairs with a lightness and cheerfulness, a smile on his face. In his hands is a box that appears to be straining his muscles with weight, over his shoulder is a large leather bag, and flung across his chest is a strap that allows a tripod, condensed to its smallest form, to hang down his back.

His hands are full and he could use some help…this door is heavy. Moira takes a deep, shaky breath and finally pushes out the door as the man approaches the final step of the staircase.

"Thanks!" he tells her sincerely but his words are premature and halted as she releases the door to crash into him as she bolts down the sidewalk that runs parallel to the parking lot. She hears him grunt as he clings to the precarious balance of the items he holds. After a moment, she hears him finally emerge from the complex, struggling with the grip on his box.

"Hey!" He calls to her in a sharp, angry bark. She stops dead, her heart beating loudly in her ears; she turns her head slightly, just enough to see him in her peripheral vision. "That was impolite." He tells her in a tone that has lost its initial anger, a tone that is matter of fact. "*You*…are impolite." He states this simple truth then goes to his Jeep, the green Jeep with the Milwaukee Brewers license plates and the retro ball and glove logo decal in the back window. While he goes about his business, she is rooted to the ground unable to lift her legs but her eyes find and watch him as he places his things carefully in the back of his vehicle then closes it up and disappears behind the wheel. She quickly turns and begins to walk down the path, shaking her hair to cover her face to avoid any eye contact but he drives by without incident so she stops and watches as he turns left out of the parking lot.

Her heart beats chaotically in her chest.

Turning on a heel, she hurries back to the solace of her apartment. Back to her clean windows, and her made bed, and her fish. With her door closed and the outside word shut out, she turns wide eyes to Leo.

"I am not impolite!" she announces. "I am a lot of things but impolite is not one of them."

"Maybe it falls under the category of neurotic." Leo offers, lounging lazily on the moss at the bottom of the tank.

"I couldn't even hold the door for him." Slowly shaking her head, she goes to sit on the sofa. "His arms were full and I couldn't hold the door. A good-looking man speaks to me, asks me to hold the door and I close it on his face.”

“I think Ted Bundy did that to lure his victims into his vehicle.” Leo points out, still staring at Moira from his bed. Moira ignores him and sighs, falling into a daze.

“He called me impolite.”

“He could have called you worse. A jerk or a moron.”

“Or a b-i-t-c-h.”

“See,” Leo floats up to the top, his fins waving back and forth gently, “impolite isn’t that bad.”

Still staring at her reflection in the black television screen, she again shakes her head, “I’d rather be called a rude name than impolite.” She turns her head to her fish, “Am I impolite?”

Leo sinks again, landing on top of the faux coral reef. “I don’t think so. I think you are just…a bit quirky.”

“I don’t want to be quirky.” She whimpers. “I don’t want to be neurotic.”

“Well, it isn’t something that someone would typically strive to be.” His black eyes burn into Moira’s dejected face, her deflating posture. She crumbles onto the sofa, curling into the fetal position wondering how long she will last in this dampened and defeated mindset. How long will she remain a rotting potato, slumped on the couch, unmoving, unmotivated.

“I can’t do this. I cannot let some guy do this to me!” she bolts up right and jumps to her feet. “No! He can hold his own darn door. He should have thought of that before he left his apartment with his hands full. He should have thought of that before he moved in upstairs from me!” her outburst causes Leo to scurry from his coral bed back to the mossy bottom with a jolt.

“What are you going to do?” he asks, barely visible through this lush plant.

“I don’t know yet.” She answers honestly with her hands on her hips. “I will not live my life as impolite though.”

Leo settles on his hammock, his eyes watching Moira as she paces her apartment. She goes through her mail, she situates the couch cushions and the throw pillows; she folds her fleece blanket, unfolds it and then folds it again in an even more perfect square. These mindless activities that she fiddles with around her home are so her thoughts can wander down a path of higher priorities.

She decides she will bake some brownies for the man upstairs as a way to apologize for not holding the door. She will be brave and go deliver them to his door when she hears him come home; she will say she is sorry and she won't be a mess. She'll put on her makeup and clean clothes and she'll smile at him, at his handsome face and learn his name because he isn't Jonathan or Charles Kent. He's just a guy who rightfully called her impolite, who didn't call her anything worse or snap at her like he could have. Like a lesser man might have.

With the brownies made and cooling, she leaves. She drives through the city where the buildings are tall, through the suburbs where the houses are large and manicured, along the shimmering lakefront of Lake Michigan where she can reminisce about the times when she was young and holding her father's hand as he let her climb the white boulders. The terns dove into the water catching fish, there were gulls and ducks, and she giggled as her dad lifted her onto his shoulders. He wore a suit and wing tip shoes; he was only taking a lunch break from a case he was working on but he always had time for her.

On her way home, she stops at a corner store, the one she used to go to when she was a teenager, where her and her friends would frequently stop for gum and smoothies. Here, she buys a newspaper, a Snapple, and a crossword puzzle book. Once home, she lays her three purchases onto the floor in front of the television and turns to Leo.

"I don't know how to look for a job." She confesses, "I don't even remember how I got the job at Skylit, but," she sits down in front of the line of goods and looks at them all in turn "I have the Want Ads. I have a drink and I have a new book to play with as a reward. We start tomorrow." She turns her worried eyes to Leo. "Tomorrow. Tomorrow I'm going to Skylit to pick up my things and that includes my last paycheck that is owed to me."

"You can do this." Leo encourages, now off his hammock and floating at the front of the tank watching her.

"Once I do that," she takes a deep breath and pauses, hesitates with her thoughts for a moment, and turns back to the paper in front of her. "Once I do that, I will be able to move forward with my life because I will have nothing left in the past." Moira blinks slowly a few times, mulling over her own words that seemed to have dripped so easily from her lips it makes her wonder if they are true.

They must be true.

But a paycheck and a few personal effects are not what holds her back. It's Jonathan. It's Charles Kent.

As long as she has Leo, though, she'll be ok…starting tomorrow. She smiles at the fish who wiggles around the water angrily as the force of the filter sucks him in then pushes him back out in a pattern his soft fins can't seem to escape.

Above her, she hears the footfall of her neighbor and her heart flutters. Perhaps she'll give the brownies to him tomorrow once she comes back from Skylit and is ready to move into the future.

Chapter 6
The Confident, The Future, and The Open Door

In the morning, when she wakes, there is an apprehension likened to a performer preparing for the stage, preparing for a sold-out show. A dancer of the Cirque du Soleil climbing to the ceiling without a harness. She is that performer, that dancer, and she is the audience holding its collective breath awaiting her fall and it almost comes too soon, almost as soon as she approaches the exit of her apartment complex.

Her upstairs neighbor is entering, his phone to his ear, laughing; across his chest is a large canvas Canon bag, his tripod hangs across his back. "No, I'll drive straight through. Sunday the latest." He says, raising his eyes to Moira, smiling at her. She pulls her purse tightly to her side and holds her breath; she's sure she notices his cheeks flush. "Hold on, hold on." He spins and pushes open the door to hold it for Moira, his eyes twinkling, a smirk on his face. She bows her head and walks through without a word.

"See, civilized." He tells her with a wink.

If only she had something witty to say, some clever come back to send his way but he quickly disappears as the door closes between them.

She will not let his presence destroy her; she will not have her confidence ripped from her heart by some guy. Some stupid guy. No, she is a performer and she can, and will, steal the show.

When she walks into Skylit, her stage, she holds her head high, fearless. Her eyes shine with confidence she has never truly known and it feels amazing especially when Leah's eyes light up to see her, though struck speechless.

"Hey, Leah." She greets, giving the girl a brilliant smile from her painted pink lips that shine.

"I...I'm so happy to see you, Moira! I...I miss you!"

Moira smiles, "I need to see Arthur." Her managerial tone is with flawless command; her work persona coming out and guiding her across the stage with grace and authority. She really does summon Work Moira the way Gotham summons Batman.

"Are you coming back?" Leah blurts out as Moira turns towards Arthur's office door. She looks back and chuckles, a knowing smile playing on her lips. "Is that a yes? Please?" Leah begs but Moira simply turns away, suppressing a laugh. The thought never occurred to her to come back, to reconcile with Arthur. Reconciliation, forgiveness, isn't really in her nature but it would mean the return of her security, of her safe way of life, and of her beloved routine.

"It hasn't been the same without you!" Leah calls to her, a voice of hopeful apprehension. Moira raises her hand to knock on the wooden door to the office, unsure of what to say to Leah; she isn't here to reclaim her past but instead to conquer her future.

"Just give it some time, Leah." She finally says, smiling sympathetically, her soft eyes on Leah's dismal face as she sinks back down into her chair heavily with a sigh.

"You look so pretty." She tells Moira, lifting her puppy dog eyes to Moira's face. "I like your outfit."

Moira smooths her hands down the front of her bell sleeved blouse, to her white denim skirt; the black fabric of her top is decorated with red roses dipped in yellow and the sleeves and collar are trimmed in white lace. The fabric is porous but soft against her skin. A Versace masterpiece her mother couldn't pass up a few years ago for Moira's 27th birthday. It's probably out of fashion by now, Moira thinks, but she smiles at Leah,

"Thank you but flattery will get you nowhere." Moira swiftly turns and raps on the door, loud enough to startle Arthur within. It's a second before he calls for whomever is at his door to enter at which point, Moira pushes open the heavy oak door. She can feel Leah's eyes on her back as she slowly moves into the office and closes the door behind her. Inside, Arthur's back is to her, looking down at miscellaneous papers on his desk, no doubt pretending to be pouring himself into his work.

"Hello, Arthur." Moira greets surprising herself with steady confidence and subtle contempt dripping like venom from her lips. At the sound of her voice, Arthur spins in his chair and casts his startled gaze on her.

"Moira!" He shakes his head in disbelief and stands, reaching a hand to her. "It's good to see you."

Her eyes flicker over his hand but she doesn't accept it; he drops his hand then quickly motions to a chair for her, which is promptly refused with a single blink of her eyes.

"I'm just here for my final paycheck. My other things would be nice, too."

"Of course." He stumbles back and sits in his chair, licking his lips incessantly flicking spit into the air. "Please sit down, Moira." His voice is imploring now, desperate.

"I don't have time to chat, Arthur." She watches in disgust as he stretches his mouth anxiously, suckling on his own lips; she can see his mind racing through his darting, panicked eyes, chasing his own thoughts.

"We've been through a lot." He finally says in a tender, paternal voice. "12 years. I watched you grow into a beautiful young woman. You were just a kid when you started here and I gave you a chance." He paws at his face then grabs his bottle of Coke and takes a large, sputtering mouthful. "No one understands me the way you do. You're the only one who understands."

"That can't be true, Arthur." Moira flippantly replies, tossing her hair over her shoulder, rolling her eyes with a scoff. "I don't understand why I got fired."

"It was a mistake." Arthur whimpers, "It was all a misunderstanding." He stands and snatches his drink and again brings it to his mouth for another gulp before falling back into his seat. He sets the bottle down and then leans heavily on his knees toward Moira. "Skylit needs you, Moira. Your office...it's still yours.

Her office. Her security and routine.

Leah would rejoice.

Moira takes a deep breath but remains silent, driving Arthur to continue a nervous babble about how her office hasn't changed a bit, no one has been allowed in there. Again, he leaps from his seat, "Come on, look." he scurries to the door and throws it open. "Come on." Reluctantly, she follows him through the door and past Leah's desk.

Her office.

Her calendar of fish wearing hats, still hangs open, the helium balloons lay deflated on the floor, sad and crushed, and what remains of her birthday presents, the ones that haven't been reclaimed by the givers, have been confined to a box on her chair with the cards. Even her mousepad, a photo of Leo, still lays on her desk.

"It's all yours." Arthur tells her. "I'll get your check." He disappears leaving her to look around her office, her old office. Beside the calendar hangs a drawing that the accountant, Bea's, granddaughter painted just for Moira three Christmases ago, and her mug from Leah still sits with a plethora of pens in it. She puts the mug in the box and then the drawing, the calendar.

The rent would always be paid; she could probably negotiate a higher wage and get a better apartment, or a house! She wouldn't have to go on the dreaded job hunt. No interviews, no new people, no new commute. She picks up her mouse pad, faded from the years of use.

"It's yours." Arthur repeats, returning with an envelope clutched in his skeletal fingertips.

"All mine, huh?" She looks out the bay window where she can see her BMW parked, but not in the usual reserved parking space then she feels Arthur comes close behind her, too close, and takes a deep breath inhaling the scent of her hair. She shudders with reminiscent disgust.

"There were some people who took their presents back but I told them off, though. I told them that they were being disrespectful and you'd come back. That you understood me and you'd come back."

"You should have mailed my check." she turns to face him, taking several steps away from him as she does.

"I needed to see you." He confesses, stepping closer; he waves her check in the air, "This was the only way."

"You couldn't call and apologize?"

"Is that what you want? You want to hear me say that I'm sorry?" A voice suddenly bubbling under with anger.

How foolish for her to have, even for the briefest moment, considered this, thought about returning to *this*. She once again looks around the office, inhaling the scent of old paper and toner. That fleeting moment of consideration makes her cringe and she holds out her hand for her check, which he hands over without a word. Gathering strength, she pushes past him, gripping tightly her box of belongings and one last time turns to face him once she is in the doorway.

"I want you to know that I won't come back here solely because you keep smelling my hair and I hate that."

"I can stop!" he calls after her as she turns on her high heel and heads towards the exit stopping only briefly to say goodbye to Leah, who pouts her bottom lip like a toddler; she asks Leah to thank her coworkers for the presents and to tell them she says "Hi."

Leah calls back to Moira and for a moment thinks about ignoring her, thinks about hurrying away but she can't. She turns back to Leah, a kind smile playing at her lips when she looks at the girl's tearful face.

"Here, I want you to have these." Leah takes her dangling golden earrings from her ears. The woven threads of gold metal in the shape of a delicate leaf, accented with green beads and long, brown and black striped feathers hanging down are heavy in Moira's hands. In all the time she has known Leah, she has never seen the girl not wearing these earrings. In a picture Leah showed her where she was in a sparkling lavender dress for a wedding, she was still wearing these earrings.

"I can't take these."

"Please. Then you can always think of me."

"Oh Leah." She sighs and they embrace over the top of the desk. She takes Leah's face in her hands and wipes the tears with her thumbs. "This is so sweet, thank you. Just know that everything is going to be okay. Okay?" Leah nods and they hug again. "Listen, Leah, you need to get out of here. Find a new job and when you do, call me. We'll celebrate." Moira pats Leah's cheeks as she nods, then turns and pushes out the door into the fresh air and sunshine. Her office is no longer her office. Her routine can no longer be returned to, her commute erased. Skylit is now just part of her past.

She wonders if she will ever let Charles Kent just be a part of her past, too, but one accomplishment at a time; she can't wait to tell Leo what happened. To recap how cool and confident she was. This is going to be the new her.

Strong and fearless.

She gets out of her car at her apartment complex grabbing her purse and the bottle of Snapple she bought at the gas station opting to leave her box of Skylit in the trunk. One day, she thinks, she will bring it inside and remember her past...maybe once she finds a new job.

For now, she is strong and fearless.

Moira, donning her new earrings, has no trepidations with looking for a new, exciting job, starting a new, exciting chapter in her life and though nothing inside the hall has changed, the antique smell still lingers and the lights still buzz and flicker, this afternoon everything seems brighter, sweeter. Even the humming lights make a triumphant music as she approaches her door.

Her door.

Her heart beats in her ears, drowning out the sound of the lights, her breath catches in her throat. Her door sits half open.

Chapter 7
The Attack, The Broken Glass, and The Two Fishes

Yesterday Moira would have run, she would have hidden in her car. She would have called the police or called John—he would protect her, he always tells her she's like a daughter to him—today, however, Moira is fearless. She may be terrified and trembling but she is fearless. Silently, gripping the wall, she slides to her door and peers inside. Armed only with her Snapple bottle, she goes inside and she sees him standing in the middle of her apartment looking down at his phone. The man with the Jeep who lives upstairs; the man who thinks she's impolite. Fury rushes over her body, her face goes hot with rage and fear and panic.

"What are you doing in here?" she screams, as she unleashes a violent tirade of verbal and physical attacks on the man who turns and raises his hands to defend himself, crying out for her to stop. She slams her glass bottle into his face several times before it shatters, slicing his temple and making him stumble backwards, one hand grabbing at his head, the other trying to hold Moira back.

"What are you doing?" she repeats, hysterically, pounding her fist into his chest, his jaw, his arms.

"Stop!" he begs, "I can explain!" desperate to block her slaps and punches and her claws that catch into the skin of his neck but she is relentless. "Stop!" he growls again, finally using all his strength to stop her assault. He grabs her hands and aggressively throws her down onto the sofa, pinning her under his weight, jabbing his knee into her groin and holding her arms above her head. Moira is startled by how easily he overcame her, how heavy his slender body is holding her down; she tries to wriggle a hand free, but the grip on her wrist is unyielding.

The stranger tells her repeatedly to calm down, to listen to him, but she won't, she can't. She struggles against him desperate to free herself just as he is desperate to keep her secured and unable to hit him anymore. He winces as the blood from a cut above his eyebrow slides into his eye. As he tries to blink away the pain, she spits in his other eye in an attempt to blind him but he only squeezes his eyes shut and groans; his groan isn't angry but pained.

"Let me go!"

"I will let you go. I will but you have to please, *please,* stop hitting me." His eyes are still closed as he says this and she's surprised by the gentle tone of his voice, the pleading. He opens his eyes and looks down at her with the lightest, most golden-brown eyes she's ever seen, almost translucent. "Please don't hit me." he repeats quietly, slowly lifting, releasing her hands and then pushing off from the back of the sofa to create distance. She quickly rights herself on the sofa, pulling down her skirt and straightening her shirt and collar as the man stumbles back towards the credenza, holding his bleeding head.

"What are you doing in here?" Moira snarls, her hands clenching into tight fists, ready to strike again.

He answers where he leans on the credenza, staring down at the ash-colored wood, "There were two guys..."

"So? You just come into my apartment?" She barks. He doesn't move, he doesn't immediately reply as he catches his pained breath. "Well?"

The man finally turns to her, "I heard a loud crash down here. Like breaking glass and it was loud. I came down and I heard voices. I was worried about you when I saw—"

"Glass? Glass..." She looks around her floor, at the mess on her floor. Gravel from Leo's tank is spread out into the carpeting surrounded by shards of glass and puddles of water. His coral lay broken, his crocodile is smashed and the plants lay dying in the rubble. A scream escapes her throat making the stranger jump as she throws herself into the wreckage, her hands pushing through the glass and water and gravel with no regard to the edges cutting into her palms, into her knees.

"No, no, no." The stranger cries, rushing forward and pulling Moira up by her shoulders. She weakly tries to smack him away, to make him let go but all she can see now is her tears. "I got your fish."

"Wha-what?" She blinks away the tears blurring her vision so she can look at him, her eyes wide with hope.

"Unless you had more than one fish, I got him out. Now listen, though."

"You got him? You saved Leo?"

The man sighs, "Yes, but…"

"Where is he?" Moira looks around her apartment searching for some evidence that Leo is still alive and that he is okay. The man goes into her kitchen where he retrieves a juice glass filled with water and Leo floating peacefully in the center. "Leo!" she cries, rushing over and snatching the cup from the man. She asks Leo if he is alright, did he get hurt, and tells him she will never leave him again.

"Could you listen to me for a minute?" The man, now slumped down on her sofa holding his sleeve to his temple to soak up the blood rushing out, asks her while staring at his feet. "Just listen."

"What? What did you come in here for? What happened?"

"I was in my apartment, I heard breaking glass and then a loud ass crash. It shook the walls so I came out into the hall and I heard voices coming from down here. One guy let another guy into your apartment so I came in. They bolted through the window when I told them I was calling the police." he motions towards the shattered window and torn screen.

"I don't understand." she whimpers, holding Leo to her chest. "I don't understand."

"I saw your fish so I got a cup of water and I called the police. They should be on their way now. I called John."

"You saved him before you called the police?" Moira raises her wide eyes to the stranger's face who nods hesitantly, unsure if that's the right or the wrong thing to have done. "You're a hero. Wait, you went into my kitchen, you went into my cabinets?" Her wide eyes go narrow, her brow furrows with agitation.

"Uh…" the man rubs the back of his head awkwardly and looks up to the ceiling hoping to possibly find the correct answer there. "Well, I wasn't going to go all the way back upstairs when you fish was all the way down here dying, was I?"

Moira finds herself unable to reply as the tears well up in her eyes, anxiety overwhelming her making her hands shake and her knees buckle. She turns and sets Leo beside the TV and disappears down the hall and locks herself into the bathroom leaving Leo alone with his savior. In the mirror, she watches herself breathe, telling herself that she is strong.

She is strong.

Then it dawns on her, the man who saved Leo, who took it upon himself to stop potential burglars—who could have been shot! —is sitting on her sofa bleeding from his head. Her floor is saturated with water and Snapple Fruit Punch, and the police are coming. What if the stranger wants to press charges on her for assault? What if he left, bleeding profusely from his head, possibly dying? He could get lightheaded and fall down the stairs. She'd be a murderer!

Her mind racing, jumping from one bad scenario to the next, she goes to her linen closet where she retrieves her first aid kit and hurries back out to the living room where the man still sits on the sofa with his head hanging low as he leans heavily on his knees. His blue plaid printed shirt is stained red from her Snapple across his right shoulder, the white t-shirt with the Milwaukee Brewers logo underneath is stained, as well. Seeing him brings a wave of tears to her eyes, a sense of panic and guilt, confusion.

Taking a deep breath, she steadies herself and then moves to the sofa where she sits down beside him, lowering herself softly to the cushions so she won't startle him. "Let me help you." she says, trying to summon the managerial tone she has taken with people so many times in her past. The voice shakes and fails.

"I'm alright." he mutters, unmoving.

"Here." She hands him the plastic container and leaves the room again, returning with a few damp washcloths from her linen closet. "You're not alright." Moira examines his face and the damage she inflicted; blood runs down the right side of his face where the glass bottle sliced into his temple and eyebrow, his lip is bleeding and puffy, and his left cheek is broken under his eye from where her grandmother's claddagh caught his skin. Without warning, she places the cold washcloth against his bloodied temple making him flinch back and pull away with a yelp; she grabs his arm and pulls him back, "Let me." He winces again as she wipes away the blood.

In silence they sit as she tends to each wound with care first applying a butterfly stitch to the gash over his eyebrow and a bandage over his temple. He whines as she applies alcohol to his cheek but she ignores him.

"I ruined your shirt." she comments, her voice is only a murmur between them. "And this will probably leave a scar." her trembling fingertips gently trace the butterfly bandage over his eye before dropping onto her lap, wringing nervously, twisting her grandmother's ring around.

"It's okay." he shakes his throbbing head and stands to stretch his back then he flops back down with a moan. "You got any aspirin?"

"Yes." Moira hops up from the sofa and hurries back into the bathroom to retrieve the aspirin, bringing back to him Tylenol, aspirin, and ibuprofen to choose from. With shaking hands that don't go unnoticed by the stranger, she hands him the bottles.

"It's going to be okay." he tells her softly, his voice calm and low; she nods and turns to Leo in his cup on the credenza.

"Oh Leo, what am I going to do?" A few tears fall to the surface of Leo's water where he stares up at her, his fins slowly waving back and forth, his mouth opening and closing slowly taking in the air. The stranger on the sofa scoffs making her turn and glare at him, "What?" she bites.

"You aren't talking to me; you're talking to your fish."

"Yea?"

"My name is Leo." He raises his eyes to meet hers and cocks an eyebrow, "Leo Fisch."

"That's not funny." Moira tells him flatly, holding his gaze with narrowed eyes.

"It is. Well, it's Elliot Fisch but people call me Leo."

"Well," she turns away, her eyes falling back to her beloved fish, "I'll just call you Elliot then...we can't have two Leos." Her voice breaks and she finds herself staring down at Leo unable to move, unable to think clearly.

The stranger, Elliot, stands making her turn to him; she is intimidated by his height and the memory of how fast he was able to pin her down makes her take a step back but he isn't paying attention to her. He rolls his neck; he looks down at his socked feet standing in puddles of water and Snapple. He looks up at the ceiling as if testing his level of dizziness, contemplating a concussion. While he's distracted, Moira picks up Leo and crosses over to the dining room where she sets the cup down and stares down at the fish.

"Thanks for all these options." Elliot tells her, remaining planted in the living room still holding the bottles of medicine. "I'll take the ibuprofen." He shakes the blue Advil bottle and sets the other two on the credenza.

"Okay." She slides over and takes the unwanted bottles from where he set them and then takes the Advil from his hand and pops it open for him. Her hands tremble as she shakes two pills out of the bottle onto his open palm and then, after several unsuccessful tries, returns the child-safe lid back to the top. The man watches as she disappears back down the short, narrow hall into the bathroom and continues to watch as she reappears and heads back over to the fish on the kitchen table.

Elliot nods and rocks on his feet, his lips pursed, eyes wandering around the room; Moira watches him sideways, her jaw tight, teeth clenched from nerves. When he settles, he holds the pills out to her and tilts his head, gazing at her with soft eyes until she looks at him.

"No thank you." she tells him, turning away again.

"Perhaps…" he says, a small smile gracing his thin mouth, "I could have some water?"

"Oh!" Moira goes into the kitchen where she retrieves a cup of water. "I'm the dumbest person I know." He chuckles, an obligatory laugh, and thanks her, swallowing the pills greedily as she looks at the shattered fish tank. "What did I do?" Her eyes fill with tears.

Elliot looks around, too, "I can help you clean up if you want. I don't mind."

"The police will probably want to talk to you."

"Probably. While we wait, we can get some of this glass—"

"I never do anything to anyone. I never talk to anyone! My best friend is a fish for crying out loud! Why would someone do this?" She spins and goes back over to Leo where she looks down at his little body drifting around the small glass. Her shoulders start to shake, the tears threaten to overtake her strength. "I'm unemployed and my only friend is a fish. What the heck did I ever do to anyone?"

Torn between sympathy and pity, Elliot watches her, unable to find any words of comfort to help soothe her as she gets lost in her own despair while his head is a symphony of drums beating him to a nauseous dizziness. He swallows hard and steps over to her and places a gentle hand on her shoulder. "It'll be okay." She flinches at his touch so he pulls back quickly and returns to the sofa where he eases himself down and waits for the ibuprofen to work. Moira strokes Leo's head and breathes deeply, trying to calm her fraying nerves and Elliot, slumped on the sofa, touches his tender lip gingerly.

"You shouldn't have come in here. They could have killed you." she states suddenly, turning to him, scowling.

He laughs, a short, unamused scoff, "*You* could have killed me." He meets her glare with one of his own.

"Are you going to press charges against me? For assaulting you?" she looks down at the cuts on her palms, willing them to stop stinging.

His glower lightens, he smirks and his eyes twinkle playfully "And admit that I got beat up by a girl? Never!" His eyes move over her, thoughtfully examining her face, her shaking hands wringing in front of her stomach, her jiggling foot, "It'll be okay." He tells her. "Not that those words are all that helpful, but it will be." Leaning his head on the back of the couch, he closes his eyes, shutting out the burning brightness around him. "I didn't know they made things in glass bottles anymore."

"Snapple is phasing them out." she replies bluntly as she goes back down the hall to the bathroom where she retrieves an armful of towels. She carefully picks up large shards of glass and places them in the bin hidden beside the credenza, conscious of the throbbing in her palms and knees. In a moment, Elliot is beside her helping, making small talk that she cannot reply to, that she cannot keep up with. The man finds anything to talk about just to keep the silence at bay from fishing to Friday fish fries to kayaking to bald eagles.

He once had a goldfish named Little Jerry Seinfeld.

Chapter 8
The Question, The Rejection, and The Whole Pan of Brownies

The police didn't stay long with their questioning and they spoke more to Elliot, as a firsthand witness, than to Moira, which was a relief to her but when they left, she was once again alone with a stranger whom she has nothing more to say to and yet doesn't want him to leave. She turns to Elliot, her mouth open to speak though she doesn't know what she is going to say when she stops and looks at him. Elliot is leaning down over Leo's cup looking at the little fish,

"How you doing, buddy? You okay? You know, my name is Leo, too."

"He looks more like a Leo than you do." Moira quips, taking a seat on the sofa.

"You think that a little pink fish looks like a Leo?" Elliot laughs. Moira nods and looks away; she looks at her reflection in the black of the television screen, to the window where a cool breeze pushes the curtains out, where Leo's tank should be. "My sister tells me I look like someone who would be a fan of Fallout Boy. I don't really know what that means but I don't like Fallout Boy."

"So your sister thinks you look like a teenage girl?"

Elliot laughs, "I don't know, but I think I look more like a Leo than a pink fish. He is cute though. He may be cuter than me." When Moira doesn't reply, the silence settles over them instantly with a heavy, tedious presence. He takes a deep breath and takes a seat next to her on the sofa; the ibuprofen has done nothing to ease his throbbing head.

At first, she is startled by his nearness but when she looks at him, at his pained eyes and tight jaw the nervousness melts away, replaced by guilt. When he smiles at her, the guilt, too, disappears. For the first time since this morning, she feels as though everything is really going to be okay.

"I'm sorry." She tells him, lowering her gaze to her feet.

"It's okay, Darlin'. It'll be okay. My head will stop hurting, John will fix your window, and you can continue doing whatever it is you do." He stands and walks over to the end table in front of the window, his eyes down at her painting of a cardinal. "You paint this?"

She nods.

"It's really good." He smiles, making her blush and avert her gaze past him to the feeder outside. Elliot follows her gaze but seeing nothing, he looks back at her then returns to the sofa with a groan when a wave of dizziness hits him.

"Oh goodness…are you okay?" she asks him, unable to look at his face for very long.

"I'm alright. I suppose I should probably get going, huh?"

"Oh, right. You're right. I shouldn't be keeping you like this." The thought of him leaving fills her with dread, compounds her loneliness and yet she has nothing to offer by way of conversation.

"You're not keeping me. It's alright. I do have some errands to run but, but it's okay." He smiles again, "I just don't want to be keeping you."

Her mind wanders to the brownies she baked him sitting wrapped up in her kitchen; she thinks she should go get them. She should apologize and thank him for helping her, for saving Leo. These two phrases seem impossible but she knows she needs to say something.

"You're not keeping me from anything but if you need to go…" There are tears in her voice and eyes as she looks at her broken window, her wet carpet, and Leo's broken tank. Her newspaper is soaked, so is her new crossword book. She jumps when he places a hand on her shoulder so he pulls it back.

"Sorry." He holds up both hands in defense. "Sorry."

"It's okay. I'm just…just jumpy, I guess. I just can't understand why this happened. You know? Just…today was going to be the start of…something. I don't know." Elliot furrows his brow as she talks, showing pity that makes her flush and look away. "I'm sorry. I guess…you don't have to wait for John. I'll be okay."

Hesitantly, he stands, his lips pursed. "Yea, I suppose. I'm supposed to be driving to Seattle tomorrow and I haven't even started to pack."

"You're going to Seattle? Just like that?"

He tilts his head, "Just like that? I guess." He shrugs. "It's been a rough couple of months so I just want to get out of town for a while."

"Oh…" She looks at him and nods with wide eyes and tight lips.

He rubs the back of his head, "My sister lives out there. I haven't seen in her or her husband in a long time so I figure now's as good a time as any."

"I've never even left Wisconsin." She sighs and looks up at him where he stands in her living room. "How long does it take to get to Seattle."

"Two or three days. Depending on what I do along the way. I guess, usually I take detours to find new things but…I'm quite eager to see them and I told my sister this morning I'd drive straight through. That's probably a lie, though. There's tons of cool shit to see on the way out there."

He gives her an indifferent shrug and crosses his arms over his chest, peering at her with thoughtful, inquiring eyes that make her shift uncomfortably and stare at his feet, his wet socks. "I don't have to leave tomorrow." Elliot now shifts from one foot the other, his fingers tapping his biceps. "What are you doing tomorrow?" He asks, planted where he stands.

"Oh, me? I don't know. Get a new fish tank, I guess." She shrugs, "Leo can't live in that little cup."

"Not a bad idea." He rubs the back of his head, scratching his fingers through his thick hair. "Since I don't *have* to leave tomorrow, maybe you'd like to go to dinner with me? Tomorrow night?" His voice is confident, his demeanor friendly, but the tilt of his head and the shine in his eyes makes her angry. Where does he get his confidence from?

"No." She answers flatly, unable to focus on any one feature of his face so she turns her narrowed eyes to the broken window. "I don't think so." The disgust in her voice surprises him, it surprises herself, and shakes his self-assured poise; his eyes betray his disappointment and once again she is guilt stricken.

"Harsh but okay." He replies in a lighthearted tone despite his melancholy smile. "Well, I'm out at six tomorrow so I guess I will see you around sometime."

"Six in the morning?" she says to the window. She can feel Leo's eyes burning into her from the juice glass, furious at her for her rejection. She's furious at herself. "You're just going to get in your car, and drive across the country?" She finally brings her eyes to his.

He shrugs. "I guess. It's what I do. Go where the work is." She nods and he glances at his watch before turning his eyes back to her face with a softness in them that makes her guilt tenfold. "There's a beautiful world out there. I would suggest you try and see some of it once. Just, you know, get in the car and go someplace. Anyplace. Get out of Wisconsin once."

Moira scoffs, "I'll get right on that." Her bitterness is thick as she looks back to the broken fish tank.

"Listen," he steps towards her, "if you need anything, anything at all, I'm right upstairs, okay?" He pulls out his wallet where he retrieves a business card that she takes with shaking fingers. "Just give me a call, okay? Or, you know, I'm right upstairs. You can come give me a knock. I'll be back in about an hour."

Moira looks down at the card and reads the name a few times over in her head: *Leo Fisch Photography*. Internally, she contemplates the odds of meeting a real-life Leo Fish, as Elliot watches her examining his card.

"You're a photographer? That explains the camera."

"Yea. I found out I can't work in an office when I was 18 and can't work retail when I was 20. I'm too hyperactive. Got to keep moving."

Moira nods, still staring at the card. "You're very kind, Leo Fisch."

He runs his hand through his hair, brushing it all the way back then letting fall back over his forehead. "I try." There is a moment of tense silence before he speaks again, "Uh, okay. I guess I'll see you around."

"Okay."

"Okay." He nods once and heads back to the door, this time there is no hesitation with his exit, it is swift without another word and with the clicking of the latch she is alone again. Her first instinct is to sob, to curl into a ball on the sofa and never get up again but with a deep breath, she steadies herself, swallows back the tears, and squares her shoulders.

"What the heck did I ever do to anyone, Leo?" she asks the fish in the cup who watches her movements closely. Moira gets up and locks the door and then scoops up Leo's glass and cuddles it to her chest. "Are you okay?" She asks him.

"That guy saved my life."

"That guy did. Elliot…Leo. That guy…my goodness what is wrong with me? He asked me out. A cute guy asks me out and I refuse and I didn't just refuse. Oh no, of course not. A hot guy asks me out, tall and handsome, *kind*, and I refuse as though I'm disgusted."

"I noticed." Leo grumbles. "You can go up there now or when he gets back."

"Oh yea. Tell him I changed my mind and he can ask me out again so I can say yes? He will laugh in my face. He has plans now. He's going to Seattle." She moans and falls over on the sofa, "I didn't even thank him." Covering her face with her hands, she groans again, disbelief dripping off her like a cold sweat. "I'm so dumb. So, so dumb! I'm not just dumb. I'm a terrible person. And where is John!"

"Moira?" Leo says quietly. "You should go with that guy. You can go to Seattle."

"You've been out of the water too long, my little love."

"I'm serious. You can pack a bag, put me in a Tupperware and we can go. I want to see the Space Needle." Leo's fins flail about the water as his little body wiggles back and forth in the small confines of the cup.

"With him?" Moira raises her eyebrows.

"With him."

"When he said get in the car and go, I don't think he meant *his* car."

"He didn't *not* say his car either."

Moira rolls her eyes and pushes back into the sofa and stares up at the ceiling. "I should have gone to dinner with him. He's cute. Did you see his eyes?"

"To be fair, it was probably the least you could do after giving him a concussion."

"And a scar and a headache and a bad afternoon. And for not holding the door or not thanking him." The tears fill her eyes and quickly cascade down her flushed cheeks. Today was the day she was going to conquer her future, to take her life back, but all she has now is a broken window and guilt lying like a rock in her stomach.

She is painfully reminded that she'll probably never see the Space Needle, or Mount Rushmore, or the Grand Canyon; she'll never go to London or Rome or Costa Rica to see the Cloud Forest.

Now, she is going to sit on the sofa and eat the brownies she baked for the cute man with the stunning eyes who lives upstairs.

Chapter 9
The Clock, The Knock, and The Hiding Spot

Sleep remains elusive even at 2AM to Moira's heavy eyes; Leo too remains awake floating silently in the little juice glass on the bedside table in the darkness of the bedroom. Moira stares up at the ceiling, seeing nothing in the blackness but straining her eyes to see anything and her ears to hear anything in her apartment or above. This evening, after John left having replaced her window, she took solace in hearing Elliot's gentle footfall from the apartment above.

The moment she looked into his golden eyes she knew he wasn't Charles Kent, she knew he was safe and even though she doesn't know what that means exactly, she could feel it—safety—when he was sitting beside her on the sofa. And she never thanked him. Such a simple phrase, meaningful and gracious, and she never said it. Now he will be heading west and she won't get the chance to say it, to tell him that she really does appreciate what he did for her today. Saving Leo.

Instead, she got annoyed with him, she shot down a pleasant offer for a date, she never said goodbye. Take care. Have a nice trip. He left in silence and now his footsteps have gone quiet; he must be asleep.

She should be asleep but right now she is certain she will never sleep again. "Leo?"

"Yea?"

"I'm frightened."

"It'll be okay. Just try to sleep." The fish replies but she is already reaching for Elliot's business card that sits next to Leo's cup. She holds the card in her hand, unable to read it in the dark, for a long time, unmoving except the uncontrollable quake of her fingers. She feels the canvas material with one hand, tracing over the embossed lettering of his name and phone number; she turns the card over in her hand, her movements slow in contrast to her racing mind. A thought hits her. She swings her legs over the edge of the bed.

Wearing only her sleep shirt that hangs to her thighs she slips into the hallway, casting a nervous glance around but she sees and hears nothing but the typical buzz of the lights. She moves down the hall, nearly tiptoeing, to the staircase where she casts her eyes up the flight and takes a deep breath continuing to creep up the stairs to his apartment. She reads the numbers, 204, on his door and waits, listening. She listens until her ears ache. There are no sounds, no movements coming from within the apartment but her heart beating strongly begins to drown out the world around her as she places a gentle palm on the worn door. Inside she is sure that he will be in his bedroom sound asleep unaware that he lay awake on his sofa watching the clock.

She knocks so softly she barely hears it but then she hears movement inside, she's sure of it. Could he possibly be awake? Her heart spasms and chokes her. What is she going to say to him? What will he say to see her standing in her nightie at his door? Before he can stumble to the door, she scurries away, back to the safety of her apartment where she can be alone with her imprudent and idiotic thoughts.

She crawls back into her bed and pulls the covers to her chin, listening to her breathing. Desperate to catch her breath, to stop her legs from shaking. What was she thinking? What was she going to do?

She shakes her head at herself and rolls over, facing Leo, and closes her eyes tightly.

The atmosphere in the room hasn't changed, it's still heavy with trepidation and thick with anxiety. A foreboding nervousness covers her like a quilt, warming her cheeks and making her sweat. It's only paranoia making the hairs on her arms stand on end, sending a chill down her spine. She can't catch her breath and her eyes dart around the darkness.

"Leo!" Moira whispers, panicked, "I didn't lock the door when I came back!"

"Go lock it now."

"It's too late. It's too late." Someone has come into her apartment; there are voices, footsteps. A man, younger sounding and exhilarated exclaims in a whisper that the door is unlocked and another man tells him to shut up and they close themselves into her home.

"Hide!" Leo hisses to Moira, who without hesitation snatches up his cup and scurries to the closet where she shoves herself into a corner and covers herself with the hanging clothes. The closet is barely two feet deep so she crushes herself into a ball bringing her knees up to her chest so tight no air can reach her lungs. She bows her head over Leo's cup and holds her breath. The footsteps and hushed voices come into her room cautiously at first but when they see the room is empty, they relax and turn on the light.

"I know this bitch has money." An angry voice growls throwing open her dresser drawers one after the other but finding nothing of value.

"She's got something." The older voice says, going through her bedside table drawer. "Fuck!" he snarls, slamming the drawer shut so hard her clock is knocked to the floor. Furious, he slams open the sliding closet door and turns on the light. Moira closes her eyes and waits. The movement of the clothes around her brings tears to her eyes but she knows she can't make a sound.

"Look at this shit!" The man calls over to his partner. They cast their gaze upon the Gucci and Prada and Versace bags lined up on the top shelf of the closet. Every birthday, every Christmas, every Please Forgive Us present she has received from her parents they snatch by the excited armful. When they can't hold anymore in their arms, they hurry like rats down the hall and out of her apartment; they don't even try to close the door quietly as one of them kicks it shut with a slam.

After the door is closed, the apartment is draped in silence. For so long, so many minutes of this heavy solitude, Moira remains unmoving in the closet only letting long, quiet breaths ease from her quivering lips.

"I have to get out of here." She whispers to Leo in a voice barely audible. "I have to get out of here."

Chapter 10
The Morning, The Monsters, and The Open Road

The orange glow from the streetlamps cast everything in a hazy light and drag eerie shadows across the parking lot in a tremulous, claustrophobic dance. There are no stars to shine as the city lights will not relinquish the sky that they have conquered and they are not to be outdone by simple nature. They offer no warmth to those who venture out into the predawn coldness like they do to those within their walls. The city never fades, not in light and not in sounds; the distant traffic still moves, an ambulance, and that stupid dog.

Moira hugs her legs just as tight, as she did when she was in the closet, listening to the sounds of the city's heartbeat mingling with her own. Every bouncing shadow causes her to jump so she tries to focus on her peep-toe espadrilles that are tied up securely around her ankle, ending where they meet the denim of her skinny jeans.

"I'm scared, Leo." She whimpers, still starting at her shoes, her fingers tugging gently on the feathers of Leah's earrings. The night is so cold, the cracked concrete beneath her stinging as though she were sitting on ice; she shivers though not only for the cold but for her fear.

Leo hides in a thick plastic plant trying to keep himself warm; he peeks out from the leaves, "It'll be okay" he says then quickly shuffles back into the plant, invisible to anyone who might glance at the Tupperware sitting on the ground beside her.

For a time, she dozes off long enough for the horizon to transform from black into pink and gold, bright with a new sun. 6 o'clock must be approaching; her hands return to tremoring, her heart swims in the pit of her stomach, and her head. Her head aches, pounding between her ears; she is sure it will explode but a noise distracts her.

The back of the Jeep opens, there is movement, shuffling, then it closes again and she goes tense against the driver's side front wheel where she rests as Elliot comes around to the front. He jumps and gasps when he sees her.

"Shit." He mutters, hand over his heart as he slumps against the vehicle, eyes wide with bewilderment. Moira jumps to her feet, her arms wrapped around herself.

"We're going with you." She takes a bold tone, managerial and commanding.

Still leaning against the Jeep, he raises his eyebrows, "We're?"

"Yes, we're." In a fluid motion, she swoops down and picks up Leo's plastic container and holds it out towards the startled stranger who runs his hand through his hair then down his face, rubbing his eyes on the way down. He rubs his unshaven chin, looking up to the sky allowing the silence to drag on, making her heart throb in her throat.

"Have you lost your mind?" he finally asks, meeting her eye and sighing, not hiding the agitation in his voice.

"They came back last night. They robbed me but I hid in the closet until they left."

His eyes widen, face dropping with concern, "Did you call the police?"

She shakes her head, "Look." She quickly and gently sets Leo at her feet then snatches up her packed duffle bag. "I packed everything I need for a week. I packed a bag. Get in the car and go."

"When I said that, I didn't mean *my* car." He says as he takes the bag from her hands. "Now, I'm going to take this, we're going to go back to your apartment and we're going to call the police."

"No, please." She begs, stepping towards him. "Please. You told me. You told me to get out of Wisconsin once."

"I'll be honest with you, Sweetheart, I didn't really mean with me."

"That's okay." She replies, watching him with pleading eyes; she bites her lip and tries to read the thoughts scattered across his face.

"This is crazy." He shakes his head and turns away from her, stopping at the tailgate of his Jeep. "This is fucking crazy." He turns back to her, the handles of her bag clenched tightly between his fingers. "You're a crazy person."

"No." She pauses, "Well, I mean, maybe a little. I'm actually pretty boring."

"Boring?" Once again, he leans on the vehicle and looks at her with contemplative eyes moving over her face. "You won't go to dinner with me but you'll go 2000 miles on a week-long trip across the country with me?"

She absorbs his words, inhales them into her lungs, tastes them on her lips; they drip with rationality and common sense. She knows it's crazy—that she is being crazy—but she's made up her mind to get out of her one-bedroom apartment, to get out, at least once, of Wisconsin. "Uh, yes."

His golden eyes burn into her then flicker over to the horizon where the sun will soon be making its grand appearance. "This is insane." he shakes his head and turns away from her and in the split second before he opens up the tailgate of his vehicle her heart plummets but seeing him throw her bag into the back, she lets out a long, relieved breath. "Get in then." He says, pushing past her to go to the driver's side where he quickly opens the door and closes himself in with his wary, doubting thoughts.

Moira is quick to grab Leo and scurry to the passenger side where she clambers inside with no thought for Leo being tossed violently into the plastic sides. When she looks over at her new chauffer, he is mindlessly fingering his broken lip while the other hand loosely holds his keys on his jiggling knee.

It's the click of the seat belt that draws his attention back to the inside of the car and to his doe-eyed passenger watching him with unmasked fear on her face. He nods at her, his lips pursed but eyes friendly, though bewildered, "This'll be fun. Like a really random adventure." There is no confidence in his voice, only apprehension. Moira tries to smile at him, she wants to ease his anxiety, to let him know he hasn't made a mistake, but her lips waiver and fail; she quickly turns to situating Leo safely between her feet.

"All right then. Here we go." Elliot jams the keys in the ignition and the pair fall into silence thick as the city's haze on the horizon. Unable to bring her eyes to his face, Moira nervously watches his hands that move with such precise fluidity, a practiced artform, that she finds every motion captivating. It is with ease that he guides them from the parking lot onto the darkened streets heading for a road—a freeway—Moira is unfamiliar with. His hands are thin and smooth with trim, short nails that drum uncomfortably on the steering wheel, both hands draped at 12 o'clock. She only breaks free of her hypnotization on his hands when he speaks.

"Well, so, I guess we'll be in the car for a while and I have some, you know," He waves his hand around, trying to think of the words he wants to say. "Things. I guess."

She raises her eyebrows but says nothing.

"So here," he raises a can of Monster Energy Drink from the cup holder between them. "This is the first necessity of travel. If you ever feel that I am getting a bit hyperactive, just take it away from me. I won't be offended if you tell me I'm talking too much. Well, my feelings will be a little bit hurt but I'll get over it. I've been told I talk too much and I can't really argue. And here," he takes a swig from the can and replaces it so he can point to a compartment behind the gear shift, "this is the candy stash. It currently has Hershey with almonds. I'm not saying this is the only candy I eat, but Hershey with almonds is the shit. Feel free to help yourself to as many as you like. Okay?"

Moira nods.

"I like the Hershey toffee ones, too. But we can add to it whatever you like."

She nods again.

"There is no smoking in my car, not that I think you smoke but I don't. I once smoked some cigarettes when I was a teenager with my sister and it made me throw up. So stupid. I smoked pot once and threw up then, too. I personally find it best not to inhale anything but, you know, air. What else? Oh, all trash must go into the trash bag…uh…" he casts a look behind her seat, "somewhere. You as the passenger will now be responsible for locating this. Ah," he laughs, "it's nice having a passenger." He takes another drink from his can. "Behind you is a cooler that is filled with Monsters and food. I don't drink out of plastic bottles of water so I have a water bottle that I refill with a gallon in the cooler. But we can stop and get you one, a water bottle. Plastic bottles are the doom of the Earth so I try to avoid them. But you can help yourself to anything in the cooler, too. You want a Monster, go for it. Am I making you feel more comfortable or irritated?"

She offers a shy smile and purses her lips, "You aren't *driving* me crazy yet. See what I did there?" She keeps her voice low, barely able to look him in the eye.

He laughs and offers his hand up for a high five that she returns with only the tips of her fingers. "Nice one!"

Smiling, she turns to look out the passenger window where she casts her gaze on the darkness that envelopes the city. There are no lights on inside the houses that they pass and no open signs on any of the store fronts. The headlights cast obscure shapes down the street, shadowy trapeze artists dancing fluidly. Moira watches in awe, not at the performance of the headlights, but that she is seeing it.

The engine purrs as they speed down the unmetered on ramp; Elliot checks his blind spot then coasts to the far-left lane. Once there, he settles back in his seat, his hands relax down at the bottom of the wheel and he turns a smile towards his passenger, "This is it. 2000 miles to go."

She looks over at him and for the first time since they got into the car, their eyes meet. "That's a lot of miles."

He nods, "Yep. There's no going back now, though. Oh yea, one more thing. This car doesn't stop until I need gas." His face scrunches with thought then he lights up with a smile, "Or until we need more candy."

Moira, leaning her head back on the seat and nods, trying to exercise circular breathing to slow her racing heart. She turns her attention back outside the window to the view of the passing city. "Do you mind..." her voice trails off, her eyes move back to his face, "Do you mind if I sleep for a little while? I didn't sleep much last night."

"Of course not." The driver replies glancing at her as she slouches down in her seat and rests her head against her shoulder and the window. "There's a pillow right behind your seat if you like."

"No thank you. You might have lice."

Elliot laughs and rolls his eyes, "Could you do me one thing before you go to sleep?"

"Sure." She murmurs.

"Would you please tell me your name. I still don't know it." After a second of silence, he looks over at her sleeping peacefully nestled into her own nest of hair. Her breathing is even and slow. "I guess not." He whispers, turning his attention back to the road that belongs to him and two semi-trucks.

When Moira wakes, she finds herself looking out the passenger window, at farmland stretching for miles, choking on instinctual panic as she desperately tries to recall where she is and how she got here. Beside her, Elliot now donning his Warby Parker sunglasses, sings along with a quiet song on the radio that Moira doesn't recognize. His fingers tap a rhythm out on the steering wheel that doesn't match the beat of the music but this doesn't affect his contentment. He moves his head with the melody, every few lyrics slipping from between his lips.

"...*Maybe tomorrow, a new romance, no more sorrow...*" his words turn to a hum as he checks his mirrors, "*If your lonely heart breaks only the lonely...*" he coos softly, his lulling and peaceful voice trailing off into a hum as he switches lanes to move around a horse trailer. Moira watches his movements from her peripheral vision, keeping her lashes low to hide her eyes, realizing that he would likely be doing this same thing whether she had emburdened herself on him or not. She wonders, as she watches him, as she listens to him sing, what it's like to have his level of ease, to be so comfortable in one's own skin, a luxury not afforded to her.

The first song ends but his drum beat on the wheel doesn't stop; it only flows into some semblance of rhythm until the next song begins when he then adjusts the tapping to the low movement of the next song. "*When you were here before, couldn't look you in the eye...*" his sighs and glances around the road letting the song play solo. "*I wish I was special...you're so fucking special...*" When he looks at her, his song cuts off and he smiles, "Good morning, Darling!"

She twists her claddagh around her finger, eyes moving back and forth between the windshield and his face. Every time she looks at his face, she looks at his broken lip or his broken eyebrow still held together with the butterfly stitch she applied only yesterday. He's removed the bandage from his temple letting the cut breathe and heal on its own. Every time she looks at him, she is hit with another, stronger, pang of guilt.

"You okay? You're not going to be sick, are you? Because...not in my car."

"I'm, I'm okay."

"Good." He looks at his phone and skips the song that's playing. The song switches to an Alan Jackson song. "I hate country music."

Elliot tells her, still smiling, "But there are a couple I like, like this one."

Moira nods, her eyes unfocused on the radio.

He pushes back in his chair to stretch his back then cocks an eyebrow at her, a crooked grin on his face, "I told you we don't stop until the tank is on E." He taps the gas gauge on the dashboard but Moira only looks at him in reply, eyes wide, fingers twisting in her lap.

His smile broadens as he turns to look out the windshield, "But I will make an exception for you since you are new to the whole road trip thing. Okay? So, if you need to stop…"

"Yes, please." Moira blushes and nods quickly looking away from his pitying eyes. She directs her attention to Leo at her feet where he looks up at her from where he lay lazily on his hammock. "It'll be okay, Leo." She looks to the fish before looking back out the window. There is only a spattering of cars on the freeway now, a couple of trucks, and rolling golden farms on each side reaching to the lush, green woods that stretch across the brightly lit horizon. Occasionally a house disrupts the vast farm fields with a hard line from gold to green grass but as they drive on, heading west, the houses all but disappear and the rolling fields are replaced by forests from the distance with towering pines and shady Sugar Maples, Oaks and Ash. The thick trees devour the horizon and run to the freeway guardrail.

But as suddenly as the forest had conquered the view, the trees disappear ending for a green pasture dotted with lazy cows, typical white with black splotches.

"Oh! Leo, look! Cows!"

Elliot leans over and looks out her window to see but when Moira scoops the fish up from the floor and holds him up to the window, he realizes she isn't speaking to him.

"Ah," he nods and looks forward to the road again, "I thought you were talking to me."

"Oh…well…I wasn't."

He turns back to her with a knitted brow, "You can talk to me, you know."

"Oh, okay." She sets Leo back down at her feet carefully and shifts her body to face him. "What do you want to talk about?"

"What? Uh, I don't know. I can talk about anything, though. The Brewers game will be on later. I'm looking forward to that. You like baseball?"

"Uh…"

"That's okay but I'm going to have to kick you out of the car then. I can only converse with baseball people."

"Uh…I mean…"

He punches her shoulder playfully, "I'm joking. I'm joking. But you should always remember that baseball people are good people." Again, they drive on in silence until, after a short distance, he nods at a sign along the freeway, "Oh good. There's a gas station at the next exit." There is some relief to his words, a thankful sigh that there will be some distraction to their silent ride. The only sound is the quietly playing song on the radio, connected to Pandora on his phone, and the click-clack of his blinker indicating his smooth exit from the freeway.

At the gas station, Elliot pulls up to the pump, saying nothing when he gets out to top up his tank, Moira heads inside without a word to her driver. The bathroom is clean and unused with plastic flowers in every corner and paintings of flower fields on each wall. The air freshener is sickly sweet and the pastel walls remind her of the nursing home her grandmother had lived in before she died. Moira was only young but she recalls the pastel green walls, minty in color, vividly, though the scent in her grandmother's room was sterile. Still, both scents are sickly.

She grimaces at the memory as she uses the toilet and again when she runs the frigid water to wash her hands. It appears that no matter how long it runs through the tap, it will remain cold against her already trembling fingers. This was such a bad idea, she thinks, shaking her head at her reflection. What was she thinking?

This is Leo's fault!

Examining her face in the mirror, the bags under her sleep deprived eyes, the freckles that dance across her nose and cheeks, her chapped lips, she thinks she should call someone to come and get her. Of course, the only people she knows would be her parents. Her father would surely send someone to get her, wherever she is. He'll send a plane, a train, an army of junior partners on foot to retrieve her and take her back to safety. She watches her reflection helplessly as her bottom lip begins to quiver, accepting there is no one in her life who she would want to come to her rescue. She only has Leo and he can't drive!

She hastily dries her hands and steadies herself to go back to him, to her driver. Elliot is already paying at the register as she approaches; when he sees her, his face lights up with a smile and he hands her a Fruit Punch Snapple.

"I thought you might be thirsty and look," he taps the bottle, "It's plastic so I should be pretty safe." She accepts the offering, keeping her gaze on his hands. "I also got an extra gallon of water." He lifts the jug, a smile still playing on his lips, "I thought we should have some extra in case your fish spills or something and I don't think cold water from the cooler would be healthy for him. He might go into shock or something. And I got you a water bottle, too. Here."

"You're worried about Leo?" she raises tear filled eyes to his, taking the metallic bottle from his hand.

His smile drops, replaced with concern, "Yea. I'd hate for him to spill and we would have nothing to refill him with. Are you Okay?"

"That's…that's really sweet of you. Maybe you're okay after all."

"I think I'm pretty decent. I brake for squirrels; I'll stop traffic to save turtles. I climbed a tree once to save a crow tangled in fishing line then it pecked me and I fell out of the tree and broke my wrist. He flew away though so," he gives her two thumbs up, "it was a win. I can also tell you jokes to make you feel more comfortable and I can sing to you all the way to Seattle, if you like?" he offers with a playful shrug of his shoulders.

"Uh…thanks, I think. I have to look for a couple more things." She shoves her Snapple and water bottle back into his hands. "I'll meet you outside."

He leaves Moira to search the gas station until she finds what she is looking for, which she is surprised and thankful to have located. At the register she pays in cash then collects the two items and returns to the Jeep where she finds Elliot washing the windows with the station provided squeegee singing along to the song playing on the station's loudspeaker. The pair, Elliot and Moira, look at each other but neither speak. Instead, they focus on their own tasks: Elliot on the windows and Moira making use of the quart sized plastic bags and shoestring she just purchased.

When Elliot turns to put away the squeegee he is dumbfounded as he watches Moira drop a handful of colored stones into the bag, the plastic plant, and then, very carefully, pour Leo and his water into the bag, too.

"What do you think of that, Leo?" she asks happily then proceeds to tie the baggy onto the handle above the passenger window. She catches Elliot watching her with raised eyebrows so she explains proudly, "Now he can see the scenery, too."

Bemused, he opens his mouth to reply but then thinks better of it and simply nods before getting behind the wheel to commence their journey. Before pulling away from the gas station, Elliot reconnects his car stereo to the Bluetooth on his phone, tuning to his favorite station on Pandora.

"Are we almost there?" Moira asks, situating herself.

"Almost where? Seattle?" He looks up from his phone.

"Mm-hm." She nods.

Elliot laughs, guiding them out of the gas station. "We aren't even out of Wisconsin yet, Sweetheart."

Moira turns a disapproving scowl towards him, "I'm not your sweetheart."

"Well, as it happens, I don't know your name. Although I can guess that it starts with an M and your last name might be Lovegood."

"Why do you think that?"

"M. Lovegood is the name on the mailbox under mine." Elliot checks his blind spot and merges onto the freeway,

"Very astute."

Elliot laughs and his ease, his comfort, irritates Moira who crosses her arms and looks out the window. "Are you opposed to telling me your name? I can try and guess. Maggie?" He suggests and she gives him a sidelong glare. "Margaret? Millie, Melinda, Megan. Oh, you look like a Megan."

"No, I don't!"

"Michelle? You could be a Michelle. What about Melissa? Mel for short?" He slides the Jeep into the fast lane and presses down on the accelerator to pass an 18-wheeler, a move that makes Moira shiver at the speed and closeness of the large truck. "You don't look like a nickname kind of girl, though. How about Morgan? Morgana! Maleficent!

"Would you stop?"

"I can just call you Sweetheart then." His smile is victorious, eyes shining with amusement. "I can go call the way to Seattle like this. Mary. Maryanne, Maribel, Maria, Mariah, Moe!"

"Moira, my name is Moira, okay. Moira."

With his left hand firmly gripping the wheel at 12 o'clock, he offers her his right hand to shake, still smiling. "Nice to meet you, Moira."

Moira reluctantly shakes his hand, "I can't believe I didn't introduce myself to you." Her gaze drifts out her window as she lets his hand go back to the wheel. "I didn't thank you for saving my fish, either. Maybe I *am* impolite."

"It's okay. You have been a little preoccupied." He suggests with a friendly smile but she only shrugs and then the conversation dies.

Chapter 11
The Driving, The Radio, and The Side of the Road

Moira finds herself drifting in and out of sleep, lulled by the smooth purr of the engine cruising along new asphalt. There's nothing but trees alongside the road now and even though the traffic is heavier the ride is relaxing with gentle music playing. She dozes and the radio is there, Charles Kent is, too. She wakes and the traffic is heavy and the radio is gone, either for the driver to focus on the road lined with construction cones or to let her rest peacefully. She likes to believe it was for her sake, although not necessary.

She dozes again and Charles Kent is there again, in her living room. He found her. He found her apartment, he let himself in—how did he get in? —and he's there, on top of her. Grabbing her, pulling her clothes off and she fights him. With everything she has, she claws at him, punches, kicks. She screams. Just like when she was in her bathroom, he grabs her and penetrates her with his fingers. His cold, rough fingers.

Please, not again.

Elliot is there holding Leo in a bowl, a goldfish bowl, and he watches. He watches and does nothing to help her even when she begs him to help her. He does nothing. She's crying and pleading and he does nothing. Nothing at all.

"Hey?"

She moans, a pained, weak whimper.

"Hey."

Her eyes shoot open to find Elliot's hand on her arm, gently shaking her, his eyes moving back and forth quickly from the road to her face. "Get your hands off of me!" she cries, smacking his hand away. Elliot holds both hands up in defense and begins to apologize when she cuts him off, infuriated, "Keep your hands on the wheel! Are you crazy!"

"Sorry! Sorry!" He laughs as he snatches the wheel.

"Keep your hands on the wheel and off me! What is wrong with you?" Moira glares, shaking her head in disgust.

"I said I was sorry." His demeanor remains humorous, unphased by her outburst, which only agitates her more; she crosses her arms over her chest and slouches down into her seat, sulking like a toddler. "You seemed to be having a nightmare…"

"Where are we anyway?" she cuts him off, still glaring.

"Just passed Alexandria, Minnesota."

"Minnesota?" She sits up, suddenly attentive, and casts her gaze once more outside her window to see what Leo is entranced by. He flitters back and forth watching the thick green woods that seamlessly turn into rocky red bluffs then back again. The woods flow into vast farm fields and rolling hills; nothing is like the Milwaukee skyline and it makes her smile for a time, relieved to be away from the city, the noise.

She watches for some time spotting a large bird at the top of a tall, spiny tree, a creek lined with Canadian Geese and Mallards. She gazes at a wind turbine farm with wonder, surprised at how beautiful she finds it. She has seen pictures of wind farms but to see it with her own eyes the acres of enormous white windmills make her forget about the strange man beside her whom she knows nothing about.

When eventually the scenery settles into fields upon fields of nothing, she retrieves a crossword puzzle book from her purse and a pencil, setting herself away to solve clues while Elliot watches the road, occasionally looking at her in the hopes of striking up conversation but never doing so.

On the radio, his Bluetooth plays the radio sounds from Wrigley field where Bob Uecker prepares to call the play-by-play of the Brewers as they take on the Cubs in a Friday day game.

"How fast are you driving?" She asks just as the radio announcer calls out the first pitch.

"Huh?"

"What's the speed limit?" she looks to the roadside waiting for a sign and, as if on cue, they pass the speed limit sign she was waiting for. "75." She states firmly, looking over at the speedometer. "You're *not* going 75."

Elliot looks down at the gauge, "Uh, no."

"90 is not 75."

"I'm not going 90." He rolls his eyes but they both know that 90 is close enough.

"Honestly! Slow down before you get us all killed." Her tone is scolding and fierce but he doesn't let up on the accelerator while she returns her focus to the puzzle on her lap. She peeks intermittently at his speed, always followed by a dirty look, which he ignores.

"Why are you going so fast?" she exclaims without warning. "And you are getting awfully close to that car in front of us."

"First, I am not going *that* fast and second, this numpty shouldn't be in the fast lane. Chump needs to move over." Elliot quickly shifts the Jeep into the center lane to pass the slower vehicle but that car moves over in front of Elliot. "What the hell man." He sighs, shifting aggressively back to the fast lane and slamming his foot on the pedal until the slower car is a distance away in the rearview mirror. He continues to drive with his foot heavy on the accelerator, unconcerned with his speed; Moira opens her mouth to scold him when suddenly the car slows down and Elliot's eyes scan the road ahead with a knitted brow. She turns to look outside too but sees nothing of interest, Elliot, however, sees the large orange signs indicating more construction ahead.

"Shit." He mutters with a sigh.

"What's wrong?"

"Constructions the next 25 miles." He tells her, clear aggravation on his soft features.

"Oh, that means you have to slow down."

He turns narrowed eyes to her, "You are starting to get on my nerves."

"Because I'm a law-abiding citizen?"

"I have no issue kicking you out of this car if you keep telling me how to drive." He grumbles, but when she doesn't reply, he turns to find her focused on the crossword puzzle book, tuning him out flawlessly. He rolls his eyes and sighs again, focusing on the orange barrels indicating the start of a very tedious journey, a journey already made tedious by his passenger's nagging. Taking a deep breath, he decides to quickly cut across the three lanes of traffic to the next off ramp, thankful Moira wasn't paying attention to his sudden departure from the freeway.

The next time Moira looks up she is surprised to find them on a two-lane highway surrounded by grassland stretching clear to the blue sky. On the horizon, clusters of trees can be seen dotting the flat land sporadically.

"What happened to the construction?" Moira asks, eyes scanning the road nervously. It's these back roads where people get murdered and dumped, their bodies never to be recovered.

"We're taking a detour."

"Are we lost?"

Elliot turns a furrowed brow to her, "Why would we be lost?" On the radio, the announcer calls out a home run for the Brewers with his trademark call: *Get up, get up! Get outta here! Gone!* Elliot pumps his fist, "Yes!"

"Impromptu detours usually lead to getting lost." She ignores the game and his joy.

Still smiling, he shrugs, "Getting lost is the best way to find new things. But not this time. I've driven to Seattle every route you can think of through North and South Dakota. We're good."

"Speed limit's 55." She says, motioning to a sign that passes in a blur.

"Don't tell me how to drive." He turns up the radio as it goes to commercial, the Brewers' inning coming to an end, "And don't talk when the Brewers are at bat if you're going to nag."

"Don't break the law!"

Elliot puts his head back and groans and turns up the radio a little louder. They fall silent, Elliot listening to the game and Moira working on her crossword puzzle.

"Laughing chocolate. What's laughing chocolate?" Moira wonders aloud.

"Are you asking me?" The driver looks at her but she is already filling in the answer and moving on to the next clue.

"Whirlpool, Sombrero, Black Eye. *Blank…*"

Elliot stays silent this time, figuring if she is talking to him, it will be about his driving skills. Moira stares intently at the words to the clue for 21 Across. Stumped, she grits her teeth then turns the radio off, slamming her hand on the power button.

"Do you mind?" he asks, eyebrows arched in astonishment. How dare she turn off his beloved baseball game, his beloved Brew Crew!

"Do you?" She counters.

He sighs, shaking his head, "Milky Way." Pointing to her book, he repeats, "It's Milky Way."

"I don't need your help and would you slow down?"

"Perhaps you would like to walk to Seattle?" He says and she sneers at him and writes in Milky Way for 21 Across. Taking a risk, Elliot turns the radio on again but she doesn't miss a beat and immediately turns it back off. "We're going to have a problem in a minute." He grumbles, clenching both hands on the wheel.

"A three-letter word for candy. Candy. Candy. A three-letter word for candy. Can-dy. Can. Dee. Three letters…"

"Stop saying candy." Elliot says through gritted teeth.

"Why don't you pay attention to staying in your lane and going the speed limit."

"I swear I will kick you out of the car."

"Why? Because you can't drive?"

"That's it!" Elliot jerks the wheel to the right and stops the Jeep on the side of the highway. Slamming the gear shift into park, he turns to her, "Get out. Take your fish and take yourself and get out."

"You think I won't?" Moira is perfectly prepared to call his bluff, not thinking that this guy, this stranger, owes her nothing but the scar on his eye and his busted lip.

"No, I think you will. I think you will because you think you are so smart. You think you know everything, Miss Goody-goody-know-it-all. The world doesn't revolve around you and good luck finding some other sucker to get your irritating ass home."

The words have barely left his lips when her hand cracks across his cheek knocking his sunglasses askew on his face but he isn't surprised but the physical outburst. He aggressively places his glasses back on his face as she hastily unties a stunned Leo and gets out of the car, slamming the door behind her. Not a second later Elliot pulls away from the gravel and disappears down the barren highway, taking with him Moira's duffel bag and purse.

On the side of the road, somewhere in Minnesota, Moira is left standing alone with her fish and a crossword puzzle book.

"You're ridiculous!" Leo scolds, racing from one end of the bag to the next, his fins furiously flailing in the water. "Do you hear me? Ridiculous!" Moira, shell shocked, looks down at her friend wide-eyed and speechless, then it dawns on her.

"Pez!" She exclaims.

"What?"

"Pez. A three-letter word for candy. Pez."

Chapter 12
The Birds, The Boy, and The Heart to Heart

The highway is empty to the east and empty to the west; the fields are empty except for clusters of oaks and maples. Moira, sitting underneath the shade of a large oak tree on the edge of a farmer's land, watches the endless horizon that stretches out for eons across the road. She's never seen so much of nothing before. The bright blue sky meets the yellow grass dotted with purple and gold wildflowers and there isn't another living soul to be seen. Miles down the road, probably already in North Dakota by now, is her cell phone, her purse, her necessities.

Leo tells her that there is no way in the five minutes she has been sat under this tree Elliot has made it all the way to North Dakota but his voice of reason has no effect. She looks behind the tree, across the fenced field towards the only house in the distance, which is a little worse for wear, in need of a paint job, but that is no indication that murderers live there.

Moira looks down at Leo who stares up at her, "We are going to figure this out." She concludes curtly with a nod but she doesn't move. Her eyes continue to gaze out towards the skyline, her mind coming to terms with her actions, with her self-inflicted predicament. After a minute, she rests her head on the rough bark and stares up into the leaves that filter the noon sun into a tango of geometric shapes across her face. Hidden deep within the foliage a bird trills, loud and dominant, owning his territory and making Moira jump with the unfamiliar sound. The bird is nowhere to be seen, his cover too perfect to be revealed but she knows he isn't a sparrow or a house finch.

In her lap, she situates her crossword puzzle book and beside her Leo is nestled safely into the grass. When the bird falls silent, she turns her attention to the puzzle as a natural ambience settles in around her: the breeze rustling the leaves, the grass swaying gently, so peaceful in contrast to her inner turmoil being suppressed only by clues to the puzzle.

A moment passes, two moments and the sudden trill of the mysterious bird calls again only now he can be spotted on a fence post not far from where Moira sits watching her. Every feather is black, his beak, his eyes, his feet, all shining black except for his red and yellow shoulders that puff out when he cries out his loud, shrill song seemingly directed at Moira.

"What?" she asks it, squinting at him and frowning; worried that it might have a taste for fish, Moira picks Leo up and nestles him into the grass between her legs, asking him what kind of bird it is.

"I don't know." Leo tells her.

"That's okay, we can *wing* it together." She chuckles in reply while Leo remains unamused. "*Owl* never give up." The bird screams, startling her. "Hey, don't *fly* off the handle at me!" She leans back on the tree, keeping her eyes on the blackbird. "Remember, *toucan* play at this game." Her smile fades as quickly as it appears, her eyes flitting back over to the empty road where not a single car has passed in the last ten minutes that she has been sitting there, under the shade of this big, old tree, protecting her from the heat of a midday sun. She removes her sweater, exposing her arms to the warmth of the June breeze. She fidgets with the straps of her tank top, adjusting her bra, and then ties her hair up with a hairband from her pocket when the bird calls out again followed by a second one warbling from the leaves above her. Her eyes move upward towards the sound then back over to the one on the fence also calling out in a shrill cry.

"I wonder what they are." She wonders out loud.

"Watermelon Wings?" Leo suggests from the surface of the water, filling his lungs with air.

"That's a cute name. I hope that's what they are." The two birds sing one after the other until a third chimes in with a baritone melody of the same sound. The trio begin a harmonious chorus of controlled chaos, vocally sparring with one another in the most beautiful way Moira has ever heard. She closes her eyes and listens to their music.

"This was such a bad idea." She whispers.

"It's okay to be afraid."

"What was I thinking getting into his car? Going to Seattle with a man I don't know at all." She shakes her head and looks over to the Watermelon Wing on the fence post. "I suppose it doesn't matter now." She sighs and closes her eyes once again. "I wouldn't come back for me either."

"You would have thrown you from the moving car."

"I'm pretty stupid. It's just…it's just…I don't know. I should have just gone to dinner with him! Then I wouldn't be here, I'd be at home…I'd be at home being nervous about dinner tonight. I'm so frigging dumb."

"I'm going to plead the fifth on that one." Leo replies, sinking to the layer of rocks on the bottom of the bag as she sighs and flops down onto the ground, using her sweater as a pillow. Staring up at the filtered sunlight through the leaves, she thinks about Leo's words and her actions, and tries to formulate a plan.

"He stole my things!" she suddenly sits up and huffs, "What a jerk!"

"I don't blame him for abandoning you. You're so difficult! And annoying! Why can't you just relax! Enjoy the ride, make a little conversation. Make friends with him!"

"Too late now." She grumbles, falling back onto her makeshift pillow.

"It's okay for you to be you."

"Annoying?"

"You're quirky."

Moira rolls onto her stomach and rests her chin on her folded hands, staring skeptically at the fish, "You might be a bit biased."

The trio of birds has since become a vicious flock of violently feuding Watermelon Wings, squawking at each other, trying to each outdo the others' ballad with no more beauty in their own notes.

"This escalated quickly." Moira comments, rolling onto her back.

"Sure did."

"We'll be okay." Moira breathes, closing her eyes. "We'll be A-okay."

After a moment, she is certain she hears a car coming down the road, from the west. She strains her ears; the car slows and pulls onto the side of the road, the gravel crunching under the tires.

She pops up from where she lay as Elliot steps out of the car; he leans against the Jeep with his arms crossed over his chest, eyes covered with his sunglasses. She offers him a sincere, friendly smile as she pulls herself upright.

"Just sitting here waiting, huh?" he says in an even, emotionless voice.

She shrugs, still smiling, though nervously, and says nothing; he shakes his head at her then moves to the back seat, she assumes to retrieve her bag. She takes a steadying breath and waits, biting her lower lip and casting her eyes down to her shoes, setting them firm on her painted toes as Elliot approaches. He unceremoniously plops down beside her close enough that their shoulders touch and their hips meet, making Moira's face go hot and her fixation on her peep toes even more unyielding.

"Here," Elliot shakes a sandwich wrapped in a cloth napkin in her face, which she accepts.

The world goes quiet for a moment, no wind in the trees, no cars on the road, and even the birds have reached a stalemate and have fallen silent. The peace goes on, stretching before them like the highway, as they eat bologna sandwiches and stare out at nothing. Moira dares a glance at Elliot first at his canvas boat shoes then back at her own feet. Her second glance travels along his long legs stretched out in front of him to his stomach where his fitted t-shirt sits flat against his skin, to the fish on his tattoo.

On the fence post the Watermelon Wing trills his song once more, solo and powerful. All other birds content to leave him on the center stage. Moira looks over at the bird, which glares at her.

"Oh dear." She mumbles, glancing at the bird. Elliot peeks around her, eyeing the bird then looking at Moira with a tilted gaze. "I thought he was cute at first." Turning narrowed eyes to the bird, "Go away you stupid bird." She frowns, turning back to Elliot, "I'm sure he is going to peck my eyes out."

He nods, then folds his napkin into a square, setting it on his lap. "Can I ask you a pretty random question?" His brow furrows. "Is your belly button pierced?" he points to her tummy where her tank top sits tight against her skin, showing the outline of her sunflower ring.

"Oh…" she looks down and runs her hand down her stomach. She's never hidden it, her navel ring, never been ashamed but she flushes by him noticing. "Uhm. Yes."

"I was just curious. Because...well I guess this is random, too, but when John first introduced us, you were looking at my arm." he rubs his tattooed arm, keeping his eyes on the horizon. "You looked pretty offended and I was going to say that just because a person has tattoos doesn't make them mean or dangerous. I'm sure not dangerous. Anyway, my thought process is that girls with piercings aren't often disgusted by boys with tattoos. From my experience anyway."

"You have a lot of experience with girls with piercings?" She gives him a sidelong glance, stiff.

Elliot shrugs his shoulders but says nothing.

"Well, I wasn't disgusted at all. I think it's pretty. Oh! I suppose men don't want their tattoos to be *pretty*, huh? I just, I like the fish." Behind them, the black bird screeches, startling her. With a grunt, she stands up, carrying Leo with her and moves to Elliot's other side. Graceless, she falls down beside him almost spilling over with Leo but never taking her eyes off the bird on the fence.

"I'll protect you." he replies lightly, offering a smile that reddens her cheeks, then he sighs, bringing his legs up and resting his elbows on his knees. "I can take you to the airport or the bus station in Jamestown so you can go home. If that's what you want. I, I guess if you don't have the money right now, being unemployed, I can pay your way. It's no big deal. I'll get you home. Shit, I suppose we could just turn around. We're not too far out, I guess." He pushes his sunglasses to the top of his head, brushing his tousled hair back, revealing his sensitive, discerning eyes. "You're clearly uncomfortable."

"I'm uncomfortable because I'm me." Moira grumbles, staring at Elliot's shoes. "It's nothing to do with your tattoo or you...well, you did tackle me pretty quick yesterday. That was kind of scary. But...I don't know."

"I was protecting myself. I still have a fucking headache." He rubs his jaw then follows her gaze to his shoes. "You got a problem with my shoes? Or is that just your face?"

She raises her eyes to his, "No. What? No." Shaking her head, "What if Leo wants to see the Space Needle?"

His smirk makes her shift and avert her gaze back to the bird on the fence post who watches silently. "I'd be happy to take him, *and you,* to Seattle."

"And back home again. You can't leave us in Seattle."

"We can make this work but for that we really got to start getting along. I.E., don't tell me how to drive and never turn off the Brewers unless you're dying. You can turn them off if you're dying but you better be on fire or something." His tone is light and friendly despite the seriousness on his face.

She forces herself to look at him, to meet his steady eye, "I want to go to Seattle."

When he smiles, his eyes wrinkle and his face lights up. "Good." His clear delight makes her face grow hotter. "This could still be a fun trip."

"It could be." She murmurs, almost to herself, as she looks to Leo then to the bird and back to the road before settling her eyes on him. "Why did you let me come with you?"

"Because why not? I like people. I enjoy making friends." He shrugs and stands, reminding her how his height intimidates her. She watches as he smooths out his pale blue jeans, his t-shirt, and finally his plaid shirt that hangs open; he rolls his neck and knocks his glasses back over his eyes. "And, you know, I've never seen someone look as frightened as you did this morning. I thought I could…help, I guess." He holds out a hand to Moira who looks at it for a moment before hesitantly taking it and letting him pull her to her feet.

"I don't understand your way of thinking." As she speaks, she picks up her things, including Leo, then turns back to him, frowning. "Seems like you took a terrible risk. And that's after I turned you down for dinner."

"Not just turned me down, turned me down like I'm scum. I honestly thought it was because of my tattoos." He places his warm palm on her back, guiding her towards the road.

"No." She shakes her head. "I think it's sexy." Her own words make her blush, regretting them instantly. "You know, I wish you wouldn't drive so fast. It makes me nervous." She says quickly, attempting to erase her words. Together they walk to the passenger side door where he opens it for her and she climbs inside.

"I'll tell you what. I will slow it down just for you. Okay?" He leans on the open door, looking down at her as she situates herself. "But I will say this: the two speeding tickets I got are bought and paid for and of the three accidents I've been in, only one was my own stupid fault and it wasn't because I was speeding." When he closes the door, she ties Leo up in the window as he comes around to the driver's side.

"What accident was that?" She immediately asks before his door is even closed.

"Ah, well," he glances at her, buckling his seatbelt, "I may or may not have fallen asleep at the wheel and rolled my truck down the side of a mountain in Montana. I *think* I fell asleep, anyway."

"Oh my! Are you okay?"

"I'm fine now!" He laughs as he throws the Jeep into a U-turn and they restart their journey west, together. "This was six years ago. I was in a coma for nine days. It wasn't good. It's why I avoid driving at night."

"Oh goodness. How terrible. How about the other two?"

"About four years ago I was driving along and I hit a deer. I had a Ford Ranger, I loved that truck, and then this buck jumped in front of me. Totaled the truck and obliterated that poor thing. Then a couple months after that I was going along the highway and a guy didn't stop at his stop sign. T-boned me, threw me into a spin, I flipped into a damn ditch and walked away with minor whiplash."

"That was pretty darn lucky."

He smiles at her, "Pretty darn lucky, yea."

They drive on a little way when he points through the windshield where there are tire tracks prominently visible in the gravel at the side of the road. "That's where I pulled over to give you some time to sweat."

"You weren't really going to leave me?"

"Of course not!" His voice is exasperated. "You really thought I would?"

Moira shrugs and casts her eyes out the passenger window, lazily watching the landscape dotted with cows go by. The sun is high in the sky and bright in her eyes making them feel heavy as she squints to block it out; her head still pounds between her ears, from the bright light, she thinks, but she can't bring herself to ask Elliot for any aspirin. Ever since she has met him, she has been demanding and needy and now she needs some aspirin.

"You know what else? The Cubs scored five runs in the first inning right after I kicked you out of the car."

"Oh yea?"

"Yea, can you believe it?" He throws both hands up in the air, shaking his head, disgusted.

"Maybe you should…" she starts but catches herself, turning burning eyes back to the landscape through the windshield.

"Let me guess. Keep my hands on the wheel?" There is laughter in his easy voice.

"Something like that."

Elliot adjusts his position, taking the wheel into both hands, and smiles at her, a jovial beaming smile, "Who's Arthur?" He suddenly asks.

"What?" Furrowed brow, narrow, mean eyes snap over to his profile. "What did you just ask me?"

"Well, see your phone was ringing. Someone named Arthur was calling you. I was going to answer it but then I thought I'd better not."

"Why the heck is he calling? What could he possibly want?" Moira snatches her phone from where it lay on the top of her purse, glaring at it with such fury she may crack the screen with her gaze. She slams the phone back down and crosses her arms, pushing back into her seat, her teeth clenched.

"Anyone who can inspire this kind of rage, I want to hear about." When she doesn't reply, he smiles at her. "I don't want to get beat up because I ran away with some guy's girlfriend. I'm pretty nonconfrontational. The last physical altercation I got into was with a Robin and the Robin won." He pauses, thoughtful eyes, "Then there was you…I kind of don't want to get my ass kicked again."

Moira relents her stubborn silence, "He is *not* my boyfriend and if you say that again, I will throw *you* out of the car! Arthur's my old boss, okay?"

"That's it?" Elliot scoffs.

"Yes. He fired me on my birthday!" she replies, disgruntled by his mockery. "My *30th* birthday!" she cries, aggrieved at his underwhelming response. "12 years of my life! Gone!"

"Well, I guess that's pretty shit."

Now she scoffs, "He used to smell my hair." She groans just thinking about him, "Why are men so disgusting?"

"We're not all bad."

She frowns, "I've had enough unpleasant experiences with the species to know they're all pretty awful."

"You know I'm a man, right? I'm that *species*." He points out, frowning but she purses her lips and remains silent. Keeping a light, sympathetic tone, he offers her a smile "I hope that I can be an exception to your past experiences."

Moira goes tense at his words as the car is enveloped by the crowd on the radio going crazy for another Cubs run scored. Even Bob Uecker sounds dejected.

Chapter 13
The Conversation, The Campsite, and The Absolute Refusal

With the Brewers trailing the Cubs, Elliot has no qualms with talking, with telling the myriad of tales from his adventures on the road, childhood friends, past family pets. There is no embarrassment telling her he worked at an adult gift and video store in college or how when he was in kindergarten, he wet his pants on stage during a play in which he played a lion.

"I'm running out of stories off the top of my head, here." He complains, after his long, meandering soliloquy, referring to her inability to join in the conversation.

"I'm just listening."

"I noticed but I am running out of things to say."

Moira grins, "I wouldn't believe that for a minute."

"Why don't you tell me something about you. Please."

"Have you ever been to jail?" She asks, curtly.

When he doesn't immediately reply, she turns to him to see him thinking, knotted brow, pursed lips, about his answer. His stiff manor makes her sit straight up and narrow her eyes.

"Okay," he begins, his tight mouth spreading into a smirk, "just twice. The first time was because I was trespassing." Moira raises her eyebrows, her lips a thin, serious line. "I would not have spent the night in jail if I hadn't called the cop a pig." He suppresses a smile at Moira's pique. Agitated, she turns her sight to the road in front of them that stretches onward where the blue sky meets the cool grey horizon.

Elliot explains how he was photographing a pair of nesting cranes on private property when he was 19 and the owners of the land called the police on him. In his defense, according to him, the landowners gave him no warning and the officer was rude, although Elliot didn't mean for him to hear the insult that he muttered under his breath.

Moira clicks her tongue at him, shaking her head when he is finished. "What else?"

"You know, spending a couple nights in jail doesn't make me a bad person! It doesn't prove or disprove anything about me." She remains silent, making him sigh and roll his eyes. "I was documenting a protest in Milwaukee about police brutality and unfortunately, it started to get a little heated and I got shoved into a cop who wrestled my ass to the ground and hauled me off. Sure did make an example of me…and what we were protesting." A gust of wind shakes the Jeep along the road causing Elliot to tighten his grip on the wheel and look out along the horizon again. Moira's eyes follow meeting the thickening clouds with her green eyes, her brow knitted with concern, lips a tight pout. A shiver shoots over her body with another tumultuous blast of wind; she grabs her bare arms and rubs them vigorously, still watching the skies ahead.

"Are you cold?" Elliot asks, immediately moving to turn the passenger heating vents on.

"No." She answers, distracted by her own conjuring thoughts. "Are we driving straight through to Seattle." She hadn't thought before of sleeping arrangements, hotels or motels, dinner. How long will they be driving? Her back is starting to hurt, her bladder is filling up. When they began and Elliot mentioned 2000 miles, that number meant nothing, it was just a number—a two with a few zeros behind it—but now there are implications attached.

"No." he says, guiding the Jeep back onto the freeway. "We stop at Theodor Roosevelt National Park. I reserved a campsite." He taps a plastic card hanging on the rear-view mirror and smiles, "I have this handy-dandy National Parks Pass. Saves tons of hass—"

"A campsite?" she interrupts, turning to him with narrowed eyes that he meets with a look of surprise.

"Yea," he nods, "why?"

"Where will we sleep?"

"In the back." Elliot motions to the back where the seats already lie flat and appear covered with a raised platform, perhaps made of plywood, with a couple of blankets laid flat over the top and pillows stuffed behind the seats. It isn't particularly spacious with two duffel bags, his camera equipment, and a cooler and with his height, Moira isn't sure how he can ever be comfortable. She eyes the set up suspiciously before scowling at him.

"I hate building and taking down a tent all the time so I turned the back of my Jeep into a bedroom." Elliot tells her proudly, explaining how he built the raised platform so he could have storage for extra shoes and supplies, how he can get a decent sleep, how cracking the sunroof offers perfect ventilation. She watches him as he talks on, beaming with his ingenuity, as she waits patiently for him to finish. "It's perfect. Although, I wouldn't mind getting a bigger car so I can stretch out more. Maybe I'll start looking after I get back from Seattle. Maybe a Suburban or a Tahoe. Something."

"This is all very cute. You are very clever and you are very insane if you think I am sleeping in this car with you."

"It'll be sort of uncomfortable since we are both tall but I can push the seats forward and the cooler can go outside. It'll be okay."

"No," she shakes her head and crosses her arms, "I don't think you understand. I'm not sleeping in this car with you. You can sleep in your car but I am sleeping somewhere not with you." She looks over at Leo who watches her, his lips moving up and down rhythmically with the movement of his fins over the surface of the water. He will scold her for her stubbornness, he will call her a fool.

And maybe she is.

But it's no crime to be cautious.

"But," Elliot pouts, "I reserved a campground and we determined I'm not a rapist. I am an upstanding gentleman." She silences him with her fiery eyes burning into his face but after a moment he looks back to her, "But this is what I do."

"Not with me it isn't."

The driver falls silent again, accepting defeat, although the passenger doesn't feel as though she has won a victory as guilt and worry courses through veins, every scenario that leaves her beaten and abandoned in North Dakota playing on a reel before her eyes.

Outside the gas station the smell of a barbeque, burgers and brats sizzling, drifts through the air mixing with the heavy scent of gasoline. It whisks Moira back to the sole camping trip they took as a family when she was a kid. Her uncle's RV always carried the stench of gas and all they did was grill hot dogs and hamburgers for breakfast, lunch, and dinner. The memory makes her smile now, though she recalls being unhappy then when night would fall and they'd have to return to the campsite lest they be stolen by coyotes, according to her uncle. Thinking about her uncle, her mother's brother, she determines that Elliot and Uncle Jake would get along quite well with their similar, outdoorsy personalities and affinity for storytelling.

As she heads inside, Elliot takes the opportunity to fill up the tank once more. Before she turns to go inside, she glances at him tapping his fingers impatiently on his crossed arms while waiting for the pump to click to a stop. She asks him if he needs anything, which he declines, then heads inside where she finds a young woman behind the counter. From her thick, red lips dangles a cigarette and her blackened eyes cut into Moira as she approaches with a friendly greeting and a wave. Moira's gesture is returned with a grunt, some primitive form of hello, as she tosses the black drapes of hair from her face.

Moira asks the clerk if there is a motel nearby and listens with little comprehension to the blasé directions mumbled from bored lips. She nods her head, faking understanding with a polite smile, "Oh, we have gas out there, too."

She pays for the gas and pushes out of the heavy double doors, escaping the dank interior of the run-down station, inhaling the cooling June air, feeling the heaviness of imminent rain. Walking back to the Jeep, she passes Elliot who gives her a tired, wavering smile but neither say anything and when Moira closes herself in the Jeep she looks to Leo and frowns,

"He must hate me."

"Could you just please relax? For once in your life just relax." He replies with little remaining patience left in his voice. "Lighten up and have a little fun while you're here."

"Oh…" Moira moans, dropping her head into her hands. "Oh, I'm so boring. I'm the most boring person I have ever met." She declares raising her eyes to the unsympathetic face of Leo, shaking her head. Her disappointment in herself is tangible, a bitter taste in her mouth put there by fear and a false sense of propriety but her pride won't let her relinquish her demands.

When Elliot returns to the Jeep, he turns to her with pursed lips but his eyes are shaded by his sunglasses, shielding his expression from her perception. "We just passed each other. Remember?" Moira nods, her brow furrows as she ponders where this conversation is going. "We even acknowledged each other as we went by. You remember that?"

"Yes."

"That would have been a good time to tell me you paid for the gas. Don't you think?"

"Oh, yea." Moira feels her face go warm as she bites her lip. "Probably." His frown breaks into a crooked grin making her shoulders ease back into the seat and a laugh slip from her lips as she shakes her head, "Sorry."

"Yea, yea." He replies lightly as he leads them away from the gas station and back to the highway. "Thanks for paying but you didn't have to."

"It's the least I can do since I have completely derailed your itinerary."

"I wouldn't go that far. I think," Elliot pauses as he thinks, visibly relaxing at the wheel, "I think you made it a little more interesting." He smiles at her, "A little less lonely." His words take her by surprise, make her search his profile for signs of jest but she finds nothing but a sincere man watching the flat road ahead, listening dejectedly to a game he is sure his team has lost.

Chapter 14
The Game, The Win, and The Failed Non-Date Celebration

The whitewashed exterior of the motel has cracked and dulled over the years standing against the elements of North Dakota, the yellow lines of the parking stalls have long since faded into nonexistence. Elliot pulls into what could be a parking spot in front of one of the rooms, all of which are in a straight line on ground level, all with two wooden steps leading to the locked door. Off to the side, disconnected from the numbered rooms, is a small building with a handwritten sign reading: Vacancy.

After paying for their rooms, Moira finds herself trembling on the edge of a solid, stale mattress in a dank, dimly lit room. It's the first time she's been alone since early this morning when the sun was barely breaking over the Milwaukee skyline. With a steady, sensitive hand, she scoops Leo out of his bag and lowers him into the Tupperware of water on the bedside table situated between the two beds, optimizing the small space of the room. She watches his big black eyes as he wiggles in circles around the container.

"I like him." Leo says, settling just under the surface, his mouth sipping at the air above.

"I…I think I do, too." She replies, keeping her eyes focused on his thin fins, tattering with age. Taking a deep breath, she lay down facing him, tucking her hands under her head when a knock raps at her door in a musical pattern that makes her smile and jump up from the bed. With shaking hands, she straightens her top, smoothing her hands down her stomach then fluffing her curls.

With a final deep breath, she opens the door to find Elliot waiting patiently outside in the filtered sunlight, looking down at his phone, while the grey clouds move in with the cool breeze. The overcast haze thickens over the setting sun but the bright rays break through and light up his blonde hair and cheerful face.

"You have to see this." He tells her, motioning to his phone as he, without waiting for an invitation, steps into her room and plops down on the bed, his eyes never leaving the screen. A moment a panic crosses her, wondering if there is some breaking news like the world has gone to war while she was sleeping in the car or an asteroid was heading for North Dakota, but before she even takes a seat next to him at the foot of the bed she hears the familiar sounds of a baseball game.

She eases down beside him and leans over to peer down at the screen where the Brewers have taken the lead over the Cubs and are now trying to end the game with 1 out in the bottom of the 9th. Elliot explains in the foreign language that is baseball how Ryan Braun smashed a grand slam after the Cubs walked in a run to bring them on top 7-6. This means nothing to her.

"He golfed it out of the park and now…" His voice trails off as he absorbs the game once again. Moira inches a little closer peeking at Elliot's eager profile gazing down at his phone, his fist clenching and unclenching nervously on his jiggling leg. His jittery movements and tense jaw while watching the sport make her smile as she urges herself to inch a bit closer, leaning against his shoulder.

"Come on, strike him out. You got this."

The camera closes in on the pitcher's intense, burning glare then it cuts to the batter's focused, burning glare. Like a movie, it moves back and forth between these two men, zooming in closer on their eyes, their furrowed brows and tense jawlines. It's a battle, a 12 o'clock showdown at the OK Corral, Burt Lancaster and Kirk Douglas fighting for victory.

The pitcher sets up and fires; the ball hits the dirt and the count goes 3-0, according to Elliot's mumbling and the T.V. commentators, it was a spiked Slider.

"What does that mean?" Moira asks but her voice falls on deaf ears. The mysterious 3 and O count remains thus so she shakes her head and turns back to the screen where once again the pitcher sets up, shaking off the catcher signs while the batter kicks some dirt, adjusts his sleeve in a ritual of adjustments. The pitcher nods to his catcher and places his gloves over his face, glaring out from behind it. He fires again, the ball flies towards the catcher's glove, slamming it with a puff of dust and a colossal thud, so loud Moira swears the catcher's finger must be broken. The batter and catcher freeze in their positions, neither moving an inch; the batter holds his bat, barely tipping his head towards the umpire waiting for the call, which is made after a moment. The umpire straightens himself, standing tall and bulky with all his padding under his black polo and he says nothing so the batter throws his bat and takes his walk to 1st base while the Brewers dugout begins to bark their displeasure.

"That was a fucking strike! It was in the zone; it was right over the plate! Look at that." Elliot jumps up, throwing his hands in the air. "Fucking ball, my ass." The commentators echo Elliot's sentiments with family-friendly language.

"Oh my." Moira flinches, scooting away allowing him to fall back beside her with a sigh.

"Idiots get paid to make that call." Elliot tells her, shaking his head. "Calls like that can make or break a game, you know?" Moira shakes her head but Elliot's attention is back on the screen. "A double play ends it."

"All they need is a double play ball, partner." One commentator says to the other right after Elliot's own commentary.

"You must know a lot about baseball. You could be with those guys." Moira smiles, gulping nervously as she leans close to him again, daring to touch him once more and forcing her eyes away from his face, from his flushed cheeks and unshaven chin, his golden eyes. Back to the game.

He nods as the clock strikes noon and the pitcher high kicks and launches, the batter swings. There's a tremendous crack as the bat splinters into a dozen shards of wood and the ball launches into the grass, bouncing into the glove of one Brewers players, the Shortstop, who throws it immediately to the 2nd baseman who fires it off to the 1st baseman who leaps to catch the high throw.

As the 1st baseman descends from his leap, he whips his glove down to the Cubs player's shoulder just as his foot lands on the base. The first base Umpire throws his fist with a grunt and Elliot leaps from his seat knocking Moira from her perch on his shoulder.

"Take that you stupid Cubbies." he spins on a heel to face Moira, "6-4-3 double play, baby. That's how you play baseball!" He throws his phone with a spin onto the bed and holds up his palms for her to smack, which she timidly does, passing a glance at Leo who watches the scene with big, round eyes. "We should celebrate!" He announces, babbling about the game with foreign terminology: The Bullpen, the Closer, and a grounder to short for the bang-bang play at 1st base. Moira listens with politeness and intrigue sitting stiffly on the edge of the bed although she doesn't understand any of it, least of all what it means for the Brewers to be straddling 500.

"Our closer needs more than two in his repertoire." Elliot comments, cracking his neck with a sharp turn before stretching his back and bending down to touch his toes.

"Uh-huh."

He leans on the bed, bringing his face close to hers. "There were five double-plays turned against us today! Five!" he holds up his five fingers to her face, pushing them towards her for emphasis. A heat tingles on her cheeks that only grows the more she focuses on it and her voice falters trying to find a reply. Elliot smiles, searching her face but this nearness, this investigation is interrupted by the rhythmic vibrating and twinkling chime of his phone. He jerks away and snatches his phone from the bed aggressively declining the call, only glancing at the screen. Moira is taken aback by the sudden appearance and disappearance of his clear agitation but he looks at her with a warm smile that reaches his eyes.

"My plan, the whole timing of my trip, is so I can go to the Brewers game against the Seattle Mariners on Wednesday. And," he waves his hand dismissively, grinning, "to see my beloved sister, of course."

"Oh." She nods, her eyes flickering over his phone as it lights up again.

He grabs the phone and silences it, rolling his eyes and shaking his head. "I hope you'll come with me. What do you say?"

"Come with where?"

"To the Brewers-Mariners game on Wednesday night." He answers with an incredulous laugh.

"Oh…" Moira stands and smooths out her shirt once again, as a way to hide her trembling fingers; she crosses the room and kneels to her duffel bag only pretending to be looking for something, anything. "You mean, like a date? Because it wouldn't be a date." She finally replies to the bag with an unwarranted sternness in her voice.

"I didn't say it was! My sister and her husband are going, too."

"Uhm." After a long pause, a drawn out, excruciating silence, she stands and turns to him, to his face where he stares down at his phone, an eyebrow cocked and his fingers slamming out a reply to someone. Once finished, he shoves it back into his pocket giving

Moira a shrug. As a man incapable of masking his feelings, whether he is playing the king or the fool, his annoyance is clear and Moira wonders if it's her unenthusiastic reply about going to the game with him or whomever he is texting with making him look so down and annoyed.

"I suppose I'll leave you alone then." Elliot says making a swift move towards the exit; he opens the door to the outside world where the clouds have extinguished the burning sunset casting the evening into a dreary grey, a mirror held to Moira's every emotion. "I'm gonna check out the town."

She opens her mouth to reply, to stop him from leaving but he's gone before she can find her voice. The door closes with a quiet click leaving her alone with Leo's silent rage, a rage so palpable she doesn't dare glance in his direction. Standing in the middle of her roadside motel room, her feet digging into the threadbare carpeting, her eyes roaming the cracks in the walls, a new fear pummels her, making her knees buckle. He's leaving and he might not come back.

"*That's* what you're worried about?" Leo scolds. "You just let the best thing that's ever happened to you walk out that door thinking you despise him."

"He knows I don't *despise* him." Her eyes wander to the door. "I don't. I just, you know. People can't be trusted. Men." As she speaks, she picks up her purse and perches herself on the edge of the bed near Leo's bowl so she can find her phone. At the bottom of her bag she locates her dead phone. Slamming her finger on the black screen and pressing the on button repeatedly she groans and slams her phones back into her purse.

"Frigging stupid girl. I don't have a charger or anything. Stupid thing stays alive long enough for *Arthur* to call me then…"

"Dead." Leo comments as he drifts to the surface.

"Ugh, and I don't want to be in here all night by myself."

"You won't be alone. You have me!"

"I love you, Leo, I do, but I want…" She raises her eyes to the door once again, her gaze unwavering, burning into the wood visualizing what waits for her outside. Him.

Leaping from the bed, she rushes to the door and throws it open, hurrying into the grey, into the wind towards the back of the Jeep. She halts, tripping over with the quickness in which her feet stop moving when she realizes Elliot is on the phone, his head bowed into the Sherpa collar of a denim jacket he pulled from the back.

"Fuck that! Don't fucking talk to me about listening!" Elliot barks when his eyes snap up to meet Moira's terrified gaze. She quickly stumbles backwards, throwing her hands up and mouthing her apologies but her heel catches a crack in the concrete and suddenly the world is rushing upwards as her body falls downwards. Moira grits her teeth and prepares for impact when Elliot grabs her arm to stop her, nearly toppling over with her but he stiffens his legs and pulls her to her feet, pulling her towards him. Unable to pull away, she freezes, resting her fingertips on his arm that still holds hers.

"I got to go. We'll discuss this later. Don't call me. *I'll* call *you.*" He hangs up and shoves his phone into his pocket, turning wide eyes to Moira's. "I've never seen a retreat quite like that." There is unmistakable humor in his tone, the anger that draped over his normal jovial visage when she first came upon his phone call erased by her presence, by the clumsy scene she performed.

"I'm so sorry." She breathes, still not moving away from his body, her eyes glued to his chest, to the logo on his shirt. She hadn't noticed it before, the clipart design of a camera lens with the words RAW People are Good People, but now she cannot seem to tear her eyes from it, wondering what it means and if she should ask, could she step into his warmth and would he embrace her.

"You alright?" Elliot asks, gazing down at her with a smile, stepping back with an eagerness to create some distance between them, an answer to her internal pondering if he would hold her, share the warmth she can feel emanating off his body. "I didn't mean to pull you up so hard."

She shakes her head, silencing him, daring to finally meet his eyes, "I didn't mean to interrupt."

"You're not. It's fine, just some drama back home. So, do I dare ask if you want to walk into town with me? It's not a date, just two people with nothing else to do."

Moira smiles and he smiles back.

Chapter 15
The Cold, The Hot, and The Very Important Promise

Together they walk down the barren, windswept streets of Nowhere, North Dakota, a town without a name but rife with old-world charm including antique streetlamps and quaint storefronts. They pass a candy store, a pharmacy, and bookstore, several bars lit with neon signs in their blackened diamond windows. Moira keeps a few paces behind Elliot, using his body to shield herself from the wind while he chats to her about the town, about the weather, how Mother Nature thinks it's October, and about anything else that pops into his head.

(Is it socially acceptable for a grown man to play with Legos and what is the appeal of Starbucks? Will the Brewers go to the World Series this year and should he cut his hair?)

It's peaceful walking down the main street in the fading light despite the blustery winds assailing them and the abysmal temperature. She's thankful Elliot was able to find a coat for her to wear, knowing the wind would have cut right through her knit sweater, though she feels foolishly intimate wearing his clothes, even a woolen peacoat.

When he looks down at her as they walk side-by-side, she blushes and a giddy feeling flutters her chest. It makes her nervous how attractive she finds him, how his eyes make her swoon, but when their hands brush against each other, she bolts, quickly side stepping away from him into a blue mailbox drop off. She grunts as she collides with it, stumbling backwards. Elliot crosses his arms and smirks.

"You alright there?"

Moira straightens her back and lifts her chin, "Who put that there?" She quickly passes him, tucking her head to hide her red cheeks. He catches up to her but now he keeps his hands in his pockets and she keeps hers wrapped around herself; she is certain he's blushing but reasons with herself that it's the cold night biting at his cheeks, nothing to do with her.

When they come up to a corner bar with neon lights half burned out, Elliot touches Moira's arm to stop her, "When was last time you went to a dive bar as seedy as this?"

Moira looks over to the blackened windows and heavy-looking door and thinks back to the country clubs of her childhood, the ballrooms, and 5-star hotels. "Never." She answers with the shake of her head.

"Let's get a drink then. I'm buying but that doesn't make it a date."

"If this is where you'd take me on a date, we'd be broken up real quick." She comments, ignoring the warmth that shoots over her body when he places his palm on her back to guide to up the steps and to the door.

"If you ever decide to go on a date with me, I promise it'd be a little better than this." He replies, laughing.

Inside is dark and smells like beer and mildew but they proceed to take a seat at the end of the bar nearest to a TV in the corner playing the Minnesota Twins game, furthest away from the handful of other patrons occupying stools. Elliot orders a gin and tonic for himself and turns to Moira who orders a cranberry and soda.

"Do you not drink?" Elliot asks, turning his attention to the game as a Twins player hits a ball that soars into the outfield, just missing the glove of the Red Sox second baseman.

"I do. Not very often though."

The Twins player turns around the first base after the outfielder fumbles it; Elliot shakes his head. "Shouldn't stretch it." The outfielder throws the ball to the second baseman who missed the ball originally and he collides with the runner. He smiles at Moira, "I told him not to stretch it. That was a straight single. No way was he going to stretch that to a double." She nods like she understands. "I don't drink too often either since I'm always driving.

Their drinks are brought to them and they sip in silence, eyes glued to the television, until the bartender strikes up a conversation with Elliot about the game, and about Elliot's Brewers hat. They talk about the MLB standings, rumors of new rules coming for next season, and the atrocious umpires. Moira watches the men converse, she watches the game with curiosity, she wonders if Leo is doing ok all alone in that roadside room.

And how many hookers have laid in that bed?

She grimaces at the thought and looks back at Elliot now that they are alone, the bartender moving back to the other end of the bar to serve the other rowdy patrons. "I've never been to a baseball game before."

He gasps, "Are you serious?" Moira nods. "We'll change that on Wednesday…assuming you'll come with." With this, he knocks back the rest of his drink and stands, pulling his wallet from his pocket. A sign to leave, Moira finishes her drink and also stands, watching him fish a $20 bill from his wallet and toss it on the counter. "Ready?" He smiles.

"Uh-huh."

As they leave, he asks her if she wants to get something to eat but she only shrugs; he asks her if she wants to walk around the town some more but she doesn't mind either way. When asked if she's hungry, she replies that she is 'ok" and when asked if she is tired, she replies the same again. With no input from Moira, Elliot leads them back to the motel, both thankful that the wind is now at their backs.

Elliot chats as they walk, his hands shoved deep in his pockets; he talks about baseball mostly, certain games he's been to, autographs he's received, rule changes from the 1800's to today.

"I'm sorry I keep blabbing on and on." He removes his hat and runs a nervous hand through his hair, each moving to the steps in front of their own room. "I've been told I talk too much. Remember, you can always tell me to shut up."

"Never!" Moira smiles, reaching out and touching his arm before yanking it back. Confusion flashes across his face but it is quickly replaced with his typical crooked smile until his phone rings.

"I'll see you later." With a clouded face, he disappears into his room bringing his phone to his ear.

For a moment, she stares in the empty space that he was just standing but when rain drops start to fall, she slips into the safety of her room where she greets Leo with a sigh.

"I wish I were more interesting." She whines, slumping against the door and knocking her already pounding head on the wood. "Ow." She pouts, rubbing her head.

"But you had a nice time."

"I don't know. I wish I wasn't so scared all the time." Another sigh, and she makes her way to the bathroom, dropping Eliot's coat to the ground on her way. Turning on the light reveals jade tiles around a rusted mirror incapable of an honest reflection and a stale shower stall fit for a prison. The water is barely warm but she cleanses her skin and washes her hair accepting the chill it instills in her long after she dries off and slips into her nightshirt.

Her stomach rumbles, her mouth is parched, and her head beats like a symphony of percussion instruments behind her eyes. For a second, she thinks she could go to his room right now like she did last night, except maybe actually talk to him instead of slinking away with her tail between her legs.

The thought makes her hands tremble so she goes to tidy her duffel bag, replacing her shampoo and body wash and tucking away her dirty clothes. She picks up Elliot's coat and lays it over the spare bed, running her fingers down the soft wool, fingering the buttons, and adjusting the collar. Taking a deep breath, she pats the lapels and turns to slide between the moth bitten sheets where she curls up and runs her hands over her smooth legs.

"If I let my legs get hairy, that would add an extra layer of warmth." She chuckles though she doesn't smile; Leo remains quiet. The only sound is Moira's stomach eating away at itself with angry, desperate grumbles until a familiar musical knock raps at her door.

Moira throws back the blankets then pulls her damp hair over her shoulders, biting her lip as she opens the door to greet Elliot who keeps his back to the wind, dressed in only his jeans and t-shirt. After she opens the door, he spins to face her, bearing the brunt of the wind and rain to his face with a grimace, but his eyes travel the length of her body down her nightshirt to her thighs, her legs, to her feet before snapping back to her face with arched eyebrows and a shameless smirk.

"Oh! I'm not wearing any pants!" She exclaims slamming the door on his face so she can hurry and put her jeans back on.

"Idiot!" Leo hisses. "Just leave him out in the cold!" He growls and burrows into the rocks at the bottom of his bowl.

"Oh!" She cries again, hopping back to the door with only one leg in her jeans, panicked and desperate to put them on but more so to not leave Elliot outside. Throwing open the door so he can come in, she hustles to get her other leg into her pants and get them buttoned up, falling over onto the bed.

"My god, woman!" Elliot laughs, "I've seen legs before."

"Shut up." Moira barks, standing so she can finally zip her jeans closed.

"Believe it or not, I've seen more than legs." He remarks, throwing a cloth wrapped sandwich onto the bed, along a Twinkie; he holds her water bottle in his hand. Her cheeks burn with a furious fire but his commentary continues, ignoring her discomfort. "I promise, I won't maul you if you're not wearing pants. You could be naked and I still won't."

"Oh goodness." She pulls her eyes away from his unflinching gaze begging for the chill that once enveloped her when she got out of the shower to return, to cool the fire that rages over her body.

"*Anyway*, I know you're hungry and I know you're not going to tell me you're hungry so I've brought you some food."

"Oh, that's so sweet. Uh, did you by chance bring any aspirin with you?" Her hands fidgeting with her claddagh, her eyes falling to her toes then to his bare feet. "Where are your shoes?"

Elliot wiggles his toes with a small smile on his lips "Eh. Who needs shoes?" His smile quickly fades, replaced by a deep frown, his eyes narrowing with concern. "You need some aspirin?" The urgency in his voice makes Moira smile,

"It's no big deal."

"No," Elliot pats his front pockets and his back pockets, pressing his lips into a tight line, "I have some. Hold on" Before she can protest, Elliot slips out of the room. After a moment, she hears the Jeep beep when it's unlocked and Elliot reappears in her doorway holding a bottle of ibuprofen. "Here. Eat something first, though."

"Thanks." Moira replies, timidly, pleading with herself to meet his eye, to show her appreciation instead of shyness. Failing, she sets the bottle between his peacoat and the sandwich Elliot had tossed on the bed.

"Listen, if you don't want to do this anymore, I can get you home. I get the feeling you're not very comfortable with me."

"Oh." Her eyes sharply meet his and she swallows the lump that has formed in her throat. "Are you saying this because you don't want me to come along anymore?"

"Not at all. I just want you to be happy so I can take you home if that's what you want."

"No, please." Moira steps over to him and lays her hands on his chest, meeting his concerned gaze. "I don't want to go home."

"Sleep on it, okay?" He tells her, stepping away but encompassing her hands with his own, hesitant to release them.

"I don't need to. Tomorrow we continue west to Seattle. We are going to that baseball game, *together,* and it's going to be great." Her words are rushed, keeping in time with her pounding heart.

"If you say so." Elliot drops her hands. "Eat something, okay. Then try and get some sleep. We're up at dawn." With this, he spins to the door and opens it, revealing a steady rain that has begun to fall.

"Can you, uh, can you promise me something, Elliot?" He turns a tilted gaze to her. "Can you promise me that…that you won't leave without me tomorrow? I'll get up when you tell me to, but if I don't right away…"

"I can definitely promise you that. I'm not going to leave you behind, okay? For any reason." She whispers her thanks, staring into his sincere, sympathetic eyes. "Good night, Moira." He turns to Leo and gives him a two-finger salute, "Good night, Leo the Fish."

Chapter 16
The Daring, The Bold, and The Friendly

In the morning, she wakes to a firm knocking at her door; she wakes discombobulated and disorientated after a night of fitfully tossing and turning from bad dreams. Elliot calls through the door for her to get up, to get going but his voice only spikes her confusion. Her heart races as her eyes dart around the unfamiliar room. The cracks in the ceiling that had become so familiar last night now seem foreign and the shadows that had become her companions now taunt her.

Elliot knocks again, harder. "Up and at 'em, Moira!"

"I'm up. I'm up!" she calls, falling out of the bed with a painful thud. "I'm up…" she moans, dropping her head against the side of the mattress. From where she sits on the floor, she taps the plastic of Leo's dish, "Are you up?"

"Ugh." He moans, sliding off his hammock.

Moira crawls to her duffel bag and tears it apart in search of clean panties and her bra. Success leads her to the bathroom where she grimaces at the puffy eyes and sunken cheeks in her reflection before sloppily brushing her teeth and putting on her underwear.

"There is no amount of make-up that can fix this." She tells Leo, returning to her duffel bag for the rest of her clothes—a white denim skirt and an off the shoulder top that she first puts on backwards. Righting it, she sighs, snatches her make-up bag, and shuffles back to the bathroom where she attempts to freshen her dampened face with a gentle veil of powders and mascara. There is extra care as she applies her eyeliner and coats each lash, dusts her cheeks with rouge and glosses her lips in pale pink. More so than the days when she would ready herself for work at Skylit.

She ties her hair into a haphazardly stylish bun piled atop her head, tied back with a handkerchief with enough tendrils falling to frame her face, refusing to admit, even to Leo, that she put extra effort into her appearance this morning.

"I feel like yesterday all over." She grumbles, repacking her bag.

"How so?" When Moira doesn't reply, he continues, "There must be some part of you that is excited by all of this?"

She thinks about each emotion fighting for dominance but the one that is losing—terribly—is excitement. Overwhelming nervousness, overbearing regret, these are winning emotions. "No." She answers firmly, zipping her bag. She looks around the room to make sure she hasn't left anything behind but seeing nothing she heads to the door. "I'll come back for you in a second."

Not waiting for a reply, she slips outside to find Elliot leaning on the hood of his Jeep pouring over a map. At first, he doesn't realize she's watching him so absorbed in his route that the world around him—Moira, the brisk morning air—doesn't exist.

"Good morning." She hesitantly greets, stopping on the passenger side of the hood. When he looks up, she is taken aback, physically startled, by the grey framed glasses on his face.

"Hey." He smiles, pleased she is awake and ready to go.

She points to his face "Glasses." She says with regrettable childishness.

"Yea, can't read well without them."

"You look good in them." Another set of words she is unable to snatch back from the air as she utters them; she cringes.

"Thanks." He grins, his brow furrowing as he peers at her. "You fall out of the bed this morning?

"Huh? Well, I mean…"

"Are you alright? Sounded painful from my side of the door." Elliot suppressing his laughter but never taking his off her face.

"That just depends on your definition of *fall*. It was more of a, a tumble and I'm fine, thank you. What are you doing anyway?"

"Marking the map with our route yesterday." He explains, running his finger over the green path back to where they started in Milwaukee. She leans over the hood and gazes down at the map; there is a frowny face in Minnesota and a black X at Theodore Roosevelt State Park. "I mark every map for every trip and every detour." He taps the sad face on the map and smirks.

Moira taps the black X, "Is this where we should have stayed?"

"Yep."

"I'm sorry but surely you understand!" She drops her bag and throws her hands in the air, turning away from him. He laughs and begins to fold his map in precise creases, a practiced artform.

"Of course I do." In a perfect rectangle, he sets the map down on the hood and moves around the car, nearer to her. "I'm not mad. I get it. I am just going to say that two people in bed, or in this case a car, doesn't have to mean sex. It doesn't mean our genitals have to touch if that's what you're afraid of."

Moira's face flares with inconsolable embarrassment and no words come racing to her defense so she snatches her bag from the ground then spins to throw it into the back seat. She slams the bag down behind the cooler and examines the back, eyes drifting from his comforter and pillows to the cooler perfectly situated behind the passenger seat so that he can easily reach it while driving. The platform he built for his bed with small storage caddies underneath are set up for the long haul, for a man on the road. Behind the driver's seat, tucked carefully between the seat and the platform of the bed, is a garment bag and a hanger with several cotton plaid shirts. Next to that her eyes settle on his camera equipment: a tripod, a monopod, and a large black backpack thickly padded with a dozen pockets; it must weigh 50 pounds easily.

"It's okay. We'll stay at motels along the way but you really miss out of the best sights in a motel." He sidles up beside her, leaning on the vehicle, his eyes cheery and playful, too much so for so early in the morning.

"I don't know what I was thinking going with you."

"I don't know what I was thinking taking you with me!" he counters in a convivial tone, his smile unwavering. "Have you slept on it? I know you said you didn't need to, but…" He shrugs, his face unreadable, "you might feel differently this morning. Are we heading east or west, darling?"

"West." Moira says gruffly to her bag.

Over the next couple of moments, they go about their separate tasks, each preparing for the tiring journey in their own ways. Elliot tucks his map away, checks his phone; Moira goes to fetch Leo and tie him up in the window. When the three converge once again in the front seats of the Jeep, belted and comfortable, they pull away from the sleepy motel in the middle of North Dakota heading west towards the dark horizon, pushed forth by the rising sun.

Moira focuses on the rising sun in the side mirror, unable to look anywhere else until a sleep suddenly drops upon her and she is plunged, as though into the deepest depths of the ocean, into darkness. The sounds of the road, Elliot's gentle, sporadic humming to the gentle radio can't permeate Moira's barrier of slumber until the air changes around her, rousing her. The traffic is thick and around them, tall buildings reach towards the sky, a backdrop of sweeping overpasses. A car horn blares behind them.

Her eyes flutter, absorbing the sudden change in the environment, but only for a moment. When she next opens her eyes, the landscape stretches out with incredible dullness, unremarkably brown and barren. The sun hangs low in the eastern sky behind them but lights the world with its warming summer rays. The world is so flat. So unfamiliar. Nothing out there is reminiscent of home, of Wisconsin, but Leo in the window seems so excited by the foreign scenery.

"Have you ever seen such flatness, Leo?" Moira asks, peering outside through her puffy eyes, rubbing a nonchalant finger against the plastic bag over his wiggling body. Elliot looks over at her prepared to answer, of course he has driven this road a dozen times, but stops himself before opening his mouth. This is a mistake, believing she is speaking to him, doomed to be repeated time and time again as everyone in Elliot's life calls him Leo. Only Moira calls him Elliot.

"Do you think it's weird that my name is Leo Fisch and your fish's name is Leo?" he asks.

She thinks for a second then smiles, "Yes, it is kind of odd, isn't it?" Moira giggles, turning her head, lazily leaning against her shoulder and the headrest, "I have two Leo Fishes in my life now. You'll have to be Elliot for a little while."

"It's taking some getting used to."

"There can't be two Leos." she says.

"Fair enough. So, what would you like to do today?"

"Who? Me?"

"Who else?" Elliot laughs, leaning back in his seat, resting his right hand on his leg, his left gripping the bottom of the wheel. She both admires and abhors his relaxed position, wishing she could be as loose and carefree. Her eyes settle on the white fish on his arm with the red and pink highlighting on its fins looking as though it shines in the water.

Be relaxed, she thinks, be friendly. Bold.

Reaching over with a steady hand, she pushes the sleeve of his plaid shirt up to reveal more of the tribal pattern surrounding the fish, the lily pads. Her touch surprises him but he doesn't pull away, he smiles keeping his eyes on the road.

After a moment of admiration for the artistic talent and beauty of the tattoo, she pulls his sleeve back down to his elbow and returns folded hands to her lap. As she watches the horizon, she thinks about all the things Elliot chatted about during their journey yesterday but she still doesn't know so many things about him. Does he have any illnesses, cancer or asthma or lupus? What about children? She is sure that if he had kids, he would have mentioned them in the monologue of life yesterday.

During his self-dialog, she learned of his three half-brothers and four half-sisters, the time he rescued ducklings from a sewer grate, and how he enjoys oat milk even though he isn't a Vegan, but he did try to be one for a minute last year. The man talked about a 17-day excursion to ingratiate himself with a band of wild horses but never did he mention being divorced or having children and she is sure that would have come up, although she was also sure he'd lose his voice from all the talking.

"What are you thinking about over there?" he asks, pulling her eyes to his; she shrugs her reply. "I wish I could do something to make you more comfortable. I guess, though, that this whole situation is a little uncomfortable."

"You're uncomfortable?" She asks with some urgency.

"Not particularly. I meant more about you. I'm fine, but I imagine you must be…" he turns a knitted brow to her. "…it's only day two. Maybe you'll feel better by this afternoon or tomorrow." Looking away, he takes his can of energy drink from the holder and takes a mouthful, his eye scanning the road. "I was thinking about you last night and I can't figure out your thought process. You seem so…" he tilts his head and looks at her with a quizzical gaze. "I don't know."

"Do you wish you hadn't let me come along?"

"Not at all. I told you, sweetheart, this can be a fun adventure for us both. I just wish I could make you comfortable to be around me. I'm not going to hurt you." He takes another drink from his can and they fall silent.

Moira watches him driving, watches his eyes roam the freeway; she watches as he opens the Pandora app on his phone and connects it to the Bluetooth, soon relaxing to the Chris Isaak station, his favorite. He taps out the rhythm and sings along to the first song that comes on making Moira look away to hide her smile.

"The world was on fire and no one could save me but you. It's strange what desire will make foolish people do...why are you laughing at me. Is my singing that bad?" He cuts off his own song, smirking at her.

"No. It's fine." She laughs, turning to the window and shaking her head. In her hands she picks up her water bottle and cradles it to her chest. He continues to sing along, moving his head to the music while his eyes watch the light traffic around them.

"What a wicked game you play, to make me feel this way. What a wicked thing to do, to let me dream of you..." He coos then, sighing, his singing ends abruptly drawing her attention to his face. Reaching over to the center compartment, he yanks it open and huffs. "Shit."

Moira watches him dig around through the loose change, an extra pair of sunglasses, and packets of wet wipes, searching for something before he slams it shut and drapes his hands over the wheel.

"What's wrong?" She asks while sipping her water.

"Hmm?" He looks at her then shrugs, "Nothing. I forgot I moved the ibuprofen."

"That's my fault."

"I'll live. We'll be stopping soon. We can find it then."

"I can find it!" Daring, bold, and friendly, she unclicks her seatbelt and twists in her seat to reach into the back for her duffel bag where she's sure she threw the bottle this morning. With her knee on the center console, she reaches into the back until her fingers grip the handle of her Prada bag.

"This is..." He clears his throat, "This is very distracting." Elliot comments, desperate to keep his gaze on the road and not on her short skirt and bare legs wiggling in his face.

"Keep your eyes on the road." She tells him, digging through the outside pockets of the bag, then digging in the center where she claims the bottle of medicine with a small cheer. She pushes herself back into her seat, beaming with her success but her face flushes when she notices Elliot's glowing cheeks as he stares, unwavering, on the road ahead. She smooths her hands over her skirt, glancing at Leo then back to Elliot.

"Here." She shakes two pills out onto her hand then transfers them to his open palm and watches as he pops them into his mouth. Elliot picks up his can of empty can from the cup holder and shakes it.

"Well shit again."

Without a word, Moira picks up her water bottle and hands it to him.

He accepts it with a perplexed and amused look. "You're an odd little duck." He tells her with the pills still on his tongue before taking a drink from her bottle.

"I'm just trying to be friendly...I guess."

"You want to be friendly?" He asks, handing her bottle back to her. "Tell me something about yourself."

She falls silent, pursing her lips.

"Anything." He pleads. "Tell me about your job you were fired from or hobbies. What about music? Maybe you'd like to put something you like on?"

"No, this is fine."

When the silence returns, he moans and throws his head back against the headrest. "Come on. Give me something here!"

Fidgeting in her seat, she spins the bottle in her palms and jiggles her foot; Moira glances around the road and forces her eyes to go anywhere but to her driver. She can sense his pique but can't get herself to speak.

"Okay." He relents holding his tongue, unable to tolerate the quiet any longer. "How about I ask you some questions and you just answer them?"

"Why do you want me to talk so bad? I was much happier yesterday when you did all the talking. I...I'm not a talker. I'm not very interesting so you should talk."

"I think that might be the most words you've strung together since we've met! Well done." He punches her arm, giving her a playful wink. "What's your favorite movie?"

Moira whines and sets her bottle in the cup holder in the door so she can cross her arms and pout while staring out the window. Her rigid posture, her visage, make Elliot laugh and give up but only for a few minutes and then he presses her again with her favorite food.

"These are not hard questions, my dear." He complains when she refuses to relinquish her silence.

Moira glances at Leo who stares at her with beseeching black eyes, begging her to say something. To offer something to this man who has shown her nothing but patience and kindness, who offered her friendship when she had no one else.

"I'll tell you what. I'm not going to talk anymore until you tell me something."

"That seems more of a punishment for you than for me. I mean, I've lived alone for the last twelve years and only a fish for company for the last five." She pets Leo's bag but he slides away from her finger, protesting her stupidity.

"That's a long time to be alone."

"You can't get hurt if you're alone."

Elliot frowns at her, "I guess you're not wrong. But…it's lonely. Don't you get lonely?"

"I have Leo."

"Ah, yes. I suppose he's about as good a conversationalist as you are. Two peas in a pod."

Turning her eyes to her fish, Moira smiles and pets the bag with tender fingertips. "He's all I have."

"You said he's five? I don't want to be mean, but I'm not sure you'll have him much longer. You might want to think about expanding your circle of companions."

The pair falls quiet as Moira gazes lovingly at Leo, at his pale fins that were once vibrant and his slow circles that were once energetic. Elliot's words have a gravity to them that he doesn't know or understand. How could he? He doesn't know the tears that they bring to her eyes as she keeps her head turned to the window, making sure her hair covers her face.

Elliot leans forward on the wheel and looks at her, his lips tight. "I'm sorry. I didn't mean…" He slumps back in his seat, "I'm sorry."

"It's fine." She sniffles, inconspicuously wiping her eyes so she can find the courage to look him in the face once again. "It's just that he really is all I have. When he's gone…when he's gone, I'll have no one again."

"You'll have me." He smiles at her, sincerity and compassion upon his face. At first, she doesn't know how to reply; she's so touched by his words. Could he mean it, she wonders? Or is this just another rouse used by a man to win her favor, to get her into bed.

She shakes these thoughts away when she looks at his gentle face, his relaxed hands guiding them down the road, when he smiles at her. Maybe he could be an exception to her past experiences. Again, she shakes these blushing thoughts from her head and tries to return his smile.

"My plan for this trip was to just get to Seattle as soon as possible but I was thinking that since you're here, maybe you'd like to see some places? We're heading to Theodore Roosevelt Park if you would like to do some exploring?" He asks when he realizes she isn't going to reply to his offer of friendship when Leo passes. She nods so he nods. "It's a nice park with some pretty good views." He explains, needing to fill the silence between them, a nervousness developing in his movements, in his tone. "I, I didn't mean to make you cry." He suddenly blurts out, rubbing a frustrated hand down his face.

And the silence continues.

Chapter 17
The Hike, The Teacher, and The Story of a Loon

With Leo tied around her neck, Moira carefully follows Elliot up the trail that winds upwards in a series of switchbacks through a rocky bluff, painfully aware that every misstep causes Leo to splash against the side of the plastic bag. Slowing, she casts her eyes to the blue June sky that shines above with wisps of mare's tails painted with artistic strokes until her feet stop moving altogether and she finds herself staring out over the Little Missouri River, glittering in the sunshine.

The river flows freely through the painted canyon; the green around the water is vibrant and in perfect contrast with the reds and browns of the rocky landscape and the purple wildflowers that grow rampantly in tufts of color. The freeway that led here, the road they traveled along since she awoke, was so bland that she can hardly remember when the landscape changed but it has and it has opened into a gem of the Earth.

Elliot turns and watches her admiring the scenery with a smile; it makes him smile but she seems to have forgotten his existence. She passes him up the trail, savoring every dimple in the ground, every kick of a stone, finding new appreciation for Mother Nature and all her flawless imperfections.

With surprising expertise, she carries Leo up a steep hill, eager to reach the summit, to see the view from the top. The overlook steals her breath as she inhales sharply the scent of fresh earth but her attention is drawn to the sound of Elliot's camera, the shutter flickering. Moira watches as he adjusts the camera, aims the lens and the shutter goes again.

"Isn't it beautiful, Leo? Aren't you glad he let us come with him?" She raises the bag to her eyes and smiles at the fish who wiggles around the bag, facing her. "Me, too."

"I'm glad you're glad." Elliot says to her, watching the interaction with Leo. "Even if you're not talking to me."

Lowering Leo, she smiles at Elliot, "I didn't want to disturb you when you're working."

"You're not going to disturb me. I'm a talker, remember? You can speak to me."

"Okay. So how long have you done this for a living? Forever?" She asks, taking a seat on the ground near the edge of the bluff. His reply comes as he turns back to his viewfinder telling her that he's been a professional photographer for a little more than ten years. It goes silent as he watches something through the lens that Moira can't see but the shutter never clicks and Elliot sighs, though he turns to her with a smile.

He moves beside her and takes a seat; when he leans back on his forearms, he casts a gaze out to the horizon and tells her about a mother loon with her chick feeding on a lake in northern Wisconsin. He explains with detailed passion about how the early morning mist was hovering over the water like ghosts, and the clouds were a pink haze, haloed with golden rays. She listens with interest to his descriptions and watches his expression, peaceful and calm as he recalls the moment that forever changed him.

He watched this mother and chick for two hours; he explains dipping off onto a tangent of his love of birds and the challenge they pose to him. In this tributary of his story, he tells her his favorite bird is the Pileated Woodpecker but he has a soft spot for Barred Owls. Still, Moira listens with intrigue, and patience, as he babbles noticing that the more he talks, the more nervous he appears to be getting.

Finally, he stops and takes a deep breath, keeping his gaze out to the horizon with hers still on his face. "Anyway." He sighs, his cheeks growing rosy as he finally meets her eye. "As I was watching them this bald eagle came down after the chick."

"Oh no!"

He nods, "Yea, it was pretty sad but that mother loon went after that eagle and stabbed it in the heart with her beak. The eagle fell face down into the water and floated downstream. The loon eventually swam away but she was making these calls that…" Here, Elliot clears his throat and looks back to the sky, smiling sheepishly. "I cried a little." Shaking his head, he adds with some defensiveness, "It was the saddest shit."

Moira looks at him, resisting the urge to pat his hand or rub his arm, and agrees how sad that must have been to witness. She admits that she has guilt issues killing spiders that get into her apartment to the point that she usually just agrees to coexist with them. Elliot chuckles, and it makes her smile to have said something even a little entertaining.

"So, how did that loon change your life?" Moira asks, turning nervous eyes to Leo.

"It was the first time that a loon killed a bald eagle, or at least it was documented. My photos were featured in National Geographic. After that, a whole bunch of doors opened all at once and suddenly, I had to quit my job to keep up."

"What was your job?"

"I was a Geography teacher at the same high school I graduated from. The same one—"

"You were a teacher?" She turns wide, disbelieving eyes to his face, searching for jest.

He tilts his head, "Why are you so surprised?"

"Oh goodness. I don't know. You seem too young and hip. I can't imagine you teaching a bunch of disinterested high schoolers."

"I was the youngest teacher at the school and that made it hard to gain the respect of my colleagues and parents, but at the same time, it helped my rapport with my students."

Silence falls over them like a curtain drawn across a brightly lit window. Moira peeks at him, as though sneaking a look through this window, at his contemplative profile, at his slightly crooked nose and the wrinkles at the corners of his eyes indicative of a man who smiles and laughs his way through life. She imagines him standing at the front of a classroom, in front of a map, desperate to gain their attention. She imagines he would be many students' favorite teacher, the center of many schoolgirl crushes.

"I bet the girls loved you." When the words leave her lips, her face lights up and she covers it with her palms. He sits up, bringing his knees to his chest to rest his arms on. "Don't look at me." She mumbles into her hands without looking at him.

"I had a student, Andrea Roenicke, who I asked one day if she was related to Ron Roenicke. He was a manager of the Brewers. She told me that there were more important things in life than baseball then she asked if I would consider dating a younger woman."

Moira peeks at him, hiding her smile with her shoulder. "What did you say?"

"I told her only if she was related to Ron Roenicke."

They both giggle, Moira thankful for his relaxed disposition, his ability to ease her embarrassment through the art of storytelling. For his coolness. This coolness sends a shiver down her spine when his eyes find her face; she shifts her gaze to the horizon wishing he would do the same.

"What did you do before you were unemployed?"

"Nothing interesting, like you."

"Teaching *was* interesting. Almost as interesting as what I do now, I guess." He lowers his legs to stretch them out before him, letting them hang over the edge. "Teaching really does run in my family. My mom teaches English and my stepdad teaches History at the same school I taught Geography and my dad is a professor of art history at UWWC. My sister, Pam," he looks at Moira, "she's the one in Seattle, is a first-grade teacher."

"I guess it really does run in your family."

"Pam is actually my half-sister but she's a whole other story. The product of my father's affair when I wasn't even out of the womb yet." He laughs, "She's my best friend though so I can't wait to see her. Maybe you can meet her when we get to Seattle and it's funny how we got to talking about me again." The last part of his sentence is stated with a hint of irritation.

"I'm just so boring, Elliot. There's nothing to me. Leo's more interesting than I am." She sighs, now hugging her knees.

"That makes me sad." Elliot gets to his feet and retrieves his camera. Removing it from the tripod, he goes to his bag and switches the long lens for a shorter lens; Moira watches him.

"That's a very big lens." She comments, hoping to change the subject and to lure him into a different conversation where he does the speaking.

"Probably my most expensive lens. It's my baby, this one." He tells her, carefully putting the telephoto lens back into its case. "You think your Prada bag is pricey…"

"Oh, you noticed it was Prada, huh? Well, I'm not a snob. I didn't even buy it." He laughs, adjusting the heavy backpack on his shoulders. "How much was that lens? Oh, I suppose that's rude to ask."

"Well," he chuckles, "if I had to choose between saving you or the lens if one of you were to fall over the edge, I would choose the lens."

"I probably would, too." Standing, she dusts off her skirt and legs, she straightens the sleeves off her shoulders then slumps against a tree, lifting her shirt to fiddle with her sunflower belly ring, not focused on her actions until she becomes aware of Elliot's gaze. Her face goes hot, "Can I help you?" she asks, tugging her shirt down, shifting uncomfortably.

He shakes his head and looks back to his camera.

Leading the way along the trail, he stops occasionally to gaze at the landscape, through his viewfinder. As they walk, he tells her—distractedly—about his dog, Molitor or Molly for short. This Golden Doodle was just about the most photogenic animal Elliot had ever seen; he practically posed for pictures. For the last seven years it was just the two of them, Elliot and Molly, going from one adventure to the next. The dog even starred in two children's books, *Molly in the USA: National Monuments* and *Molly in the USA: Wisconsin's Seven Natural Wonders*, the pride of Elliot's career, and a calendar.

There is no hiding the sadness in his voice as he talks of his dog when he admits this would have been his first trip without Molly since he adopted him from a rescue in Illinois. Melancholy quickly overtaking him, Elliot shakes himself and changes the subject.

"I always loved Paul Molitor. I loved that he was such a great player but I loved most that his middle name is Leo and that's my name. You know what I think, though?" He stops and turns around to look at her. "I think we should document you and your Leo. The story of a girl and her fish."

"Us?" She raises Leo to eye level, "What do you think about that, my little love?" The fish swims back and forth, drifting to the surface and back down again. "He thinks it's an okay idea. But he doesn't know if I'll be as photogenic as he is."

Elliot smirks.

When they return to the car, Elliot changes from his hiking boots to his boat shoes, commenting to Moira that he thinks she should get some hiking shoes, too, if she enjoyed this stop and would like to do more. She agrees, commenting how her feet are sore since her espadrilles are for style not hiking.

"There are so many places I'd like to share with you, that is, if you want to." As he speaks, he stows away his hiking boots under the bed, only passing a fleeting look to her where she stands beside him watching him.

She smiles and turns her attention to the sunlit landscape dressed in trusses of green grass and wildflowers in between red bluffs and towering rock formations. Everything seems to glitter, like Pavarotti himself, from the white flutters of clouds to the cutting, jagged hills. She turns back to him, now securing his equipment, and watches his movements, letting her gratitude sink in, wondering why it is so hard to tell him a simple 'thank you'.

The desire to reach out and touch him, his arm or his hand, is overpowering to the point that she clenches her left hand into a fist, squeezing her thumb until it throbs. She wants to kiss him, his cheek or his mouth. This thought, this craving, makes her hold her breath and turn desperate eyes down to Leo, pleading for advice. The fish only looks at her.

"I'd like to see whatever you're willing to show me." She murmurs, blushing profusely as she makes her way to the passenger seat where she can tie Leo up. While she works, Elliot slips behind the wheel and waits for her to be ready before pulling out of their parking space in the gravel parking lot.

Not before long, they're walking around a store side-by-side in search of some shoes and a fishbowl. Walking beside Elliot reminds Moira of less lonely days when she had a boyfriend, someone whose hand she could hold. Elliot isn't like Jonathan or any of the boyfriends she had in high school as he playfully leads Moira around the store, helping her pick out a pair of decent shoes for hiking and the best fishbowl, which they decide should be a glass canister with a screw on lid so they won't waste water. Where Jonathan was condescending and serious, Elliot is silly, smiling at Moira often, saying hello to every worker with overt friendliness, explaining to Moira that his greeting may be the only kindness they receive that day.

Once they've paid, they cross the parking lot back to the Jeep where Moira immediately sets away tying Leo to the window again. As her fingers work to secure her fish, she can feel Elliot watching her, making her self-conscious and causing a tremor to shake through her fingertips.

"We should get something to eat. I could stop at a gas station and find some local secret if you like? Or we can eat in the car while we continue on our way? Up to you, sweetheart. Moira. Sorry."

"Whatever you want." She replies.

"I wish you'd say what you want to do for once."

"I'm the stowaway, though! I do what you do."

"Except sleep in the car." He retorts with a playful wink that makes her face flush.

Chapter 18
The Farmstead, The Questions, and The Photoshoot with a Fish

The drive is mostly quiet as Elliot focuses on his memory of the directions he was given from a gas station clerk while Moira silently ponders how he can so confidently know where he is going. The two-lane highway leads them to the "lovely old tree" as described to Elliot where he was told to take the next right turn afterwards onto a suffering country road, nearly washed away into the fields that run alongside it. Eventually, through the maze of dips and potholes, they find the turn that leads them to the farmstead.

"This is perfect." Elliot comments thoughtfully, his eyes scanning the area. "Fucking perfect."

"What is?" Moira's eyes search for what he sees. He parks the Jeep in what is presumably a parking space in the dirt lot then turns to her with an enthusiastic grin.

"Look at this place. It is straight out of a painting. Picture-freaking-perfect."

Moira looks around with a furrowed brow, "It looks like a house."

"Ugh." Elliot moans, clasping his hands over his heart in feigned shock. "I am going to make you see! Prepare the fish!" he commands like a king readying his army for battle then leaps from the Jeep. When Moira doesn't move, he spins and stares into her confused, unmoving face and shakes his head. Leaning in, he tells her in a low voice, "That means put Leo in the bowl. We're going for our first photoshoot."

"Oh!" She blushes not only for her inanity but for his nearness, though he doesn't stay close for long as he bounces away to get his camera.

"I like his enthusiasm." Leo whispers.

She nods, her straight, pursed lips spreading into a smile as she does as she was told, prepares the fish, by lining the bottom of the bowl with the river rocks, settling the faux moss into the center. With water from the gallon that Elliot had purchased yesterday morning, she fills the glass bowl and then adds a few drops of Stress Coat from the bottle she keeps in her purse.

Once deemed "picture-freaking-perfect", she scoops Leo's little body into her fingers and carefully lowers him into the water. He doesn't flail when in her hands, doesn't flop chaotically in a panic like typical fish out of water, but instead lays peacefully on her fingers.

"Here you go, my little love." She coos as he wiggles off her fingers into the freshwater. He soars around the open space stretching his fins and rolling around; he comes to the surface to let her stroke his head.

"You sure do have some kind of bond with that fish." Elliot says, approaching with a smile.

Moira gives a Mona Lisa smile in reply but remains quiet, not wanting to repeat her sad sentiments that this fish is her only friend in the world. Accepting her silence as final, Elliot removes Leo's bowl from her hands.

"Let's do this then."

Moira watches as he situates the bowl for the first photo of the tour, setting it down on a retaining wall holding a raised garden of Mona Lavender, Elephant's Ears, a rainbow of Asiatic lilies, and a spread of annuals—Petunias, Snap Dragons, and Dusty Miller.

On his haunches, he takes the first couple shots.

She stands behind him watching him, watching his fingers manipulate the settings on the camera with silent interest, stepping back as he lay on the ground, his camera pointed up at Leo. Her face flushes while she clenches her legs together and holds down her denim skirt but Elliot is focused only on the lens of his camera, on zooming in on the details of Leo's flowing fins.

"This is such a perfect fish." He exclaims, getting to his feet and dusting off his jeans.

Moira beams with pride moving over to Leo. "You're perfect. I always knew you were perfect but now someone else realizes you're perfect."

Elliot clicks his fingers, a smile on his face, and he swiftly steps over to Moira and pulls her arms gently. "Sit here with your fish."

"Me?" she asks startled, setting herself down on the retaining wall where Leo was a moment ago.

"Yea, yea." He kneels before her and adjusts the bowl in her hands, moving her like a frightened mannequin. "Hold him like this. Both hands, here. Bring your feet in." The warmth of his touch on her knees makes her jump but he just keeps working, pushing her feet against the retaining wall until she is in a regal pose. She blushes and he steps back, looking at her, calculating, then moves back to her and places his fingers on her chin. He moves her head slightly, "Look over there. Chin up. Don't be nervous!" He grins, pointing in the direction he wants her to be looking. "Look that way, please." The shutter clicks and he stands upright with a nod signifying success. Now they can eat.

Inside, the waitresses and customers pass quizzical glances at the couple taking pictures of a fish, but no one comments so they're left to enjoy breakfast in peace with, once again, Elliot offering the only commentary until it's time to get back on the road again.

Elliot waits patiently for Moira to situate Leo in the window, his brow knitting with concern, "Is he going to be okay?"

"Yea, why?" she doesn't look at him as she focuses on her task.

"Aren't fish sensitive?"

Moira shrugs.

"So, he's going to be alright? He's not stressed?

"No." She finally turns to Elliot, a grateful smile gracing her soft face. "He's good but we appreciate your concern." As she says this, she buckles up and snuggles back into her seat, indicating to Elliot she is ready to depart.

Elliot navigates down the country roads that lead them here while Moira watches out the window purely content, at peace, with how the morning is shaping up. The quiet contentment doesn't last long before Elliot presses her to talk, to tell him something about herself. She groans and rolls her eyes, turning her head further to the right, further from making eye contact.

"You can look out that window as hard as you like." He begins, suppressing the urge to laugh at her unnecessary exasperation. "We're still in the same car."

She turns irritated eyes to him, "What exactly do you want to know?"

Undaunted by her biting tone, Elliot smiles and shrugs, "Anything. This is how people get to know one another. We talk."

"*You* talk." she retorts, with a huff.

Now he rolls his eyes, "I've had better conversations with my dog."

Moira crosses her arms, refusing to make eye contact. Inside, she struggles with the desire to be personable, to be likeable and friendly but something more than shyness keeps her chest locked, something near to bitterness. He's a stranger, she justifies, a man. Men can't be trusted.

While she internally battles to be social, Elliot turns on the radio, keeping it low, and begins to tap out a beat on the wheel, singing without qualms to Bruce Springsteen's *I'm on Fire*. His head moves with the rhythm, a charming smile playing on his lips.

"Ah!" He interrupts himself, his smile spreading across his face. "Tell me about when you got your fish." His expression is that of a man who has come up with an extremely clever idea.

"Leo?" she asks, turning her attention to the fish that gazes out at the passing world. To the unknowing eye, he stares blankly, thoughtlessly, but Moira sees him for what he is. Bewildered and enthralled by the rugged, flat landscape framed by rising red bluffs speckled with colorful flowers as far as the horizon. "I got him from a pet store."

Elliot shakes his head in a disapproving manner, "There's more to it than that. Why did you get a fish?"

"I don't know."

"Fine." He concludes with a frown. "We'll just sit here." Resigned for silence, he leans back in his seat, draping his hands over the top of the wheel after turning the radio up, and presses forward with an indifferent visage greying his normally sunny face.

"I was lonely, so I got a fish! What more do you want?"

"So you've been alone for 12 years and had him for five? I'm just trying to figure you out. Like, are you a nun?"

"No, of course not. I mean, I was raised Catholic but...well, I guess." She hesitates, looking at Elliot with a sidelong glance. "I guess I don't have much use for religion."

"Woman after my own heart." He mutters, grinning as he maneuvers around a tractor bumbling down the highway. The move makes her shiver but, as agreed, she doesn't comment on how fast he drives or how close she thinks he was to the tractor. Instead, she chooses to try making conversation, friendly and unassuming.

"I bet you've skydived." She smirks as though it is her turn to say something clever, as though she has him all figured out.

"Hell no." He replies to her surprise. "I'm not jumping out of any plane. I'm not climbing any part of Mount Everest, I'm no Jimmy Chin! And I'm not tying a rubber band around my waist. I'm also never going on that fair ride that flips you around," He motions with his hand like a windshield wiper blade and shakes his head.

"The Hammer?"

"Yea, that's the one!" he confirms passionately. "The Hammer. Fuck that."

Moira laughs lightly and focuses her gaze outside, "I always liked fair rides."

"You're stupid." He says, flatly, his eyes on her with surprise and disapproval in them but still they sparkle with his humor. She only laughs then lets her eyes drift outside where countless rocks and flowers on the side of the road pass by along with the minutes. The music accents a peaceful, comfortable quietness between them only dipped in awkwardness when driver and passenger make eye contact.

They are quiet until they merge onto the freeway and Elliot settles them into the fast lane. Once cruising along, he turns back to her with inquiring eyes and a mind, a tongue, which will not rest.

"What's your favorite movie?"

"Why do you want to know so bad?"

"And why are you so opposed to telling me? I'm glad you turned me down for dinner because I think that may have been painful. At least with breakfast, we had the fish to talk about."

"You don't seem to understand." There is no hiding her agitation; she turns to him with narrow eyes, "I'm not good at this. I'm used to being alone! Besides, when I was thirteen, I went on my first date and my brother told me that men only want to talk about themselves. They don't care about women, they only care about what's in their pants." She crosses her arms and looks outside.

"Your brother said that to you when you were 13? When my littlest sister, Lainey, went on her first date last year, she was 15, my advice to her was to make sure she didn't tuck her dress into her nylons. She didn't think that was funny but she doesn't think anything I do or say is funny. We had an incident when she was 11 and now, she doesn't really talk to me."

"What incident?"

"Okay, so about five years ago, I took her camping and she got her first period. This seems to have traumatized her."

"Oh dear. That poor girl."

"Poor girl?" Elliot looks at her, eyes wide, mouth open. "Poor me! I didn't know what to do so I took her home and she hasn't spoken to me since." He shakes his head and leans back in his seat, keeping his eyes focused on the road.

"There's a big age difference between you and your sister, right?"

"19 years to be exact." He answers before sighing and looking at her with narrow eyes. "I want you to know that I don't want to talk about myself, I'm not trying to get into your pants. I just want to get to know you since we're going to be in this car together for a while. But I'm going to stop trying." His voice holds no anger, no irritation. Instead, it's dejected, quiet and slow, his brows knitted in thought. "You want to be alone, fine. You think I'm a bad guy, that's not fine but I can't force you to see that I'm not."

For a moment, Moira remains speechless, unable to form a coherent thought, or speak a coherent sentence. Elliot turns up the volume on the radio and adjusts himself in the seat, watching the building traffic around them as they head south. She wonders how long he would last not speaking but she also knows this isn't fair, after all the nice things he's done for her since they met.

"My favorite movie is Die Hard, I love Josh Groban. I can eat macaroni and cheese all day, and I don't think you're a bad guy. I'm just…I'm just nervous. I'm the type of person who is nervous in my own skin."

"Die Hard? For real?" His brows arch, ignoring her other confessions.

"Well, Die Hard with a Vengeance. It's the best one." She keeps her eyes on his hands.

"Will you marry me?" His words startle her and she pulls her eyes to his face, to his serious eyes but his mischievous, crooked smile. "We can go to Vegas because I don't think I want to let a woman go whose favorite movie is not only an action movie but one of *the* best action movies ever made."

Her face grows hot as he smirks at her, making her turn her gaze to Leo who watches her, urging her to relax.

Chapter 19
The Falls, The Bird, and The Versace Spider

The morning disappears into the afternoon with a hundred stops along the way, heading back east, south, north again and finally west. Moira's concerns for his timeline are dismissed each time they stop and get his equipment out. As long as Elliot keeps his sister updated on when to expect him in Seattle, he is carefree, addicted to the wanderlust.

Detours, he reiterates, is how you find the hidden gems, the diamonds off the beaten path. A one-day trip should always take five, he concludes, grinning broadly at her. This is something Moira can't comprehend, how he can live like this, how he can have a home life.

A melancholy smile crosses his face, "It can make things difficult." He confirms, not taking his eyes off the road. "I used to spend weeks or even months on the road living out of my car. I migrated with Whooping Cranes, I spent a year staying at every State and National Park. But...I've been trying to keep it closer to home. Thinking about settling down, I guess. It's hard to do that when you're always traveling."

She wants to question him further, to prod into his life the way he keeps trying to do with her but she isn't sure how. She isn't sure how to ask or even what she wants to ask. An open book doesn't always divulge its secrets that remain between the lines.

"What's on your mind?" He asks her suddenly, flicking his eyes over hers briefly before turning them back to the highway. His perceptiveness startles her and she realizes she is staring at him, examining his features.

"You told me yesterday that I can ask you anything, right?" He nods. "Why do you look so sad?"

"I'm not sad." He tells her, frowning. "I'm just contemplative, I guess." She glances outside at the scenery so far removed from what she is used to in Milwaukee that she should be awed, however her concern and attention is on her chauffeur. "I'm okay." He tells her as though reading her thoughts. "I just sometimes wonder what my life would be like had I kept teaching."

"Oh no!" Moira cries, aghast at the thought. "But think of all the wonderful things you've seen!"

He turns his golden eyes to her, serious, his lips a thin, terse line. "Can't help but think about it sometimes. When I get lonely. But I'm glad you're here." She meets his eye but only briefly as she pulls her gaze outside, her face flushing. He reminds her that this would have been his first trip without Molitor since he adopted him seven years ago. "It's nice to have someone to talk to." He says, then adding with teasing eyes, "Even if that someone is you."

"Oh ha." Her hot cheeks reveal her flattered bashfulness, though she tries to hide it by turning her attention to the landscape of red and gold geological history that is the Black Hills of South Dakota. She's not even sure when they got to South Dakota, or how, but around them tall spruces cover vast sections interrupted by granite obelisks that stretch along the horizon reaching to the heavens with jagged fingers. They pass an acreage of rolling plains covered in fairybells and star lilies, and tufts of milkvetch.

She points out a lone tree in the distance, standing tall on a steep hill, to Leo and a flock of what she assumes are vultures circling so high in the sky they appear to be simple black dots. Elliot refrains from interrupting her conversation, reminding himself internally, again, that she isn't talking to him. So lost in the beauty of the scenic road, Moira appears to have forgotten his presence entirely, which makes him smile, content with showing her more than the walls of her apartment.

After some time of driving, they pull off the scenic route and onto the side of the byway. A large brown sign indicates Bridal Veil Falls and a little way from this is a viewing platform for the best view of the falls. The moment they get out of the car, the sounds of rushing water can be heard like thunder in the distance.

Moira can hardly take her eyes off the falls, astounded by the amount of water and the booming noise. She confesses to Elliot, pulling him down by his collar towards her to talk into his ear, that this is considerably better than the little falls Leo's tank used to have over his filter.

"Come on." He motions for her to follow him as he heads to a trail head. She eagerly follows him down the trail, careful of her footing on the uneven ground while Leo hangs around her neck and still attempts to absorb the beauty surrounding them. The canopy of the towering trees sings in the wind, the sounds of the falls keeping the rhythm.

They reach a point where Moira is no longer sure that they are on a trail, but still she follows Elliot to a stream, which he surveys the area then takes off his hiking boots and socks and steps into the frigid water. She watches, annoyed, as he crosses and turns to her.

"Well?"

"You've lost your mind. I am not walking barefoot in this water. There could be a lobster waiting to cut off my feet. A barracuda!"

Elliot sets down his equipment and comes back for her, first taking the shopping bag that has Leo's bowl from her fingers, "Give me Leo."

"Oh…"

"It'll be okay. Trust me." With hesitant fingers, she places Leo around Elliot's neck, telling herself internally that it's fine. Elliot then turns and kneels before her. "Jump on my back, I'll carry you over, Your majesty."

"Uhm, okay." She wraps her arms around his neck and he lifts her up, grabbing her thighs and pulling her against him. As they cross, he hums a song as though attempting to ease his own embarrassment or perhaps hers, which rages.

Once across, he sets her down and turns to return her fish to her. "See, Leo, that wasn't so bad." She mutters; Elliot chuckles then leads the way down the path.

The three follow the increasing volume of the waterfall until it is before them, pouring down over the edge from 50 feet above. Elliot waits patiently for Moira to ponder the beauty of this subsidiary of the main falls that stretches wide and tumbles like lace over the rocks. When she is ready, they prepare Leo for another photoshoot.

After a few shots from different angles, Elliot asks Moira if she will sit for a few photos with Leo, which she hesitantly agrees to. Elliot holds her hand as he helps her over some rocks to where she can sit on a boulder in the middle of the river. He tells her where to look, up to the falls, down at Leo, to the sky, and compliments her for her natural talent and ability to follow instructions as well as her fish.

"Is Molitor as good a model?" she asks, smiling and blushing while he adjusts the settings on his camera.

"He's the best. I swear he has a human brain."

"You adopted him from a rescue, right?" She asks and he nods. "He knows you saved him. He wants to say thank you."

Elliot smiles, "Maybe."

Moira closes her eyes and relishes the gentle spray from the cascading falls. How peaceful such a tumultuous roar can be, she thinks.

"Pretty cool, huh?" He asks her, sloshing through the water to be by her side. She nods, handing Leo's bowl to him so he can get the fish back to shore.

When she is safely back on solid ground, under the canopy of towering pines and elms, she smiles at Leo, sitting down in front of his bowl. Elliot moves a little further down the river, watching the woods above, watching the river beside him.

Listening to the pure sounds around her, Moira closes her eyes and lets them all sink in. Each individual bird, each murmuring leaf. Each and every sound a lullaby soothing her worries even as Elliot disappears down river with his camera.

"How are you, my little love?" She peers down at Leo, love in her eyes, when she realizes she's alone with him.

Leo swims to the surface of the water and inhales deeply, filling his tiny lungs. "This place is great. This guy's the best thing that ever happened to you. Look how happy you are."

Her face goes hot, "Happiness is overrated."

"One day you'll see that happiness isn't overrated. You'll see that you can be happy and maybe, just maybe…this guy can help you."

Flushing, she shakes her head vehemently, "We should go find him, anyway." Composing herself, she heads down stream to find Elliot waist deep in the middle of the river, his camera pointed downstream, though at what, Moira isn't sure but he motions for her to be quiet, to not move. She peers down to where he is looking and sees a Great Blue Heron wading in the water, fishing, not 10 yards away.

She watches as Elliot adjusts the lens, spinning different dials, then hears the fluttering of the shutter just as the bird stabs its beak into the water, returning with a sparkling fish in its mouth. The camera shutters again and the fish disappears into the heron's belly.

"Oh! That poor fish." Moira gasps, looking down at Leo with a pouting lower lip.

"Circle of life." Elliot whispers, unmoving, following the bird with his lens as it wades through the flowing waters.

For ten minutes Moira watches Elliot silently watching this bird through his viewfinder; she listens to the shutter and wonders how many photos he needs to take of one bird. Deciding it isn't her place to question—she is his guest, after all—she plops down on a fallen tree, setting Leo down beside her in his glass bowl. For a while, she can be thankful for the beauty that surrounds her and for getting new shoes that protect her feet. There is so much to be thankful for, right here, right now. The wind in the canopy, the sound of the babbling river, and the birds warbling in the trees. Her feet don't hurt and they aren't wet.

She takes a deep breath and looks around, she looks down at Leo, up to the sky, then at Elliot standing barefoot in a river, getting his pants and shirt all wet for a picture. Gazing at him, she lets her thoughts wander until movement in her peripheral vision draws her attention to a spider making its way down her shoulder. Panic hits her and she screams, flailing her arms and falling backwards off the log. The heron, frightened from the sudden noise, takes flight, disappearing into the trees before Elliot can get another shot off. He looks over at her with arched brows and taut mouth as she attempts to right herself.

"There was a spider." She explains, rolling off of the log then popping up from behind it and looking at Elliot, her face burning. "He had striped legs!" She hollers, panting. "Like he was wearing socks. Fuzzy socks. He was like, like a Versace spider!" He stares at her, mouth agape as she climbs over the log and straightens out her skirt and top, brushing the dirt and leaves from her backside. Elliot shakes his head and wades back to the shore where she waits for him to climb out, offering to take his camera from his hands. "Now you're all wet."

Picking up his shoes and socks from under a tree with his tripod, he flashes her a confident smile, "I have more pants." He then leads the way back to the jeep, Moira following closely behind him incredibly conscious of the way his wet jeans hug the curves of his body. She forces her eyes to the sky to avoid staring at him as he walks. When they finally reach the byway where the Jeep is parked, she is thankful to no longer be walking behind him.

She returns Leo to his bag in the window but Elliot hasn't returned to the driver's seat like normal so she slips back out of the passenger side and moves to the back of the Jeep where she can see the back is popped open. Upon seeing him standing there, in the road, bare feet on the concrete, in his boxers, she exclaims and scurries back to the front seat where she plops down with her head in her hands. Elliot, unphased, continues to change into dry clothes before sliding behind the wheel.

"Sorry." She mutters, unable to look at him for fear he'll see her flushed face.

"You like my Snoopy boxers?" he asks, laughter in his voice.

"Uh, hey I'm gonna change my clothes so I'll be a minute." Moira says in a mocking male voice, impersonating him poorly. "You couldn't tell me that?"

"Is that what you think I sound like? *Is* that what I sound like?" There is feigned alarm in his voice, an impish grin on his face. "Sorry, sorry. Next time I take off my pants, I will let you know."

Moira shakes her head, her face turning yet a deeper shade of crimson.

"I'll tell you a story, okay? To help you get over your embarrassment. Okay. So, my stepdad, the history teacher, he will not and I mean will *not* stop buying me socks and boxers. I swear to you I could wear a different pair every day for a year."

"That's…that's really fascinating." She turns an unimpressed face towards him, though her cheeks still burn.

"It is. I think it is. I have so many boxers and so many socks, I just don't know what to do anymore. I've asked him to stop but he thinks I'm being polite."

"My mom buys be purses. I am not a purse person but she doesn't stop."

"The moral of the story being that our parents are annoying."

"Well, mine are for sure." She kicks her purse on the floor at her feet. "If it isn't Gucci or Coach or, I don't know…Givenchy, it isn't worth owning."

"Ahh. Your parents are rich."

"Oh yes." She confirms. "Very."

"Okay, so tell me something then, Miss Lovegood." He cocks an eyebrow, "How the hell did you end up in our shithole apartments? No offense to John. I've been friends with John's son since middle school so I love the man like another father, but still."

"Well, Mr. Fisch, if you *must* know." Casting her eyes outside, she takes a deep breath and chokes down her bitterness, "I moved out when I was 18 determined to never speak to my parents again."

Elliot thinks for a moment letting his confusion sink in and saturate his expression. "Oh wait, wait, wait." He waves his right hand, left hand still holding the bottom of the steering wheel, "I get it. I get it now. You moved out when you were 18 because you're *you* and I can see you doing something like that. Stubborn, fiery, whatever the opposite of levelheaded is. But…you'll still take your parents expensive presents even though twelve years later you're still holding a grudge for whatever stupid thing they said or did?"

She thinks about her answer, long and hard, aware of Elliot looking back and forth between her and road, waiting. Memories of Charles Kent flood back to her, his reflection coming behind her in her bathroom mirror, his dry hands grabbing her waist, pulling her legs, her skirt. His fingers, his cold ring and her parents' deplorable words. She shudders and pulls her view to the landscape outside of her window, her breathing deepening, heart racing.

"I'm sorry. I was only kidding about…"

"It's okay." She looks at him trying to smile, to ease his guilt trodden face. "It's okay. I'm all those things. I'm fiery and irrational and definitely stubborn. It's probably why I'm still single and my only friend is a fish." She laughs, sardonically, and leans back in her chair adjusting herself for the maximum amount of comfort the front seat will allow then reaches for the volume and turns it up ending their conversation.

Chapter 20
The Tire, The Cat Skills, and The Fight

When she wakes, she is alarmed that the Jeep is stopped on the side of the highway, pulled over onto the gravel. Her head snaps around looking for any sign of Elliot but she can't see him though she can feel movement under her seat.

"What happened?" she asks Leo, hanging in the window.

"Flat tire?" he suggests.

Moira whines and hastily undoes her seatbelt so she can throw herself out of the car to find her driver. She stumbles on the steep gravel side having to balance herself using the vehicle until she comes around the back to find Elliot changing out a flat tire.

"Rip Van Winkle awakes!" he cheers.

"Wha…what?" she pulls her headband off her head and runs her nails through her hair, staring at him, blinking heavily.

"Oh, Rip Van Winkle. It's a 19th century story—"

"I know who it is." She cuts him off in a piqued tone.

"Okay." He replies, briefly pausing from his task of removing the nuts from the flat tire to glance her way before busying his hands once again. She watches him work, as he babbles, almost nervously, about a kid who fell asleep in his class so he let him sleep all through the lesson and the next one, too. His hands move with fluidity, experience. She can tell he's been through this many times before and still he talks as he pulls off the flat and swaps it out for the spare. He tells her how the kid was furious, red faced and threatened to tell his dad.

Elliot laughs at the memory, amused by his past antics. From that point, he explains, he called the kid Rip but was appalled to find out that not one of his students understood the reference. He tightens the bolts, spinning the tire iron and still talking. As she observes him working so easily, she examines the softness of his hands, the normal cleanliness of his trim nails now covered in dirt. She hears him talk about how he incorporated Rip Van Winkle into a lesson on the Cat Skill Mountains and how one of the English teachers, Mrs. Davig, was furious that he was stepping into her domain of literature. Her eyes move to his biceps as they flex under his shirt sleeves when he tightens, once more, the bolts on the spare tire.

His movements are as flowing and liquid as his conversation, his memory of the evil Mrs. Davig transitioning seamlessly into how the spare tire won't get them too far, how he should have gotten a new spare tire a long time ago but could never be bothered.

"We'll have to get it changed." He concludes, finally standing. "I can't believe you slept through that." He wipes his dusty hands on his jeans then goes to put the flattened tired on the back where the spare should be hanging. Again, he wipes his hands on his jeans, smearing blackness onto the light denim. He's talking about something, she can hear him, but her attention is on the setting sun, on the orange bleeding into night like a watercolor painting.

"What do you think?" He asks, stepping beside her, peering at her distracted face. "You're still half asleep."

"I must be really *tired*. Get it? *Tired*?"

Elliot chuckles, "Nice one." Then places his warm hand on the small of her back, guiding her back to the passenger door. Her face glows like the sunset and a shiver shoots over her skin, fading as soon as he removes his palm to open her door. She clumsily takes a seat, stumbling as she plunks down.

"Aren't you irritated?" she asks him suddenly as he's about to close the door.

He pulls it back open, and cocks his head with some confusion, "Why?"

"That you got a flat tire? I would be so mad."

"You weren't awake when I called the car a c—" He slams the door cutting off his expletive with comedic timing.

The drive into the nearest town isn't long but given the late hour, Elliot determines that the tire will have to wait until the morning. He tells her, to her secret relief, that their current option is to stop at a motel and wait until morning before they can move on.

In the parking lot of a motel, a near duplication of where they stayed last night, Elliot's phone begins to chime but he quickly dismisses the call only to have it start ringing again moments later.

"People." He gripes, rolling his eyes. Moira chooses not to reply, knowing that whatever People he is referring to is probably the same from last night's argument that she overheard. Instead, she follows him inside where they each pay for their own rooms, again Elliot in room One and Moira in room Two.

At the Jeep, his phone rings again as he snatches up his duffel bag from the back, "It must be 9 o'clock in Wisconsin." He mumbles, letting the phone ring in his back pocket.

"I should call someone." Moira says, thoughtfully, as she picks up her bag. "Just to let someone know where I am."

"Yea, you should. I don't want your parents to accuse me of kidnapping their daughter. I spent two nights in county jail; I won't do well in prison." With this being said, he goes into his room and she goes into hers where she drops her bag down and sets Leo's glass bowl down on the dresser.

With Leo draped around her neck, she casts her view around the room, at the single full-size bed in the center of the room, the two nightstands on each side. She looks at the window and the door to the bathroom, then down at Leo.

"This is the part of the night that I hate." She sighs, moving to get his bowl so she can make him comfortable for the night.

"You should go over to his room and see what he wants to do tonight. Don't repeat yesterday where you made us all miserable." Leo tells her, sliding onto his hammock.

"I suppose." she answers, her eyes on the door, wishing Elliot would come knocking.

"Don't make him come to you."

Moira forces herself to stand, urges her feet to the door, and swallows the lump of nerves in her throat as she pushes herself out the door into the darkening evening. She approaches his door but seeing that it is ajar, she stops in her tracks. When she hears the anger in his voice, she creeps towards it, knowing she shouldn't listen, that it's wrong. She doesn't, she can't, stop until she can hear his words.

"What do you want from me, Lauren?" He asks the person on the phone. There is a pause as this Lauren says something then Elliot bites back with shocking venom, "You should have thought of that before you fucked him in our bed!" His voice is low but enraged.

Lauren must be speaking now for Elliot has gone quiet except for the occasional scoff.

"That's not going to happen. I'm in South Dakota." He tells her flatly; he listens some more, "You're not going to do that. You're not taking him anywhere. Shit, Lauren, you've held him hostage for a fucking month." Again, he listens. "I'm in South Dakota. I cannot and will not be there at 10 tomorrow to pick him up. You will have to wait until Sunday when I get back." He sighs, annoyed, "Oh, don't start crying...now you miss me? You fucking miss me? Don't call me anymore, I'm fucking busy. I'll call you on Sunday." He listens again, "Whatever." At last, Elliot ends the call.

There is weighted silence.

Moira's heart beats in her throat but she won't get caught listening; she is going to be bold and risk an offer of kindness. She knocks on his door and lets herself in, finding him slumped on the bed, leaning on his knees, head hung low.

"Your door is open." she simpers, wringing her hands.

He nods but doesn't move from his position until she sits beside him on the single bed, only then does he look at her.

"Are you okay?" she asks him, steadying her hand and placing it on his back, rubbing gently. "I'm sorry to...to bother you. I didn't mean..."

"She says she's going to take Molitor to the fucking pound if I don't pick him up tomorrow. She cheats on me, kicks me out of our house, holds my dog hostage and now..." Elliot shakes his head and pushes from the bed with a groan. "It was a really bad breakup."

"Sounds like it." Moira twists her fingers in her lap as she watches Elliot pace the room, she listens as he tells her what happened. His usual vivacious tone is solemn, heavy with dejection, and his eyes fixate on his feet. He tells her how he came home from an engagement photo shoot that was canceled because the couple broke up. He tells her how he was going to surprise his girlfriend by cleaning the whole house and making her favorite meal for dinner. Lauren is a nurse and often would be stressed so he wanted to do something special, be thoughtful and romantic since she so often told him how he wasn't.

"When I came home, she was in bed with another guy. So, me being me, I waited in the kitchen for them to finish." Finally raises his eyes to meet her, and he sneers, "It was a traumatizing two minutes." His tone is dry, hinted with humor.

Moira can't help it as a laugh escapes her lips, "I'm sorry." She covers her pursed lips. "It's not funny. It's not…I'm sorry!"

He shakes his head and shrugs, returning to the bed where he drops down beside her and sags forward. "It's a little funny. But I tell you what, I will never forget what I was doing on May 19th…listening to some guy fuck my girlfriend."

"My birthday!" She blurts and, again, covers her face, wishing she could sink into the floor and disappear. "You wanted me to talk now I can't shut the heck up."

"You're good." He smiles weakly, his eyes only passing over hers for a moment before finding his feet. "So, you mean to tell me that you got fired on your birthday and that's the same day that my relationship of three years fell apart?"

"What a terrible day for all."

The pair fall silent, each staring at the floor in front of them, at their shoes, at each other's shoes, at the stained carpeting, until finally Elliot pushes off his knees and crosses the room with a sigh.

"She misses me. Can you believe that?" He spins to face Moira, his hands on his hips. "She fucks some guy in my bed and now she misses me. I swear too much don't I?"

Moira shrugs, "I don't know. I don't swear so I would say anyone curses a lot compared to me."

"That's right. I haven't heard you swear. I'll…I'll try to cut back." Elliot rubs the back of his head and casts his eyes back to the floor to hide his shamed expression.

It isn't like him, she thinks, to not hold eye contact, to frown so much or to blush. His embarrassment startles her.

"Oh, goodness no. Don't change anything on my account, Elliot. I don't even notice. It's just words, right? Uh, so, are you worried about your dog? Do we need to go back?"

"Nah." He turns from her, removing his wallet from his back pocket and tossing it on the table. "She's not going to. She's just trying to get her way. If she does, I will fucking kill her and then I really will go to prison." He moans and runs both hands over his face. "I am so fucking stupid! I should have taken Molly with me. I should have…" On a heel, he spins to face her, shaking his head, "I couldn't take him with me. I had a commercial shoot in Mexico that weekend. I-I didn't want to burden my mom with the dog when my stepdad is allergic!"

Moira wants to tell him he doesn't have to explain himself to her, his reasons, whatever they were for leaving Molitor with Lauren, surely made sense at the time. She doesn't say anything; she watches him pace around the room.

"When I came back from Mexico, she refused to give him back. She said some bullshit how she paid for his vet bills; he's her dog. Like a fucking pu--" He cuts himself off, his face flushing, "I'm not good at not swearing. Like a *pansy* I walked away. I always just walk away."

"I'm sorry."

"35 years old moving back in with your parents fucking sucks, Moira. It sucks. And, you know as much as I love them both, my mom and stepdad, they drove me nuts. That's how I ended up at John's. By you."

"I can only imagine."

"I mean, Lauren had my stuff packed up and ready to go not eight hours later. What else was I going to do?"

"You did what you had to do, I guess."

Elliot slumps on the bed beside her, "Yea. I guess." Standing suddenly, he crosses the room, again running his hands through his thick blonde hair. "Listen, I'm going to take a shower and get myself cleaned up. Try to calm down a bit."

Moira jumps from her seat with an abrupt nod. "Sure. Well, you know where to find me…if you need anything or…okay." He thanks her as she heads to the door and when she leaves, she doesn't look back.

Chapter 21
The Call, The Ceiling, and The Night of the Many Confessions

Moira sits on the edge of the bed listening to her stomach gnaw away at itself. The peanut butter and jelly sandwich she ate sometime after the falls has long since satiated her and now, she truly believes that if food were placed in front of her, she would drop her head into it like a pig at a trough.

There's no guarantee, and she explains this to Leo, that Elliot is going to come see her when he has finished his personal business. He may not want to see a female; he may be so angry that he's not thinking about food the way she is. For a moment, she thinks she could just go to the Jeep and get something from the cooler but the next moment she remembers that he always locks it.

When all hope is lost and she is about to collapse into the bed and try to sleep away her hunger pangs, a knock raps at her door, a most beautiful sound that causes her heart to race. She hurries to open it, almost tripping over her own feet but she recovers, straightening her night shirt and wishing she brought some shorts to wear underneath them but she won't make a fool of herself tonight. She'll let him look at her legs, it's fine. She can't help but blush at the heat she feels over her body.

"Hey." Elliot greets, stepping into her room, His hair is damp and brushed back allowing Moira an opportunity to see the cut on his eyebrow and temple better, since his hair is usually tumbling over his forehead. Elliot moves to the bed and throws himself down, covering his face with his elbows.

"How are you?" She asks, rocking on her feet.

"Ugh." He groans, dropping his arms to his side, staring at the ceiling. "Mirrors on the ceiling." He points, wearing a cool smirk. "Classy place."

Moira follows his gaze, "I never understood the point of that." Her face ignites, "Oh, I wish I wouldn't say such stupid things!" She shakes her head, "Don't look at me."

"That's the second or third time you've told me not to look at you." He chuckles then sighs. "Did you call someone? To let them know what you're doing?"

Moira shakes her head.

"You really should." He props himself up on his elbows and gazes at her, "I'm sure someone out there loves you and is worrying about you."

"My phone's dead and I have no charger, nor was I planning to buy one."

"Hmm…" Elliot rubs his jaw, casting his eyes to the ceiling in mock thought, "if only there was someone you knew who had a phone you could use." He pulls his phone from his back pocket and unlocks it with his fingerprint before handing it over to her. "Just let someone know where you are. I don't want people to be worrying. Do you want me to leave?"

Moira shrugs, "No. It's okay." It seems like an eternity that she stares down at the phone in her hand, staring down a Milwaukee Brewers background covered in the many applications downloaded to his phone. The one app that taunts her, though, is the blue phone icon.

She swallows a lump that has formed in her throat and dials in her parents' home phone then brings the phone to her ear, keeping her eyes closed; Elliot busies himself by staring up at the ceiling, at his reflection, and twiddling his thumbs that rest on his stomach.

"Hi, mom. Hi, dad." Moira begins when the voicemail kicks in. "It's just me. I just, uh, wanted to let someone know. I, uh." She sighs, and swallows again, strengthening her voice, "I'm taking a road trip with a friend and I'll be back in a few days. Just doing some sightseeing. So, yea. Just wanted to let someone know. My phone's dead so…" She raises her eyes to the ceiling and breathes deeply, leaving a long pause. Elliot looks over to her with some concern but she ignores him and continues, "So, I got to get a charger. Anyway. Letting you know. In case, I don't know. In case you were looking for me. Okay. Okay, bye." She ends the call and hands the phone to Elliot without meeting his eye. "Voicemail." She mumbles, taking a seat on the bed.

"You okay?"

With her hands folded in her lap, she stares at the window, unable to find her voice, to reply to him. She only reacts when he reaches over and places gentle fingers on her back making her jump.

"Oh, I'm fine." She smiles, "But thank you. I just prefer not to speak to my parents. But I suppose if you do murder me, it's best someone knows where to look for my body." As she speaks, she timidly moves to lie down beside him, keeping her eyes on her own reflection. "This is awkward."

He looks at her in the mirror, "I can go if you're uncomfortable."

"No, no." She turns to look at his face, "It's fine. I'm hungry, though."

"Oh shit! I'm sorry." He pops up from the bed and turns to her, asking her what she wants to eat but she only shrugs. Nodding to her indecisiveness, he tells her that he'll be right back and heads to the door, leaving it ajar so he can get back in.

While she waits, she fiddles with her claddagh, then her belly button ring, flipping the sunflower back and forth as she gazes up at herself, at her flushed cheeks. She asks Leo, whose reflection on the table can be seen in the mirror, how he is doing but he doesn't have time to reply before Elliot reappears holding a backpack in his hands. Quickly, she pulls her shirt back down over her stomach and her panties hoping he didn't see but the red on his cheeks suggest otherwise, but he makes no comment.

With his foot, Elliot closes the door and moves to the bed where he throws the backpack to Moira's feet then throws himself over her, flipping to the other side. She squeals, going tense at his abrupt actions, as he sprawls out next to her and she feels embarrassed for her fright, for the secret flush of warmth that spread over her at the thought, the sight of his nearness.

"I brought some food. It's not fancy but it's food."

Moira nods, sitting up to take the backpack so she can get the couple of sandwiches out, along with some Twinkies, her bottle of Snapple, and his water bottle. They each unwrap their sandwich from the napkins and begin to eat, silently at first but Moira knows from her short acquaintance with the man that the silence will be killing him.

"You look tired." She says, as she tears crumbs from her sandwich and feeds them a begging Leo.

"So does your fish. Is he okay?"

Moira looks at Leo, examining his paling complexion. The fish isn't as vibrant as he once was in his youth as he now pushes into five-years-old. She tilts her head, face contorting with concern, "He's old, I guess." Shaking her head briskly, she blinks away her tears.

"Aw, no. Don't cry, please. Please don't cry." He sets his sandwich down and reaches over, placing warm fingers on her knee. "It'll be okay. I-I'm sorry. I shouldn't have said that."

"It's okay." she pats his fingers and forces a smile. His reluctance to pull his hand away, his guilt is evident in his emotive eyes. It makes her smile how he wears his emotions so blatantly, so freely, while she has spent her life learning how to keep her own hidden.

Elliot gruffly stands, smoothing out his t-shirt, his jeans; he runs both hands through his hair. "Let's talk about something else." He begins to pace around the room. You got anything? To say?" His voice is flat and she wishes she had something to say, something to make him smile or laugh. Anything to possibly intrigue and entertain but there is only silence. "Okay." He nods, sitting back down and taking another bite of his sandwich. As he chews, he stares at the square television bolted to the dresser.

He nods and the pair fall quiet but Elliot can't stay quiet long, a trait he worries will drive her crazy. She smiles at him with an encouraging gaze so he continues, jabbering with an air of unease. He talks about his littlest sister and how he was close to her throughout her youth, until that fateful camping trip. He tells her how he used to take her everywhere as soon as she was able to walk.

His phone chimes on the table making him sigh and shake his head with rolling eyes. "This might make me a bad person. In fact, I'm sure it does, but I'm going to tell you anyway. I never missed Lauren when I was gone and my trips got longer and longer the longer our relationship went on. Even though I was trying to stay local and settle down...I couldn't with her. I didn't want to." Slumping back, he stretches his legs out and gazes upwards, his eyes unfocused. "I knew after a year that I didn't even like her."

"You didn't like her?" Moira raises her eyebrows at his comment, glancing at Leo who silently watches, floating near the surface.

"Yea. I mean, she's pretty. She got hit on everywhere we went and she loved it. She fucking loved that. She'd rub my face in it." he exhales, falling onto his back. "A year in I realized she was lazy and self-absorbed. On our one-year anniversary, she was mean to our waitress and I really, *really* hate that. Cashiers, waitresses, customer service reps. You have to, *have to* be nice to these people. I was genuinely ashamed. But Lauren, she never had a nice thing to say about anyone really. She's always the smartest one in the room, the expert on any subject. Even," he laughs, "telling me how to take the best photos. "He turns his sad eyes to Moira's face, "I knew after she was mean to that waitress that I should have ended it. I didn't do that, though. Oh no. Of course I didn't. We moved in together. Fucking idiot."

"So, why did you stay then?" Moira sits up and hugs her knees but stares forward at the wall. When Elliot doesn't answer, she looks back over her shoulder at his drained face and lifeless eyes.

He shrugs his sagging shoulders after a moment, "It was nice having someone to come home to. Even if it was her. That makes me a bad person, doesn't it?"

"No…" Moira begins, thinking about her words, "I think it makes you lonely."

Elliot makes no reply; he closes his eyes and drapes his arms over his stomach. They each let the silence reign for a time, sitting together but alone with their own thoughts on loneliness and love. Their pasts. Moira lays back and runs her hand on the blanket, in the space between their bodies, contemplating opening up to him. To tell him, he is not alone in this lonely world, she's been where he is.

"I've been cheated on."

Startled by her sudden voice and the confession itself, he turns wide eyes to her. "Really? I just assumed you've never...you know what, never mind."

She gives him a wry smile, "Am I really so virginal?"

Elliot blushes, shrugging his shoulders. "Are you going to tell me about it? Or is this a Moira Lovegood half story?"

"I'll tell you."

It's a hard story for her. To admit that her ex-boyfriend found her so dull that six months into their year long relationship he started seeing other people. To confess that in her devastation when he left her that she didn't even know she went into a pet store. And it all started because she refused to go skydiving.

"That's why you asked me about skydiving." Elliot realizes, nodding as his understanding creeps over him. As she speaks about how he, this *man*, called her boring and told her to lighten up, Elliot listens with a furrowed brow, unable to hide his disgust, and his pity. She has to laugh, she has to turn away from Elliot's burning gaze, boring into her, revealing her in such a way that she cannot stop now.

The show, her story, must go on even as her shame is cutting with his eyes. Jonathan controlled her weight, told her what to eat because she needed to worry about her belly button ring looking foolish; he already told it made her look whorish but she refused to give it up. It was her last sign of independence and she couldn't give it up.

Her diet, her clothes—nothing too low cut in the top and nothing too short on the bottom—and her shoes. He wouldn't tolerate his woman being taller than him and anything more than a 2-inch heel was unacceptable. She had resigned herself to flats and flip flops. Turtlenecks and cowl necks and crew necks. When she found a used condom in the trash can of his bedroom, she bought his lies without question, she believed she was in the wrong for seeing it.

"You were with him a whole year?"

"Don't talk." Her words hit the wall. "You stayed with someone you didn't like for three years. I at least thought I liked him. I thought he might be right. That I am intolerable. Neurotic to a fault. He had me convinced that I was lucky to be with him. And you know, he did make me feel safe. He would keep me warm when I was cold and hold me when I had a bad day. That was always worth it, I guess."

Moira lays back down, mimicking Elliot's posture with her hands crossed lightly over her stomach, staring up at herself. She swallows hard, her pride, her bitterness and recalls, in a slow voice, how one day he called her. He told her she was unbearable and neurotic; he said he was done with her and moving on to someone else, someone exciting and wished her luck finding a man who was willing to deal with her baggage.

She remembers the hot summer Saturday like the memory of a dream. Driving around, aimlessly, sobbing. She parked the car and she wandered from store to store with no focus, no attention. Until she saw Leo.

"I was done. I found my new man."

"I'm sorry, Moira. You should know that what he said, it's not true. You're not boring. You're great and I'm not just saying that."

Shrugging, Moira averts her gaze, sending it to the window, "Well, men will say what they will to get a woman's clothes off. Jonathan was good at that. Say what I needed to hear until he got what he wanted then he'd leave me cold."

He clicks his tongue, "That's not what I'm trying to do." Then he covers his eyes with his elbows and sighs. "I'm sorry you've had such bad luck with men, Moira."

"It's why I'm done. I'm better off. I can be neurotic all by myself. I don't have to skydive or straighten my hair. I can get fat if I want to and still keep my belly ring. I'm just…I'm fine being by myself. Loneliness is underrated."

Dropping his arms back down from his eyes, he looks at her, not in the reflection on the ceiling but at her beside him. "So, you just plan on being alone forever then?".

"I'm safer that way." Moira mumbles.

"Safer but not happier."

Moira shrugs but inside she mulls his words, weighing them and their truth.

In the night, Moira wakes to find Elliot asleep beside her, still on his back with his hands resting on his stomach. She rolls to face him letting his words flood back to the forefront of her mind. For a long time, she watches him sleep, daring to place her hand on his warm forearm. She ponders how he can always be so warm when she herself is shivering, though she refuses to slip under the covers; it feels too improper, too embarrassing.

Sitting up to look down at his peaceful expression, she wonders what he dreams about and are they sweet or tormenting like her own. Moira gently sweeps his hair from his face and runs her fingers along the cut over his eyebrow; she's drawn to him but she doesn't know why, moving nearer to his mouth with her own. Just a feathery touch, she brushes her lips against his then she lays down, daring to slide a little closer to him, to smell the skin of his neck. She'll caress his arm until she finally dozes off.

Chapter 22
The Temperamental, The Phone Call, and The Ill-Timed Joke

The knocking is aggressive and persistent. Why won't it stop? It isn't knocking, it's pounding. Her name. Her name is being called. Opening her eyes, she looks around the room, confused and dizzy, wondering how or when she tucked herself under the blankets. If asked what her last meal was, Moira wouldn't be able to answer but she might have eaten like a pig at a trough. She remembers wanting to eat food like a pig at a trough.

Stumbling, she clambers to the door, fighting a wave of nausea, and throws it open not waiting to register who it is, who's knocking, before she turns and throws herself back onto her bed with a painful moan.

"Are you sick?" asks the man who enters her room. Of course, it's Elliot in her doorway, but in Moira's sleep induced delirium, it could be anyone from her father to the Pope.

"No." She groans into the pillow.

Elliot looks over to Leo, barely able to tear his gaze from her bare legs, her thighs, to her lacy underwear, and shakes his head at the fish. "Then let's go." He shakes Moira's foot but her only reaction is to pull her feet in, tightening herself into a ball. He sighs and moves up from the foot of the bed and jiggles her shoulder. She swats him away but misses so he tries again to give her shoulder a firm shake. This time when she swings her fist, she makes a solid connection with his hip, the contact jolting her awake, as Elliot totters back with a grunt.

"Oh!" she exclaims, sitting up and pulling the blanket over her legs, her face growing hot.

"Let's go, Sunshine." Elliot grumbles.

Moira pulls the blankets to her chin, "How'd you get in here anyway? What do you want?" While these questions escape her dried, cracked lips she recalls, suddenly as a wave breaks on the shore, petting his arm last night while he slept beside her and she wonders when he left.

Elliot, impatiently tapping his fingers on his crossed arms, tells her that he wants her to get up so they can go to which she replies, whining, for him to get the tire fixed. When he comes back, she'll be ready.

"I already did that."

She moans and rolls off the bed, "This is so unfair!" she exclaims as she stomps to the bathroom.

"She sounds like my 15-year-old sister!" Elliot, plopping down on the side of the bed, says to Leo who swims around the bowl in small circles.

She returns briefly from the bathroom to retrieve a change of clothes, "I heard that." She mutters, spinning away to get changed. Her face is flush and no amount of powder will conceal it, her eyes are hopelessly baggy. Frazzled, desperately overwhelmed, she tries to cool her cheeks, to calm down so she can pull herself together.

"Is she always this putzy?" Elliot asks of the fish, leaning forward on his knees, turning his eyes to Moira who emerges from the bathroom in an unconcealed and inconsolable state of panic. "Or this crazy?"

"Shut up." She barks, repacking her bag with hasty disarray.

"And rude, too! Oh, Leo, how do you put up with it?"

Moira's eyes snap over to Leo's face, watching her with big black eyes, a gaumless mouth slowly opening and closing. She knows he has many answers to provide but he'll remain silent.

Once Moira appears to have finished packing her bag, albeit sloppily, Elliot picks that and her room key up pausing to peer at her.

"What?" she asks, her face going red.

He looks as though he wants to say something, as though he is gazing into her and reading her thoughts but he shakes his head, a crooked smile on his face as he turns to go outside to check them both out of their rooms. When Elliot is gone, she scolds Leo for not waking her up; his only excuse is that he was sleeping, too.

All Moira wants to do is close her eyes and go back to sleep, as they head west with only the radio for noise. She thinks about doing it, about closing her tired eyes, shutting off her disgruntled mind as it races from last night's conversation to sneaking so close to him as he slept, his lips. What must he have thought when he woke up with her clinging to his side? Grimacing, she retrieves a crossword puzzle book from her bag to distract her roaming thoughts, but she knows Elliot's tongue won't stay idle for long. By his air, the way he is passing glances at her, fidgeting behind the wheel—moving his hands from the top to the bottom, to ten and two—he has something to say, which he does with a frown.

"I'm sorry about last night." He says but she only glances at him, keeping quiet.

Elliot shifts uncomfortably in his seat and brings his left elbow up to rest on the windowpane. As he drums his fingers on the top of the window, he focuses his attention on the curvature of the road.

"It's okay. Whatever you're sorry for." Moira tells him, trying to be casual, friendly, but her voice is heavy with the desire to keep sleeping.

"I just talk too fucking much. And I keep swearing." Elliot grips the wheel in both hands and looks at her, his face serious, cheeks turning rosy. "Just prying into your life, falling asleep in your room. So, I'm sorry."

"Oh, uh, it's fine. You don't have to be sorry. For anything."

"Well, there might be something." He mutters, taking a deep breath. She looks at him, concerned and confused, her heart plummeting into her stomach as her mind jumps to every dark scenario it can conjure up.

"What?"

"Your, uh, your folks called me this morning."

"I'm sorry, what?" The dark scenarios of last night she conjured are replaced with anger; how dare they call him and how dare he speak to them. She clenches her jaw as she watches his nervous eyes.

"Yea. Caller ID, it's a curse and a blessing. They were looking for you. They wanted to talk to you."

She can't keep the unfathomable dread from her voice as she asks what was said.

"I told them, and you'll probably be mad at me, but I told them that you couldn't come to the phone because you were tied up in my trunk."

"You *are* a bad person!" she cries into her palms.

"Yea well, I then got to explain myself to your sobbing mother and your furious father for the next ten minutes so I got what I deserved."

"I'm so sorry. I'm *so* sorry." Moira whines and drops her head against the window with a thud. "What else?"

"Nothing." He shrugs, "I told them you were in your room and I didn't want to go waking you up. We talked for a while. They seem nice enough. You know…once they calmed down enough to listen to me."

"I can't believe you said that to my parents." Again, Moira covers her face with both palms, her head shaking, her shoulders quivering.

Elliot laughs, "It just came out. It was like a reflex!"

"It's not funny." With both hands, one clenching her puzzle book, she smacks his arm several times, "What is wrong with you?"

"I'm sorry, okay?" Elliot smirks, slouching in his seat with both hands resting on the top of the wheel; Moira turns her gaze to the sunlit valleys and peaks passing by in a blur.

Her mind races.

Chapter 23
The Novelty, The Eggs, and The Girl at the Gas Station

They speak for a while about Moira's parents, what her father does as a lawyer and who he has represented in the past, and the different charities her mother volunteers for. She tells Elliot about her two older brothers, Ian and Cole and how she still talks to them but she keeps the conversation to a minimum, how she won't see them but she'll take their phone calls. They aren't allowed to talk about their parents and if they try, she hangs up. She isn't sure anything she says is interesting but Elliot listens as if it were.

She tells him about the house she grew up in and the apple tree in the backyard; she tells him how she played softball in high school and he tells her that he played baseball in high school. His nose is a little crooked because he got hit by a pitch right in the face. Moira is immensely amused by his telling of the story with his wild hand gestures and clear, and admitted, exaggerations. He wanted to stay in the game, he *insisted* he take first base but no one would listen to a sixteen-year-old with a broken nose and they took him to the hospital instead.

It's something she admires about Elliot, his talent for talk, the way he weaves a truthful tale with only enough fabrication to make it hilarious. She wishes she had that ability but everything she says is bland, straightforward and factual, though he doesn't seem to mind or notice. He smiles at her and encourages her to be open, to talk, and apologizes for interrupting with his own related stories. And of course, his foul language.

Moira laments that she is boring and Elliot defends her, saying she is shy where he is a hyperactive, which she doesn't disagree with, passing him a teasing smile. In a sincere voice, honest eyes, he tells her she is not boring; he reassures her that she is delightfully quirky as exampled by her traveling across the country with her fish. While she appreciates his sentiment, she will continue to believe she is just, sort of, boring.

How many crosswords has she completed now—three, four? — while Elliot sings along to the radio, his voice has become a soothing constant on their journey together. No qualms, he just beats out a sporadic rhythm and serenades her to whatever song comes on next.

"How much longer are we going to be driving?" She asks, slamming her book closed.

"A long time." Elliot replies without missing a beat. He looks worn out himself, as his eyes continuously scan the road ahead where it winds through steep cliff sides with only thin steel guardrails to keep them on the road.

Moira sighs again and falls heavily into her seat. The sun is shining bright as it begins to fall in the deep blue sky, cloudless except the horizon where billowing grey clouds tower and build. It reminds her, painfully, of a painting in Charles Kent's foyer of a ship on a rough and stormy sea. The clouds painted in the sky could have been modeled by the storm front brewing in front of them, they might have been foreshadowing to her 18th birthday.

She always hated that painting. So old and dull.

"Has the novelty worn off?"

"Novelty?" She looks at him, thankful for the distraction from her wandering thoughts.

"Yea. Driving across the country with a stranger." They are nearing an exit sign so he peers down at the gauges set in the dashboard, "We'll get some gas."

She waves off his assumption, "It's not a novelty. I'm driving across the country with a stranger to avoid certain murder."

"That doesn't even make sense. I could have murdered you."

"It made sense at the time."

Elliot pulls off the freeway and guides then down the exit, scanning the signs on each side for where the nearest gas station is. Moving into the left turn lane, they come to a stop at the intersection where Elliot looks both ways, as does Moira, before turning into the far-right lane.

"You're supposed to turn into your own lane not just slide over." Moira informs him with a frown.

"Blah, blah, blah." He pulls into the gas station. "I still could murder you."

"You don't look like a murderer."

Elliot rolls his eyes as he removes his seatbelt, "I think you were just looking for a good time. Unfortunately for you, you put all those good time eggs in this basket," he points to himself, "and I am just a guy, a not very exciting guy, driving to Seattle to see his sister." He hops out of the car and turns back, leaning in, onto his seat, "Day three isn't even halfway done yet and I've broken all your eggs."

Leaning across the center console, bringing herself nearer to him, she looks into his golden-brown eyes and almost loses herself in them, almost forgets what she is about to say, but she recovers with a giggle and a grin,

"That's okay. I don't really like eggs anyway." It isn't clever or witty and it is said with her typical awkward air but still, her tone carries with it an appealing, though unpolished, charm. The tilt of her head, the batting of her long lashes, her shy smile gives Moira a grace all her own. She hesitates, her eyes flickering down to his mouth, his moving down to hers, each with a hitch in their breathing. She's drawn to him, moving forward just a fraction.

Her cheeks ignite, her heart leaps into her throat; she pulls back into her seat with such force, she knocks Leo's bag sending him into a nauseating wave pool. She exclaims her apologies and tries to soothe him while Elliot watches the fiasco with a smirk, his own cheeks burning, his heart racing.

Once Elliot leaves to fill up the tank, Moira drops her hands in her palms.

"You should've kissed him." Leo comments.

Moira whines her reply, keeping her face buried.

When the tank is full, Elliot opens the driver's door and pokes his head inside, "Do you want anything?"

"No, thank you." She mutters, settling her eyes on Leo's pink scales.

In only a few minutes, he emerges from the gas station talking to a woman, all smiles and laughter.

"How can he meet people so quickly?" Moira whispers to Leo, glowering in Elliot's direction.

"Because he's likable…unlike you." Leo informs her. She puffs out her lip and watches through the windshield at Elliot's interaction with fascination and, unexpectedly, jealousy. She recognizes the feeling immediately, envy, for this woman's wavy blonde hair, her petite frame and a cropped top. When the woman turns her back to the Jeep, Moira can envy her flowery tattoo inked onto her lower back.

Certainly, Moira rolls her shoulders and looks off to the side, at the pump screen where it shows how many gallons for how much money, this feeling is for Elliot's carefree mannerisms. It's not this strange blonde woman's flashy smile and perfect hair.

Moira tries to shake it off but her eyes wander back to the station where Elliot says goodbye to the petite blonde in the painted-on jeans and heads back to the car.

"Who were you talking to?" She immediately asks once he seats himself behind the wheel. Her tone is unintentionally combative, rife with possessiveness. She quickly shakes this accusatory manner off, covering it with innocent observation. "How you can just talk to people!"

"I like people." He shrugs. "I like talking to people."

"Yea, pretty people." She rolls her eyes and motions to the woman now washing the windows of a 4x4 truck a few pumps over.

Elliot smirks and confirms with a nod, "Pretty people are easier to talk to." He pauses and looks at her with a thoughtful expression, "Except you."

Moira blushes, aware of his eyes searing into her face. Shifting, she picks up her purse, "I'm not difficult but I have to go potty so I'll be right back."

"You should have done that already!" he shouts after her. Moira flaps her arms at him but doesn't turn around so he gets comfortable and waits for her to back. When she does come out, after a few minutes, she is alone.

"There were people in there, but I didn't feel the need to strike up conversations with any of them." She announces as she gets in.

"Whatever." He says, chuckling, "Anyway," he continues in a pleasant, dipping into enthusiastic, voice, "There is a street festival not far from here. About an hour. That girl, her name is Josie and she's from *Alabama*." he emphasizes the state name with a faux southern accent that makes Moira laugh, "She told me about it. Want to go? There's a motel in the town that we can stay at."

Moira looks at Leo, her cheeks beginning to glow. "Sure." She finally answers, looking at him with shy eyes that make him smile.

"Good. I'm glad you were able to make a decision." He nods, pulling away from the gas station. "You're getting better."

Chapter 24
The Tattoo, The Fair, and The Masterful Conversationalist

After driving for an hour, time filled with general conversation mainly by Elliot, they arrive in a minuscule town called Mercy where the street fair is being held. The main street is closed so they wind their way around side streets looking for a place to stop for the night. Eventually they find a small motel not far off the main street.

Elliot retrieves her bags from the car leaving his own behind for now and follows her into her room.

"This is nicer than the last two places." Moira comments, her eyes on Elliot as he tosses her bag onto one of the two beds. "Do I have time to shower before we go out?"

"As you wish." He moves back to the door, "Just come give me a knock when you're ready, you know where to find me."

Moira is conscious of her extra efforts in showering and brushing her teeth, putting on her make-up and doing her hair. It's not a date, she reminds herself as she moisturizes her freshly shaven legs. It's not a date. She is a stowaway and he's only on the rebound from a failed relationship.

Besides, he asked her to dinner once, after her apartment was broken into, and she denied him that pointblank; he isn't foolish enough to try again. She slides into a blue and white striped dress, soft cotton and low cut, hanging above her knees.

"Too short?" she asks, but Leo doesn't reply.

She hates herself for being nervous, hates her quivering tummy and her overly prepared appearance; she hates that she must keep reminding herself that this isn't a date, just an event she happens to be present for. He would be doing this with or without her.

With practiced care, she hangs Leo around her neck and moves down the hall to knock on Elliot's door. When he answers he is wrapped in a fluffy white towel. The sight makes her blush but he is unfazed and confident.

"Sorry. I decided too late that I should shower." He tells her, turning away. His tone skin glistens from his shower and his damp hair is tousled and messy, dripping with water down his tattooed back. He crosses the room and looks through his bag giving Moira an opportunity to examine the intricate inking of a dragon that stretches across his shoulders and down his spine. She's impressed with the detail and how the design flawlessly blends in with the sleeve tattoo of the koi fish. At the tail of the dragon is Japanese writing, darker, newer looking than the rest of the tattoo.

"Two seconds." He tells her, after retrieving a pair of socks and boxers from his bag, then he disappears into the bathroom, leaving the door open so he can speak to her, offering her his apologies. He was on the phone with his sister for a while before he decided to shower.

"It's okay." She calls back to the door. "Hey, what does the kanji mean, on your tattoo?"

"What?" he steps out and looks at her, his plaid shirt open over his skin, his fingers working to fasten his light jeans.

Moira blushes and looks away but her eyes will not stray for long finding his flat stomach, his toned chest. "The Japanese on your dragon. What's it mean?"

"I…I don't really want to tell you." He says, vanishing into the safety of the bathroom.

"What? Why?"

"I'm too embarrassed."

"Why get something you're embarrassed about?" She asks, going to the doorway and peeking in at him drying his hair with a towel.

"I'm only embarrassed to tell *you.*" He sighs, and tosses the towel onto the sink, turning to her. "It means luckless in love."

"What happens when you get married?"

Elliot shrugs and pushes past her. She smells cologne that she has not smelled on him before and it makes her body go hot.

"Ready?" he asks, pulling a Brewers cap onto his head then turning to get his wallet and phone from the bedside table.

"Sure. But I still don't understand."

"I did some pretty stupid things when I went to Mexico. I was doing a photoshoot for a magazine at a Yoga Resort and…I can't even remember the name. I did some things and…" he shrugs, his face glowing; he won't look at her but she won't take her eyes off his face. "I did some things, okay. Then I got drunk and got that addition to my tattoo."

"What things?" She asks, watching him secure his equipment over his shoulders and attaching a short lens to his camera.

"I was upset about Lauren, okay? And then there were these two girls…and I did some things and got a tattoo. And no! Fucking hell! I wish I could shut up once in a while. Forget I said that. Forget this conversation."

"Oh…" Moira turns her reddened face, unwilling to look at him after such a confession that makes her own heart sink.

Elliot groans, his face flush with embarrassment and shame, "Sorry, just forget this, okay? We should bring the fish's bowl with us."

Moira nods, neither able to make eye contact with each other.

Guided by the dazzling lights, the smells of everything deep fried, and a mixture of different music, Elliot leads the way through the crowd. A band plays songs from Robert Plant to George Michael while several couples dance around a spattering of picnic tables. There's a Ferris Wheel, a Tilt-o-Whirl, a carousel.

They pass a dunk tank, a man guessing weights, and a balloon artist but they keep walking until the crowd gets thinner. Elliot leads them away from the festivities until he finds a spot on a hill where he sets up his equipment to start his series of shots.

The shutter snaps, slower than she has heard it click before, then Elliot moves over and again takes another shot. He lines up another. The lens captures in perfect flare the dizzying lights of the slowly turning Ferris Wheel in the background lit against a charcoal sky. Dozens of nameless fair goers are frozen in their laughter with just bought corn dogs and ice cream cones. A victorious child holds up a stuffed dog won by popping half filled balloons with darts. His perfectly round and innocent face lit brighter than any other light.

Elliot's camera cannot grasp the music dripping with poetic enticement through the air, nor can it waft the scent of everything that is happiness, but Moira can and she does. As Elliot relocates, she stares and drinks in all that she can.

There is so much joy here with the spirits of people soaring, the air is cheerful. Moira casts her gaze skyward at the billowing grey clouds threating rain but for once, she is at peace. For a moment she watches the sky when a thought crosses her mind and her peaceful feeling dissipates.

A plane could just fall from the sky right now.

"What's wrong?" Elliot asks, noticing her concern, his eyes moving to the sky, searching.

"Oh…I was just thinking how terrible it would be if a plane were to fall from the sky right now."

Elliot's eyes widen and he laughs, "Uh…yes, yes that would suck. I don't *think* that will happen though." With this, they walk back into the crowd and they set up Leo's bowl to take his picture by the Ferris wheel and with a clown walking around on stilts, though Moira isn't happy about letting him hold her fragile best friend.

At a picnic table near a band, Elliot positions Moira with Leo then hops on top of the table to take her picture. While he adjusts the settings, her eyes travel up the length of his legs but quickly shoot back to gazing at Leo like she was instructed.

"Keep your eyes on *that* fish." Elliot tells her with a smirk, lowing his eye to the viewfinder; the shutter goes and he raises his gaze. "You guys make a good pair. You're really pretty."

"I think he's talking to you, Leo!" Moira says, both her and Elliot blushing.

He jumps down from the table and begins to put his camera equipment away while the band plays *The First Time I Saw Your Face*. Moira watches them play entranced by the music when Elliot plops down next to her on the seat. "We could go put Leo back into the hotel room if you like. Then we could explore the area some, maybe go on a ride or play a game or something?"

"You don't like rides and the games are only a rip off."

"Perhaps you'd like to check out the vendors and buy something shiny?"

"Oh! Only to turn my skin green! I think not."

Elliot leans back, his elbows on the table, "You're impossible." For a moment, they listen to the song, slow and romantic; they watch the several couples sway to the music, holding each other closely. They pass shy glances back and forth but say nothing letting a strange tension electrify the air around them.

Moira sighs, turning her back to the band, to the happy couples, and wraps her arms around Leo's bowl, resting her head on her arms. "Jonathan was right. I am dull as eff...except he wasn't so polite."

"Hey." Elliot leans down to meet her eye level, using gentle fingers to force her eyes to his own, "Don't ever listen to him. Not ever." She nods, her eyes searching his face as his does her, a pause in their nearness for a moment and he moves closer; she tilts her head in anticipation for his lips to touch hers, her breath caught in her throat.

But the touch never happens.

Elliot jerks away, standing abruptly and pulling his hat off to run a hand through his hair, a nervous habit. "We should put Leo away before we do anything else." Moira nods, trying to steady her breathing, to slow her hammering heart and to calm her burning cheeks.

They walk back to the motel in silence, side-by-side, shoulder-to-shoulder. Elliot disappears into his room and Moira into hers where she sets Leo on the nightstand between the two beds.

"Oh, my little love." She coos, going into her purse for some Stress Coat and blood worms. "I'm so nervous." She strokes his head when he comes to the surface for his meal. "I think he was going to...to...goodness, I wish I wasn't so nervous." As she whispers to Leo, Elliot knocks at her door. "Maybe I'll just invite him in. We can stay in for the rest of the night. We can..." Her face flushes, "Oh goodness, what am I thinking?" She mutters, quickly wishing Leo a goodnight, kissing him through the glass and hurrying to the door, still unable to calm her heart.

Chapter 25
The Drunkard, The Rain, and The Venom in Her Voice

As they walk on, Elliot tries to get Moira to tell him what she wants to do, if she wants something to eat or drink, a ride on the carousel or even have a dance with him by the band. She shrugs, her usual reply, but he won't be deterred. He walks backwards in front of her with impressive precision pointing out different things they pass.

"You're going to fall!" She laughs, reaching out and taking his wrist, pulling him back towards her. Elliot only laughs, then drapes his arm over her shoulder, expecting her to pull away but she doesn't so he leaves it there.

"The fair is your oyster!" he tells her passionately using his free hand to motion to the space in front of them. "We can do anything you want, my dear!

"I'm not good at this sort of thing. I haven't been to a fair since I was a kid. I've hardly left my apartment to do anything but go to work."

"Jonathan never took you to the State Fair?" he asks, pulling away from her so he can look at her face, which scowls and she rolls her eyes.

"Yea, we did once. I was the designated driver. We went to watch the bands play and he just drank until he couldn't remember my name." As they slowly walk beside one another, a light rain begins to fall; Moira looks up to the sky, letting the cool rain calm her cheeks.

Elliot clicks his tongue and shakes his head but before he can say anything, they are called to from behind. When they turn, they see a group of five people, three young men and two young women all in their early twenties, approaching them led by the blonde with the perfect hair and tattooed back from the gas station.

"You came! This is so exciting. I can't believe we ran into you!" She cries in a thick southern accent as she throws her arms around

Elliot like he's her long-lost friend. Elliot is taken by surprise but he hugs her back and passes a bewildered smile to Moira who raises her eyebrows at him.

Introductions are quickly made around the group, all smiles and laughter, friendly, and the conversation flows as steadily and as naturally as the Bridal Veil Falls leaving Moira to wonder how strangers can have so much to say to each other but Elliot has clearly entered his realm of enjoyment. Adult conversation.

They talk about Montana and Wisconsin; they talk about Josie's home state of Alabama and how she moved here a little over a year ago. The group eventually drifts into a conversation about Elliot's job which enraptures the group with his anecdotes.

With everything he says, Josie, who Moira irrationally decides she hates, touches his bicep with her striking blue manicured fingernails that glitter in the fair lights and giggles. Moira wants to punch her in the throat; certainly, that's unreasonable—right? —but this girl won't keep her hands off him and while Moira has no claim to the man, she's still annoyed.

"Your boyfriend is so funny, Myra. You're so lucky." Josie says when Elliot says something Moira didn't hear since her mind is wandering. She does a double take and swallows hard against her parched throat.

"Oh, he's *not* my boyfriend." Moira corrects, shaking head, glaring.

"Well, that's surprising." She chirps, laughing politely, her touch lingering on Elliot's arm.

"You know what, we should actually be going here. Do you guys know where we can get a drink?" Elliot says suddenly, stepping back from the group, adding distance between Josie's eager hand and Moira's indifferent expression. One of the guys points them down the block to where a bar is set up in a white tent that can't be missed. Josie begs first that they don't go then, when Elliot insists, that they come back to hang out some more before the end of the night. Elliot says they might then turns to head for the beer tent, Moira right behind him.

"Why do you keep doing that to me?" He asks with a furrowed brow once they get inside the tent.

"What?" She tilts her head.

Elliot orders a gin and tonic from the bar then finally brings his eyes to her face. "Dismiss me with such disgust. I'm not sure if I should be amused or offended."

"Neither." Moira's face contorts, expressing her confusion. "Aren't you going to buy me a drink?"

"No, that's a boyfriend's job."

Moira moans and slumps her head against the bar, into her arms, "I don't have my purse with me, though!"

"Aww." Elliot takes an emphatic sip, smacking his lips, "Very refreshing." She laughs and rolls her eyes while admiring his golden-brown ones.

"I just didn't want to hinder you hooking up with some…hot chick." She tells him, looking up at him from where she rests her head on her arms.

He chokes on his drink and scowls. "Hook up? With her?" He points outside, referring to Josie and Moira shrugs. "Oh, for fuck's sake." He shakes his head, not hiding his agitation. "She's a fucking kid. You can for sure buy your own drink now." He averts his angry gaze, still shaking his head.

"A woman should never buy her own drink." A man on the other end of the bar chimes in, smoothing his hand through his ginger hair and beard as he approaches. He leans over the bar, pushing into Moira, and calls for the bar tender to bring Moira a glass.

"No, no!" she calls, wide eyes on the young man tending bar who stops and looks at her. "Just some water, please, if you don't mind."

"That's not a drink." The stranger bellows with laughter and again leans into Moira, breathing the stench of a brewery down her neck. "So, where you staying, baby doll?"

A signal goes up and Work Moira is summoned just as the thunder outside starts to roll in, ebbing and flowing with flickers of lightning.

"Nowhere." She answers in her most professional tone, commanding and firm. The bartender brings her a plastic cup of water that she graciously accepts and takes a mouthful, turning furious eyes to Elliot, who leans on the bar, facing the exit watching the scene only in his peripheral vision. The stranger reaches over and touches an unruly tendril of her curly hair, bringing his nose near to it. She is whisked back to Arthur.

She remembers Charles Kent and her skin begins to crawl, a panic rising in her chest.

"C'mon, baby doll. Let me show you a good time."

"I'm already having a good time, thank you." She snaps her eyes back to Elliot who stares ahead at the door, listening to the world around them. The rain is heavier now and the pressure in the air is tight on the chest; there's a storm coming and not just here in the beer tent.

After several minutes of dodging the drunkard's advances, she spins back to Elliot, to find him staring down at his drink, looking nervous and uncomfortable, fidgeting fingers on his cup.

"Can we please…"

"Yea." He pushes away from the bar and places a firm hand on her shoulder to guide her to the door but the man grabs her around the hip and crushes her against him, pulling her away from Elliot's hand.

"C'mon baby. This guy's nothing!"

She growls and throws herself with every ounce of her strength to pull away from him. "Don't touch me!" Gritted teeth, she glares at the man who leers at her, "Don't touch me!"

Storming out of the tent, with Elliot close behind, she clenches and unclenches her fists but she doesn't stop walking until she reaches the edge of a small lagoon a distance from the bar tent, and the fair grounds.

"Jerk!" she cries, spinning around and shoving him backwards. "What is wrong with you? What is *wrong* with you?" she launches into a tirade of slaps onto any part of his body that he weakly tries to defend against.

"Stop." He tells her, trying to push her hands away, though her attack is more of an annoyance than a genuine threat to his wellbeing. "Stop hitting me!"

"You stupid jerk. Why didn't you do something? You couldn't say *something*?"

"You seemed to be handling yourself just fine." He grumbles, looking to the sky as the rain's pace begins to quicken.

"Well, I wasn't!" she barks. "You should have done something."

"Listen, sweetheart, I'm a non-confrontational individual. Okay? Remember the robin story? Remember when you did this to my face? I didn't win either fight."

"Aren't men supposed to be the mighty protectors?"

"You know what?" he turns sharply towards her, "I'm not getting my nose broke again because you don't want to get hit on. He's harmless! Why can't you take it as a fucking compliment?"

"Take it as a compliment?" There are tears in her voice as the memories flood back, taking her back to her confession. When she told her parents what happened to her. What happened to her in her own bathroom on her birthday. What Charles Kent did to her. "Take it as a compliment." She growls, spitting venom; Elliot remains silent knowing he's crossed a line. The heavens now open, drenching them and the world around them in a vicious down pour but each are rooted where they stand.

"That's what my parents said to me." She steps towards him, her eyes narrow and mean. "Oh, he was just drunk, they said. Just drunk." Her voice almost breaks, but she raises her chin and glowers at him, "Take it as a compliment, they said. It's nothing. Nothing! Pig!" she shouts, pushing his chest but he remains still—wordless—startled, regretful eyes on her face. Her hands drop to her sides, drained of all energy; the rain washes away her anger leaving only sadness behind. "It's a compliment what he did to me? How he groped me? How he pushed me against my vanity, how he shoved his fingers..." she swallows hard but refuses to break eye contact, "how he shoved his fingers into me as I screamed? He grabbed my throat and made me look at him in the mirror. He told me I'm a goddess. That's quite the compliment, isn't it?"

"I'm sorry." Is all Elliot can reply, his eyes dropping to the ground, ashamed.

"That's all it was though. He let me go because I wouldn't stop fighting, because I threw my head back into his nose. So, it was nothing really. *Minor* sexual assault. Just minor. It could have been worse, right?" Her voice is drenched in condemnation and sarcasm. The memory disgusts her, infuriates her, but as she looks at Elliot shrinking in front of her, his eyes filled with pity and shame, she deflates.

"I'm sorry."

"Yea, so are my parents." She says calmly.

"We...we should get out of this rain." He stutters, unable to look anywhere but his feet.

She looks up and the sky dropping fat rain drops onto her face. Elliot raises his hand intending to place it on her back to guide her towards the motel but he lets it fall back to his side. He wants to comfort her, to take her hand or to hug her. To let her know how infinitely sorry he is for what he said but he can't. He doesn't know how so he just walks a little in front of her, head hung low, pulling his baseball cap over his eyes.

As they near the festival the drunkard appears before them making both Moira and Elliot groan and roll their eyes.

"Baby doll, why are you letting this boy keep you in the rain?"

"Boy?" Elliot scrunches his face.

"Take is as a compliment, Elliot, it means you look youthful." She sneers, turning indignant eyes onto the stranger with the ginger beard as he places his heavy arm around her shoulders. She accepts this contact with exhausted indifference.

"C'mon, bro, get your hands off her." Elliot's voice is calm but bordering on irritation. He only wants to get Moira somewhere safe and warm, somewhere he can profusely apologize and spend the rest of the night groveling at her feet. Elliot's words are ignored and the man pulls Moira towards the street, "I can take you somewhere and get you real wet."

"All right!" Elliot grabs the man's arms and pushes it off Moira. "Get the fuck out of here."

There is no warning before the guy throws his fist against Elliot's cheek; Moira muffles a scream with her hands as Elliot smashes backwards into a tree, dazed. Pain shoots into his head and he grabs his face and groans. Moira hurries over to him.

"You want some asshole?" the drunk throws his arms open and steps towards them. "You want some?"

"What's with this guy?" Elliot grumbles, wincing as the pain throbs through his jaw.

"What'd you say? What'd you say? Trying to protect your little bitch. Stupid whore."

Moira helps Elliot to his feet, "Are you okay?" The stranger hurls more insults at Moira, calling her a slut and a whore, and she desperately tries to ignore him, to pull Elliot away. "Let's get out of here. Please?" she whispers to Elliot who meets her eyes and examines her face, searching for something. He only finds sadness.

"God dammit." he grumbles, yanking his arm away from Moira's loose grip then, without hesitation or thought, throws a right hook into the drunkard's eye socket that crumbles the man to the ground.

"Oh my god!" Moira gasps. Elliot snatches her arm and pulls her towards the fair.

"We got to go. We got to go!" he makes no attempt to play it cool, to hide the panic laced in his normally composed voice. They rush through the festival ignoring all the other people who also hurry to find shelter.

"I want to go home." Moira simpers once they near the motel.

"I'm sorry but that's not possible right now." He tells her but she reaches over and spins him around to face her.

"I don't want to stay here. I'm not staying here. Please, let's just go. Somewhere else, anywhere else!"

He looks up at the black sky sheeting down on them.

"Please." She begs.

Chapter 26
The Wrong Turn, The Beacon, and The Thunder All Around

The headlights reflect bright white against the heavy rain making it virtually impossible to see past the hood of the Jeep. Elliot's knuckles are white on the wheel as his eyes frantically scan the road. He won't admit to Moira that he's taken a wrong turn and they didn't make it to the interstate like he had planned. Instead, they travel down a puddled gravel road in the wrong direction.

Moira holds Leo's bowl to her chest as she squints out the windshield trying to decipher their whereabouts. The lightning flashes and the thunder roars around them yet somehow Elliot seems to be in control of the situation, of the road. She casts her eyes at his dimly lit face and sees no wavering confidence.

"I hate to tell you this…" he passes her a glance when he notices her watching him. "…but I have no idea where we are."

"Are you serious?"

"I must have taken a wrong turn."

His confession makes her slump back in her chair, defeated, "And I was just thinking how smart you are."

"Not smart enough not to hit that guy." He mumbles. "Ah! What's that sign say?" He slows down to read a large brown sign reflecting in the night like a beacon in his headlights. "Thank goodness." He sighs. The sign points them in the direction of Ylobbí State Park two miles away. "We have to stop, I'm sorry. I can't drive like this."

"It's okay." She tells him, her voice soft, her eyes looking down at Leo.

"Well, no. I'll be able to find the park on the map and from there I can get us back to the main road."

"Honestly, Elliot, it's fine." She keeps her eyes down at Leo who looks up at her with wild confusion. "It's okay, my little love." Stroking Leo's head, she shifts her gaze outside her window, watching nervously as the blackness illuminated with flashes of lightning goes by.

Two miles later, they arrive at the ranger station of Ylobbí park to find it closed, though Elliot is not surprised given the time and the weather, so he proceeds to find a campground, determined to pay in the morning.

They drive a little way into the park until they find a campsite where Elliot backs the Jeep in, up the narrow gravel path to where it opens into a wide space. The car is barely stopped before Moira sets Leo onto the floor and throws herself into the elements, relishing the cold rain on her burning skin, certain she might throw up.

The trees above sway violently in the strong winds and still the thunder quakes the flooded ground. She walks to the middle of the campsite and turns her gaze skyward, staring at the silhouetted treetops dancing in the light of the storm. Her emotions, like the storm, crash over her.

Elliot cuts the engine and gets out to check on her. "This doesn't seem like a good idea." He calls to her over the noise of the slashing rain and wind.

"Neither was hitting that guy. Why'd you do that?"

He leans against the Jeep and crosses his arms with a shrug, looking away from her intense stare. "I wanted to protect you."

"You wanted to prove something."

"Yea, maybe. To prove that I'm not useless. That I didn't lie. I can protect you. I will keep you safe."

"Get into a fight, get hurt and go to the hospital or go to jail? I don't need any of that from you." She's pacing around the campsite now, looking from him to the sky to her wet feet standing in an inch of water.

"As long as you are on my Seattle Tour Bus, I'll keep you safe. Even if you don't need it." He shoves his hands into his pockets and shrugs his shoulders again. "Or want it. But you can't..." he rips his hat from his head and wipes the rain from his eyes, pushing his hair back through his fingers, "...you can't tell me you want me to interfere and then get pissed off when I do. What do you want then?"

He's looking at her for an answer that she does not have and can only look around in hopes of finding one. "I don't know, I guess." She pulls her eyes away and turns to look at the camp, what she can see, through the darkness. There's a picnic table near a fire pit. When the lightning flashes, she can see the rust worn metal of the fire pit, years in the making with a hundred memories around a hundred fires.

In the forest around them, the limbs of trees can be heard snapping with the force of the wind making her eyes snap up, back to the silhouettes bending in the sky.

"I'm sorry, Moira, for what I said. I'm so sorry." Elliot tells her but she doesn't move.

She wants to be safe.

And protected.

Isn't that all she ever wanted? Isn't that why she has kept the same routine, the same awful job, for 12 years? She takes a step towards Elliot but steps back just as quickly as she moved forward.

What can she do when she has secluded herself from people for so long thinking that is what has made her safe and happy? She meets Elliot's pleading, bewildered eyes, her chest heaving.

He starts to say something, some beseeching words to get them out of the rain but she closes the distance between them, she can't hear him. Then she presses her lips to his. His mouth is warm against hers, his cheeks, too, are fiery in her palms holding him to her. There's a tremor between them, but she can't tell if it's her body or his.

Perhaps it is the thunder bellowing around them.

When they finally separate, she gazes into his shocked eyes and she knows, with confidence, what she wants, whether it's right or wrong. She finds his lips again and pulls him into the Jeep, her fingers pulling him by his shirt, finding the buttons, with trembling fingers.

He closes the door behind them, shutting out the storm and the cold. She pulls him down on top of her while pushing the shirt off his shoulders, feeling the warm skin of his chest, of his arms and shoulders, against her palms. She slides her hands down his stomach, feeling him shudder in the wake of her fingers, moving swiftly to undo his jeans while he buries his face in her neck. She can feel his hesitation, his insecurity; she can see it in his eyes when the lightning flashes outside. It makes her smile, makes her kiss him— his mouth, his neck, his chest—and rip off her dress; he pulls her panties off, accepting her certainty, tossing them to the front seat with her bra.

When there is only skin for their hands to wander along, teasing and trembling, she savors his every touch that burns her skin, his breath in her ear. It's been so long since she's felt a man's touch and Elliot knows where his hands need to go; he caresses her breasts, her neck, her stomach following every stroke with his soft lips. Her body quivers, her breath taken, as he finds her with his mouth, his grip tight on her waist. She grabs his hair and gasps, unable to catch her breath. When she is overwhelmed with the desire to kiss him again, she pulls him up so she can taste his lips. Her heart beats, deafening, in her ears, even the thunder is drowned out.

He asks her, panting in her ear, if she's sure and she is. She has never been more certain about anything in her life. He groans against her neck when they finally join as one. She arches against him, pulling his hair, wrapping her arms around his neck; he slips his arms around her waist, enveloping her in his embrace.

Breathless but fervent—wild— they move together, panting. She rolls on top of him, pulling away to lay a trail of kisses down his body with her warm mouth. It makes her blush, the way he moans and runs his hands through her hair; it makes her shiver.

Tomorrow when the percussion of the rain and the chorus of thunder move on, she is certain there will be regret but for now there is no seeing past the sheen of glistening sweat, all that separates their bodies. Letting her lips and tongue move her back up to his mouth, she stifles her moans into his neck, her hands grabbing at his shoulders, at the chairs of the front seat, pulling into his hair, as she sinks back into him.

The storm has long moved on when they finally separate, collapsing breathlessly next to each other, their fingers still caressing each other's skin. Outside, the wind sings them to sleep as they catch their breath, laying with their quivering bodies entwined.

The only light is the afterglow.

Chapter 27
The Night, The Morning, and The Idiotic, Irrational, Bald-Faced Lie

Moira doesn't immediately open her eyes when she wakes; she lets the quiet and the panic set in before daring to look morning in the face. The light penetrates the dark tint of the Jeep's windows enough for her to tell that it's early in the morning.

Her heart palpitates in her throat like a hummingbird's wings as her eyes move around her surroundings from the roof of the Jeep to the cooler above her head, down to the toes. Alone and shivering, a wave of nausea hits her.

"What have I done?" she whispers.

"From the sounds of it, you had a good night." Leo answers from his bowl on the passenger side floor.

"Oh god!" she moans, covering her face with her palms. "What was I thinking?"

"You were thinking…he's cute, I think I'll have a piece of that."

"You're not taking this very seriously." She barks.

"It's no big thing. You had a good night." Leo replies, his nonchalance aggravating her.

"Good nights don't always mean good mornings!" Moira snaps, starting the frantic search for her clothes that are found at the "foot" of the bed in a soaking heap along with Elliot's except her personals, which she finds on the passenger seat. She groans, pulling the garments towards her and slapping them into the pile with the rest of her clothes, she then runs her fingers through her hair until they get stuck in the tangles.

"I'm so stupid!" she gripes, snatching her duffel bag from beside her so she can attempt to throw some clothes on, a task made more difficult by her clammy, unclean skin.

When she finally does throw herself out of the Jeep, fighting back nausea, she finds Elliot with damp hair looking over a map so casually seated at the picnic table, so unphased, so cool.

"Good morning." He greets upon seeing her, standing, straightening his back then smoothing his hands down his t-shirt and his khaki cargo shorts. There's nervousness to his movements, but his eyes shine, crinkling like tissue paper, with his smile.

"Hey." She replies, moving to the passenger seat to get Leo out of the stuffy car and into some fresh air. Without looking at Elliot, she crosses over to the picnic table and sets the fishbowl down, desperate to quell her churning, anxious stomach and racing heart.

She's going to throw up, she's sure of it.

"I went and paid for the campsite. I paid for tonight, too. The rangers were nice. Look," he waves his map in her direction and beams, "they gave me a map and told me about some hidden gems." The whole time he speaks, his voice is chipper and enthusiastic; it makes Moira angry that he can be so normal, so calm. He's always so relaxed.

When he approaches, she scurries back to the car where she snatches her duffel bag and pretends to busy herself with her things. "Are there showers here?" She asks, still staring into her bag.

"Yea. Just up the path to the right. Just under the bed there you'll find a towel. Should be one there. And," he goes to the passenger side of the Jeep and pulls out a damp towel from her seat. "I got this one, too. I used it so it's a little wet, but you might find it useful." Going to her, he holds it out, blushing.

She doesn't look at him, but she takes the towel from his hands.

"Uh, are you okay? I get the feeling…"

"I just don't want you to have the wrong idea about me. I mean, this might be normal for you but—"

"This isn't normal for me." He interrupts, his voice suddenly anxious.

She swallows and finally raises her eyes to meet his. "You just always keep condoms in your bag?" The bite in her words surprises them both.

"No, no I don't." His face flushes and he looks away quickly before snapping his gaze back to her. "I bought them at the gas station because I thought…I thought I felt something happening between us. I just, I just wanted to be prepared is all. Did I do something wrong?"

"I just don't want you to…I'm just…I'm not that kind of girl."

Elliot's eyes narrow, "What kind of girl would that be exactly?"

"The kind who has one-night stands."

"You know, that's not typically the kind of guy I am. Well, except for the time in Mexico but that wasn't my fault and I'm not proud. Fuck me, shut up." He closes his eyes and shakes his head before turning to her, his face hot.

"I just, I just need to shower. I feel so disgusting." She cringes at the thought of her own filth, as she throws the two towels over her shoulder and yanks her bag out, gripping it to her chest like a life preserver and the campsite is the ocean.

As she heads down the path, she thinks about taking Leo with her since she is in desperate need of consoling words and advice but when she turns, she stops. Elliot rests his head on his folded hands bringing himself to be eye level with Leo.

"You hear that, Leo the Fish? I made her feel disgusting. That's real great." He mutters and a wave of guilt floods over here, the ocean that surrounds her threatening to drown her. Before she can be overwhelmed, she turns and hurries down the path until she finds the bathrooms.

The stream of the shower is weak and cool on her burning skin. She relishes the water but her mind won't turn off from the turntable of images of last night. Even the three Daddy Long Legs in the corners of the shower stall, mocking her, aren't enough to distract her and neither is her missing earring from Leah. When she saw one was missing from her ear, she nearly cried but she reasons that it must be in the Jeep somewhere in the tangled mess left behind.

Intent on moving forward, she steps out of the cool water and goes to work on her hair, first wrapping it in the dry towel then tousling it wildly. On his towel, the one he used this morning, she can smell his body wash when she brings it to her face and it reminds her, painfully, that she is a woman, that she enjoyed every second of his caress. It reminds her that she cannot wash away last night and pretend it never happened.

Anger at him swells in her chest, not for last night, but for his high spirits this morning, his cheerful disposition. For him to rent the campsite for another night. Does he expect a replay? She slams her makeup bag onto the stainless-steel counter, spilling the contents into the rusted sink. With little care, she applies her makeup, throwing the mascara and blush and powder back into the bag when she's finished.

She convinces herself that he's still on the rebound, that he's only using her. She convinces herself that once they get back to Wisconsin, he'll leave her all alone. He'll hurt her the way men have hurt women for millennia, the way all the men in her life have hurt her. There's no point to allowing herself to believe that he might actually like her.

Or that she might just like him.

She dries her hair in the air dryer against the wall, only after determining that it is spider free but, despite her resolution to despise Elliot and his presumptions, she can't stop thinking about his hands and where they touched her, the heat they brought her last night and now in memory.

Looking around the dark bathroom, she wishes she had brought Leo with her; she could use a good pep talk, not that his guidance was much use this morning, anyway. For now, she can only look to herself in the rusted mirror, barely able to maintain eye contact with her own reflection.

"Why are you so stupid?" she asks, leaning in and examining her eyebrows, her lashes, her lips. She thinks about the places her lips had wandered last night and her face lights up, burning. The places *his* lips touched her—had Jonathan once done those things, made her moan, scream, that way? —and how is she going to face him? How can she go back out there and look him in the eye? She moans and pulls her hair into a high ponytail, letting loose the curly tendrils in front of her ears.

"At least you acted by your desires." She says, arching her brows at her reflection. "You like him. You know you like him and you think he's cute." With her hands resting on the countertop, she sighs. "That's what Leo would say. And Moira would say, he'll only hurt me in the end. That's what men do. Even if they are seemingly nice guys."

Returning to the camp, she finds Elliot sitting at the picnic table with Leo, his eyes covered with his sunglasses, frowning down at the fish. Neither speak. Moira goes to the back of the Jeep and is mortified when she sees the back of the Jeep has been cleaned, the bed made, his bag and equipment organized, and her things, her wet personals, folded into a tidy, embarrassing pile, including her missing earring. Relieved, she puts her earrings back in, sighing, and thinks of Leah. All the misdirected phone calls and invoices sent to the wrong customers, the mug she bought Moira for being nice and the time she begged Moira not to hire a guy for the factory because she had a one-night stand with him not even a year earlier.

Moira touches the soft feathers of one of the earrings.

"Do you feel better?" Elliot's voice is flat.

"We both know that last night was a mistake." She says sharply, locking her eyes on his face. The man recoils, as though hit in the gut; he turns away, pursing his lips.

"I didn't know." He tells her, standing and holding both hands up, "But I know now. I guess…" he rubs both hands on the back of his head, "I guess I'm sorry. I should've known better. And I sure ain't going to try to convince you that I'm a great guy, really. That last night wasn't a mistake or that I really thought there was something between us. That we might've had something, a future starting here. No." He casts his eyes to the sky. "No. I'm sorry that I made you feel disgusting."

"It-it wasn't you that made me feel gross. I just felt gross. It wasn't you." Her words are said to his feet.

"Well, either way, there's something about me you don't like, which is pretty sad because I like you. I've liked you the moment I met you. But it doesn't matter. I'm sorry and I won't say another word about it."

His words startle her but she can't find the courage to look him in the eye and to tell him that she really does like him, too. That it wasn't a mistake. If she could tell him she's scared of being hurt, he could reassure her. They could live happily ever after.

"We just need to move on." She says instead.

The sounds of the natural world surround them, a woodpecker hammers away in the forest, the canopy of leaves still sashays with the wind. The right words elude each of them but finally Elliot pushes off from where he leans and throws his arms out to the side, surrendering.

"Well, what do you want to do then?"

"I don t know." She replies, downtrodden eyes on the ground. She's afraid to look at him, afraid to meet his eye, to see his sadness and when she does look up her heart flutters in her throat as every image from last night flashes through her head. Her face goes hot and she must resist the urge to reach out and touch him—his cheek, his untidy hair—to kiss his sad lips. It was these emotions that got her into trouble last night.

"I guess it doesn't really matter what you want to do. I asked you that last night and you regret that decision, so I'm going to make a decision for myself and you can..." His voice trails off with his eyes that move to the tree line. "You can do whatever."

"Okay."

"I'm going to check this place out." He says, shrugging and walking to the Jeep. He pulls open the driver's side passenger door and grabs a backpack and begins shoving supplies into it. "You're welcome to come with me. You're also welcome to stay here and do a crossword or whatever it is you do."

"What would you prefer me to do?" She asks, watching his hands shove granola bars and bags of trail mix into the bag.

"You're here." He says without hesitation. "You might as well see something cool. Make staying here last night not a total mistake."

"Okay."

He stuffs his water bottle into the bag along with several cans of Monster. "I don't know what that means. Do you want to come or not?"

The thought of being alone at the site fills her with dread, to be alone with a murderer lurking in the woods, or a bear or a skunk. The thought of not being by his side. "Yes please."

He nods, curtly, and reaches for her water bottle so he can fill it with cold water from the cooler. "I wouldn't recommend taking your fish. Terrain here can get pretty rough. I'd hate for something to happen to him."

"Okay."

"Is that all you're going to say?" Shoving her filled bottle into the backpack, he raises his shaded eyes to her.

"I'm sorry." She raises her chin and looks at his face, desperate for her gaze to hold, but it fails and she snaps her head away.

"No, *I'm* sorry."

Chapter 28
The Hike, The Hesitation, and The Beautiful World

By noon, her feet and legs are killing her, her back has gone tight and stiff. The steep hills and jagged pathways make Moira thankful that she didn't bring Leo along, although it's lonely without his face, as Elliot seems content capturing each view of waterfalls and scenic panoramas with his lens in silence.

More than an hour is spent following a family of river otters, another thirty minutes with a playful mountain chickadee, and they found his favorite bird, the Pileated woodpecker, who was surprisingly eager to have his picture taken and Moira can't help but watch Elliot work with intrigue and admiration for his patience making sure to capture the bird's speckled wings, his red mustache, and his long tongue as it searches the bark for a snack.

They work their way up a bluff along a series of narrow switchbacks until they reach a viewing platform comfortable enough to take lunch. Moira takes a seat on a wooden bench bolted into the rockface while Elliot plops down across the platform, near the edge, leaning against a tree. In Minnesota, she recalls as she watches him, he sat so close that their shoulders touched and it made her blush. Now she blushes for the distance he keeps, for his quietude.

He appears to be more comfortable with his leg dangling off a 1000-foot drop into a sea of trees than he would be sitting beside her on the bench. She grows envious of his indifferent visage and resting alongside that envy is a bubbling anger that suddenly he can be so silent. He spent the entire trip talking to her about anything and everything that came to his mind, desperate to get her to open up to him and now he stares out into the distance. His eyes are constantly scanning his surroundings.

She could ask him something, maybe about how many times he's been to Montana or about the Brewers—did they win last night? Are the team they're going to go play in Seattle any good—or she could just apologize. Tell him how she feels? That he's cute and nice; she likes him and last night was the best night she's ever had.

He'd be happy to hear it; he said he likes her…he said so.

So why the hesitation?

And why won't he talk? If he would open the dialogue, she could fill in…she thinks. She watches him watching the world in the distance willing him to speak to her.

"You have something to say?" Elliot asks, first to the horizon then turning covered eyes to hers.

She shakes her head and he looks away again, with a sigh. She bites her lip, wishing she could find some words to bring back some semblance of normalcy to their short acquaintanceship.

They don't appear to exist.

For another two hours, they follow the meandering trail through the forest. They climb up bluff faces and navigate jagged paths back down into valleys. Moira, on the verge of death by exhaustion, observes Elliot as he hops around the trail with a 50-pound backpack and an endless supply of energy, climbing trees to get the best shot, scaling down cliff sides to get new—and dangerous—perspectives. She wonders, as she watches, what interesting things he would talk about if she had reacted like a rational adult this morning. If she had embraced their intimacy, a new relationship, if she had listened to her heart and his.

They could hold hands and smile.

Following the sounds of rushing water, Elliot leads her down a narrow path, a sharp dip in the rocky ground. Elliot steps down the path first, sliding then stopping himself, getting his footing, and continues with caution, telling her to watch her footing. Moira watches his descent down the steep decline, assessing how she is going to follow without dying and once again feeling thankful she didn't bring Leo with her.

With a deep breath, she takes her first step down the slope, feeling her foot slide with the dirt and leaves. She pulls her foot back and looks down at Elliot who continues to make his way towards the bottom. Another shrill inhalation and she moves again to mimic Elliot's careful movements.

She sees him stop and raise his lens at something, it could be anything as she often can't see what he sees when he sees it but when she sees him stop, she knows she, too, must stop.

It shouldn't be a hard thing to do.

But the dirt and the leaves, the slope and Moira being Moira, she stumbles down, gaining momentum and unable to regain her stability; she crashes into his back with a cry knocking his camera from his grip and scaring a Barred owl from its perch. Together, they drop down the vertical hill until Elliot is able to regain control of his feet.

She presses against his back, her hands firmly on his shoulders, panting. "I'm sorry."

"You okay?" He turns and puts his arms around her waist with his right hand, his left securing his camera to his chest.

"Yes. Yes." She balances herself using his shoulders, "Is your camera? I thought you dropped it."

He tugs at it pulling on the strap around his neck and tries to smile.

She exhales and looks to the sky, "Thank goodness." She sighs again and bows her forehead to his arm. "I'm sorry I scared your bird."

His nearness, his warmth.

"It's okay. Let's go."

She nods her head against him and looks up to find him scanning the tree line, searching perhaps for the owl; she watches him swallow, hard, and look down at her.

"Let's go."

They walk until they reach a staircase built into the rocky terrain that seemingly reaches to the heavens. A brown placard informs them that Ylobbí Peak is only 350 steps above. With a smirk, Elliot grips the railing and places one foot onto the first step.

"Want to race?"

Moira's mouth drops open as her eyes travel up the length of the staircase until it disappears, hidden by the leaves of the trees surrounding it. Elliot doesn't wait for her reply before beginning the ascent to the top, which Moira genuinely believes, though she doesn't tell him, will take them forever. They will never make it to Seattle in time because they will still be here, climbing these stairs!

Probably until they die.

But she doesn't tell him this; she remains silent.

By the time they reach the top, Moira has tied up her cotton button-down to let the skin on her back breath. She wipes the sweat away from her brow with the fabric of the bow not caring how slovenly, or wanton, she may appear in Elliot's eyes. She is too hot and sweaty to care about anything except the view of mountains dominating the horizon with jagged, snowy peaks and forests thick with deep green pines and verdant maples, stretching for miles around them.

"This is totally worth all them stairs." She says, breathless but awed. He brushes past her and sets his equipment, his monopod and camera bag, down onto the ground. Going through his bag, he changes his lens out and begins his routine of shots.

She gazes out at the waterfall cutting through the rocks just beneath them; if she leans over the wooden railing, she can feel the spray of the water. She closes her eyes and relishes the cool mist but it crosses her mind that this rickety railing could fail any second and she would go plummeting to her death. Would Elliot take care of Leo?

"You're not listening at all are you?"

"Huh?" she turns to Elliot who looks at her from over the top of his shades, kneeling on the ground, cleaning his lens. "Uh, I'm sorry."

"It's okay. Lauren always said I talk too damn much." Elliot throws the microfiber cloth into the bag.

"No, no!" she steps towards him, her head shaking vehemently. "No, I was just thinking something. I was thinking something stupid."

"Yea?" he doesn't look at her, he moves past with long strides and sets up his next series of shots, pushing his glasses to the top of his head.

"If I fell off this cliff, would you take care of Leo? Or would you dump him out somewhere?"

He looks up from his viewfinder, his head tilted but he doesn't look at her, though she knows he's thinking of the question. "I would take care of him. But nothing is going to happen to you." He sighs and lowers his lens, turning to her. "You told me about something absolutely horrific that happened to you. When you were young."

Moira's face goes hot, her body freezes. Suddenly, the logo on his shirt is mesmerizing but not enough to stop her heart from sinking; she starts to crack her knuckles and twist her ring, she bites her lip and looks to her feet.

"Truly awful and I want you to know that…I just want you to know that…" his voice trails off and he finally breaks away from her face, turning instead to the sky. "I don't actually know what I want you to know." His eyes move back to her, his lips are pursed and nervous. "I guess that I didn't mean to add to your trauma last night. I didn't mean to hurt you in any way or make you feel any sort of pressure…"

"No, please don't…"

"I'm sorry that I made you feel that way. It was never my intention. I just thought, wrongly, that you may have felt the same way about me as I do about you.

"Stop. Please, stop."

Elliot puts his hands in the air and nods once, "Sorry."

She tries to focus on the beauty around her, on the wind in the trees and the sounds of the finches within them. The fluffy clouds. But to think she could make him feel this way, to make him feel guilt when that burden should rest solely on her. To make him feel responsible for any part of her trauma and to not make it right. To be silent!

She tries to find her voice, her courage to be honest, but she fails and leans against the wooden railing unable to find any joy in the splendor of the view.

"There's something else, Moira. That I need to tell you." He lowers his camera and turns to her, dropping his sunglasses from his head to his eyes. "Your folks called again this morning, when I was heading over to the ranger station."

"What? Why?"

"They're worried about you. I guess they feel I'm some sort of conduit to your well-being. I-I was mad, I was so mad at them. For what they said to you. But, but…" Elliot walks over to the railing and looks over it, focusing his eyes on the waterfall beneath them. "They said you didn't tell them."

She snaps her head over to him, livid, "What?"

"They said you never told them what happened to you." Elliot can't bring himself to look at her. "I didn't think it was my place…to tell them anything. But…I felt I had to. Moira...they didn't know."

"I didn't tell them? Of course, I did. Of course, I did! How can they say that? And then they made *you* tell them. To make *you* repeat it! How could they? Of course, I told them. I remember, I remember where we were standing. I remember…"

Elliot puts his hands up, "I'm just telling you the conversation I had with them this morning. Trust me, it's not one I wanted to have."

For a time, they are silent as she thinks back to the memories she has tried, for 12 years, to repress, to bury so deep she'd forget. She brings her quaking hands to her mouth; her legs fail and she falls onto the ground. "Oh god." In the foyer, she can see it as clear as the scenery around her now; she was begging her parents not to make her go with them to Charles Kent's house.

How he grabbed her.

That's all she said. He grabbed her and she repeated this sentiment over and over. They didn't understand what that meant. Grabbed.

Nothing about his fingers.

He was drunk; he didn't mean any harm when he grabbed her.

"For twelve years." she says, burying her face into her knees, hugging them. Elliot kneels before her and places a hesitant hand on her leg, his fingers trembling. "You're the only person I ever told, I guess. The details. I-I couldn't tell them. I couldn't. Why didn't I tell them?"

"Well," Elliot stands, "I don't know that my minor in psychology is going to be much help here but I think that might be common with victims of, uh..." He takes a deep breath, shaking and nervous, "I think it's pretty common."

"I couldn't say it. I couldn't tell them, make them understand."

"I'm here if you need to talk, Moira." He says, backing away, giving her all he can offer: space.

"Thanks." She murmurs, looking up at him, her eyes only reaching his chest. She hugs her knees for a while, tightly as though they might breakaway if she lets them go. She replays the scene in the foyer, on repeat. Over and over. Over and over.

What she said to her parents and how they replied, how she sobbed and decided that she would never speak to them again. They left her alone and she began to plot her escape.

If they weren't going to protect her, she would protect herself. The memories continue until she can't breathe. Elliot continues to work, although hesitantly, glancing at Moira with thoughtful eyes but she ignores him, his concern, and steadies herself against the railing and gazes out at the horizon wishing her mind would slow down enough for her to get a grasp on her own thoughts.

Her thoughts are a jumble, a cryptic mass of emotions, heavy baggage of the psyche. Her parents didn't think it was so bad, their daughter being grabbed. It was a different world 12 years ago and she didn't tell them…they couldn't figure it out, though? Maybe they did…all those cards over the last 12 years, all those missed calls, and deleted, unheard voicemails.

The world around her goes quiet except for the bird song and the sound of Elliot's shutter. When she finds the courage to look at him, thinking she may say something, though she isn't sure what, she's bewildered to find him photographing a fallen leaf. He takes the time to rearrange the leaf onto a grouping of rocks and photographs it again.

Moira watches him work until he nods with satisfaction then looks over to her. He tries to give her a reassuring smile but it falters and his troubled eyes give away his tormented emotions but she has nothing to say to make him feel better, or herself.

Glancing at his watch, he looks out to the horizon, "It's getting late. We should maybe start heading back."

Nodding, she watches him gather his equipment. Before moving to follow him down the trail, she glances at the fallen leaf he was photographing.

She leans over the leaf and gazes down at it, transfixed. Its center is puddled with water and the edges are frayed like lace but it's still vibrant, it's still bright with life that pops against the greys of the rocks beneath it. Moira touches the leaf, brushing over the surface with her fingertips.

The world must be more beautiful than she realizes.

Chapter 29
The Milky Way, The Crash, and The State That Hates Them

Moira plops down on the picnic table with a sigh, kicking her shoes off and rubbing her sore feet. Elliot heads to the Jeep and stores his equipment leaving a trail of silence behind him. She looks to Leo, who stares back offering nothing by way of advice or guidance so she scrunches her face at him. She's startled when Elliot approaches, looking at her with a cocked eyebrow.

"Don't you make faces at your dog?" She replies, coolly.

"Probably." He shrugs. Two days ago, he would have launched into a story about Molitor but now, only the one word passes his lips. Elliot looks down at his watch then up at the sky where the sun is beginning to set. Her eyes follow his to the sky where they each watch a flock of birds pass over the coral clouds, disappearing into the trees. Elliot removes himself from her side, retreats to a safe distance, to the Jeep, as soon as the birds are out of sight.

She turns her attention back to Leo who stares at her with disappointment written all over his pouting face. "Are you mad I didn't take you with me, my love? Well, be thankful I didn't. I slid down a cliff and almost knocked Elliot right over. You might have died."

"Here." Elliot interrupts her conversation with Leo by throwing a sandwich down in front of her before moving to take a seat across from her. While she is thankful for the food, since all of the hiking has drained her energy, she isn't sure she can eat another sandwich. She finds herself gazing at Elliot who stares off into the distance beyond the Jeep thinking that this diet is likely why he is so thin.

"You must have something to say now." He says, suddenly turning his eyes to her face.

"Why?" She asks, dropping her eyes firmly on her sandwich.

"Because you keep staring at me. What's on your mind?"

"There's a lot on my mind," She confesses in what may be the first honest statement she's made to him all day. "My parents and you. How you can eat sandwiches all day, every day. How thankful I am that I didn't take Leo with us." She shrugs, keeping her eyes locked on her sandwich. "A lot."

"Makes sense." He nods and they fall quiet for the rest of their meal. When they each are finished, Elliot picks up the cloth napkins and goes over to the Jeep leaving Moira to stare at Leo.

"Elliot?" Moira asks, still gazing at Leo's pink fins. In her peripheral vision, she sees Elliot close the back door of the Jeep and turn to her. "Can, can we still be friends? For now? I mean, you can hate me when we get back to Wisconsin but for now..." The fear is too great to look at him.

"I don't hate you."

"I would if I were you." She finally looks to him, meeting the sadness in his eyes with her own.

"I don't. I only have myself to be upset with. You've done nothing wrong."

"That's not fair." She shakes her head and pulls her gaze back to Leo's flowing pink fins. "I was not a victim last night. Don't think for a moment that I was. I just want things to go back to the way they were."

"That's hard. I mean, I'm trying and I'll stop acting this wounded eventually, I'll get over you and you can just be another, uh, notch in my belt, right?" She looks back over to him where he leans against the Jeep with his arms folded, staring down at his shoes. There is no conviction to his words, a weak attempt at humor but his downtrodden face gives away his heart. "It'll be easier when we get back to Wisconsin." He concludes, finally raising his brown eyes to meet her green ones.

"Do you want to take me to an airport? Then you can—"

"Of course not." He cuts her off, shaking his head vehemently. "I promised to take Leo, and you, to see the Space Needle so that's what we're going to do. Unless you want me to take you to the airport in Missoula."

"No."

"Good. I'm going to pee then we can head back to town." He doesn't waste any time slipping to the other side of the Jeep, out of sight. Moira blushes, jealous of his carefree style; she can't even use a public restroom if someone else is in there let alone go in the woods with someone not ten foot away.

"Tell him you're sorry." Leo hisses, drawing her attention to where he hovers. "Tell him how you feel."

Moira shakes her head, glancing towards the Jeep. Whatever she's feeling isn't what she wants it to be, what Elliot is feeling is only temporary.

A love—is it too soon for love? —of convenience.

It's easy to think you're in love when you're alone with that person but you can't fall in love in three days, or four.

"You deserve to be lonely, Moira." Leo growls, "This man is the best thing that has ever happened to you and you are being willfully blind!"

"All right." Elliot says, coming around the Jeep rubbing hand sanitizer from the center console around his hands. "We should go."

Moira nods, captivated by his movements, by the way he shifts from one foot to the other staring off beyond her, checking his watch. Finally, he takes a deep breath and fishes his keys from his pocket, turning away from her while her mind races with Leo's words.

The ride into town is much easier in the day than the ride into the park was last night in the dark and rain. In the falling light, Elliot sees the turn he missed that would have led them to the freeway, the turn that would have kept them from Ylobbí park and prevented their disastrous morning together.

"I was thinking…" He begins, exhaling slowly, "I was thinking that I'll drop you off at the motel. I'll come back for you in the morning." He looks at her, "I promise."

"I don't understand. Where are you going?"

Elliot doesn't answer right away; he keeps his eyes on the narrow road. Finally, he answers in a low voice. "I'm going to go back to Ylobbí. I want to go back to the top tonight."

"Which we could have done together if…if…" she loses her voice and turns her eyes first to Leo, still in his bowl and placed snuggly between her feet, to the trees along the roadside.

"I didn't think you'd want to go all that way again. I guess I just assumed. And I'm sure you don't want to spend another night in the back with me. Seems inappropriate considering." Moira doesn't answer, which draws Elliot's attention to her stony face. "I mean, we can go together…if you wanted to. I'd love to share it with you, the Milky Way. I just didn't think you'd want to."

"The Milky Way?" She wonders what that would be like, seeing the edge of the galaxy. To set her eyes upon a sky so uncorrupted by city lights you can see every star that was ever born. No jets or radio towers.

Another night with Elliot.

Her stomach trembles with the thought, making her hands wring and toy nervously with her sunflower navel ring.

"What's this guy's problem." Elliot grumbles, pulling Moira's attention to the here and now, drawing her eyes to the side mirror where she sees a blue SUV move close to their tailgate then drop back some distance only to speed up again, pulling near them. This blue vehicle straddles the solid yellow line, slows down, and speeds up again.

Elliot looks at Moira, arched brows, slack jaw, "Montana is not our state."

"For real." Moira replies, looking in the side mirror to the erratic blue SUV, making her hands twist for different reasons than tonight.

"We'll let them pass." Elliot decides at the next straightaway in the road with hatched yellow lines. Easing off the accelerator, dropping his speed to the speed limit, he guides the Jeep near the side of the road in the hope that the guy behind them will pass. Instead, the blue SUV stays close on their tailgate. "For fuck's sake."

The road begins to curve, the hatched yellow line turning into a double solid line, and now the SUV veers into the opposite lane. Elliot shakes his head, though his grip stays loose on the wheel, his posture slouched and comfortable where Moira is rigid, passing nervous glances back between the mirror and Elliot's irritated face.

Elliot slows their speed down even further, resting his foot on the brake, when the vehicle revs his engine and swings into the oncoming lane, blowing past the Jeep with a roar. Just after the bend, the road straightens out into an undulating straightaway, dipping high and low through the tree covered landscape. The SUV bestrides the center line, weaving and swerving,

"I think we should call the police." Elliot tells her, glaring at the vehicle in front of them.

Over the top of a small hill, a white pickup truck blares its horn; the SUV throws itself back in his own lane, in front of Elliot and Moira. The sounds of three sets of screaming brakes echoes through the peaceful evening.

Moira pushes against the dashboard, and squeezes her feet together desperate to secure Leo, as the car screams to a halt. They watch as the SUV spins wildly and hits a ditch, flipping over once before hitting a tree with a deafening crash.

"Shit!" Elliot shouts, jerking the Jeep to the side of the road and smashing the button for his hazard lights. "Call 911." He tells her with incredible calm, leaping from the Jeep. With trembling hands, she grabs his phone from the center compartment but it's locked with a passcode or his fingerprint. She scrambles out after Elliot,

"What's the PIN?"

"2913!" he shouts back to her. The driver of the white truck is sprinting towards her, already on the phone with the emergency services so she slides Elliot's phone into her pocket and hurries over to the accident to see what use she can be.

Elliot has the driver's door open but he's unresponsive except for slurring unconsciously. On the other side of the vehicle, his passenger stumbles out sobbing and gasping for air. Blood gushes from the girl's head, the blond girl with the pretty blue nails.

Moira gasps when she recognizes her, "Josie!" she cries, taking hold of her arms and pulling her away from the wreckage.

"Myra? Oh, Myra! I was so scared! I begged and begged him to stop." She wails, falling into Moira's arms. Moira leads the girl back to the Jeep where she situates her in the passenger seat with motherly command then hurrying to the back and getting one of the bath towels. As she applies pressure to the girl's wound with one hand, Moira pets the other side of her pretty blonde hair, rubbing her arms and embracing her with her other hand.

The girl, Josie from the fair, who kept touching Elliot's arm, who laughed at everything he said, quakes uncontrollably no matter how tightly Moira tries to comfort her.

Moira raises her eyes to Elliot and the driver of the white truck who have managed to rouse the driver of the blue SUV but now can't get him to sit still and wait for the ambulance. She is horrified to see the man, the drunkard, now donning a black eye courtesy of

Elliot's fist last night, stumbling around, spitting out blood as he slurs.

"I'm fine." He staggers around, shoving Elliot's shoulder. "Look what you did to my car, man." Elliot looks at the driver from the white truck, a man in his fifties wearing a flannel shirt and blue jeans with greying blonde hair and a grey beard, who addresses the drunkard:

"Come on, Karl, settle down. The ambulance is coming."

The Drunkard, Karl, pushes the older gentleman while speaking incoherently and tumbling around the wreckage. The drunkard curses them, he curses God. Screaming and spitting blood, tripping and sprawling out on the ground, he curses them again, calling them every insult he can think of, he shouts at the car, blaming that, too.

"He does this all the time." The older gentleman says, he and Elliot approaching the two women. "Josie, you should know better than to get messed up with him." Josie sobs, burying her face in Moira's neck.

It's another 20 minutes before they hear the sirens racing toward them from Butte, the nearest city with a hospital and real police department, and another five before they arrive but once they do, it's a chaotic mess of yelling and movement; a spiral of confusion and blue lights. Officers moving back and forth, asking questions of Elliot then Moira. They ask questions of the driver of the white truck. The blue lights are dizzying, the noise and watching Josie get loaded into an ambulance.

When she is free, she finally goes to find Elliot who she hasn't seen since the police arrived. She is surprised he is not at the Jeep, assuming he would be waiting for her there, so she leans on the hood and waits for him.

The red and blue lights are hypnotizing but the whole situation feels surreal. In her head she thinks about the sight of the blue SUV flipping, of Josie's bloodied head. Moira shivers and hugs herself, dropping her gaze to her feet. Rubbing her shoulders, she fiddles with her shirt that is still tied up over her tummy. Slowly, she unties it and lets it fall down in a wrinkled curtain over her sunflower.

If only the images would stop, these turbulent thoughts rioting through her head. Last night at the fair to last night in the Jeep. Elliot's sad eyes this morning, his silence. And now. In her despair, she doesn't hear Elliot approach, his camera around his neck, his tripod in his hand.

"Are you okay?" When he speaks, he startles her and she jumps with a gasp. "Sorry." He mutters, slumping back against the hood.

"Oh, Elliot!" she moans, dropping her hands to her sides and turning to him, "Are you okay?"

"I just asked you." He tries to smile and she realizes that she doesn't think she's seen him smile all day. He is normally so smiley, always laughing. Not today, though, and she knows that it's her fault.

"I'm fine." She sighs. "I'm really okay, but I hate this state. I frigging hate it."

"I hear ya."

If only she could make him smile again.

Chapter 30
The Phone, The Passcode, and The Curious Eyes

By the time they are released from the scene, it's after 8 o'clock and the sun is touching the horizon, leaving behind it a trail of gold bleeding into the navy night. It's decided that they will go back to town and hunker down for the night at the motel. Elliot's decision is not met by Moira with any resistance, though she is torn between feeling bad they didn't get back to the peak and being thankful that she can shower in a real bathroom.

And it's the single greatest shower of her life.

When she finally appears, she smiles at Leo, situated in his bowl and swimming in small circles happy to have been fed, happy to have survived tonight. The two remain in silence for a while as she dresses in a clean night shirt and fresh panties and cleans up her duffel bag to prepare it for tomorrow, to lay out an outfit so she can be immediately ready to go when Elliot knocks. She shakes out her jeans to fold them up when Elliot's phone falls from her pocket. Picking it up, she turns it over in her hands, slowly, then shakes her head and sets it on the bedside table. Her eyes flicker over the phone.

Next door, she can hear the hiss of Elliot's shower through the thin walls. Her mind wanders to images of the water sliding over his body. She thinks about his tattooed back and his trip to Mexico. She thinks about how she felt him tremble under her fingertips, she could feel his skin, his muscles.

Rolling to her back, she stares at the ceiling and lets the What Ifs slip in. What if the SUV hit their Jeep, or the white truck? What if Elliot had been killed; what if anyone had been killed. She remembers Elliot's face, his fury, when he spoke to the drunkard, his sadness when he was standing beside her leaning on the hood. Her eyes well with tears.

If she could have a cuddle.

What would Elliot do, she wonders, if she knocked on his door. If she asked to stay with him.

"He would laugh at you!" she answers herself aloud, hostility in her voice, "That boy isn't so dumb he'd risk another night for you to regret."

"I don't think so" Leo mutters but is ignored. Blinking her tears away and tossing her head side to side.

"I wouldn't bother with me but I shouldn't bother with him. We both know he'll just hurt me. I guarantee you once we get back to Wisconsin, I'll be kicked the curb. You heard him. I'll just be another notch in his belt." She rolls to face Leo's bowl, tucking her arm under her head.

"You know he didn't mean that seriously!" Leo scolds.

"He'll just hurt me."

"So, you hurt him first. You're going to be lonely for the rest of your life."

Moira wraps her arms around herself, biting her lip hard enough she thinks it may bleed. She doesn't want to listen to Leo. "And then…and then there's my parents." Her voice comes as a whisper. "I-I don't even want to think about this. I can't. I'll think about the car accident!"

"Moira, go next door. Go see Elliot, tell him you're sorry. Go hug and kiss him and tomorrow morning, don't be afraid. Just…be you being in love."

She sighs and begins to roll to her back again, pulling her eyes from her preaching fish when his phone starts to chime beside.

She picks it up and feels her heart plummet into her gut when she sees her parents phone number on the screen, she sees that Elliot has inputted their names into his phone, Patrick and Shawna Lovegood. He knows their names. Shaking her head, she sets it down on the table and waits for it to go to voicemail so she can listen to what they have to say.

They greet Elliot as Leo and ask for him to let Moira listen to their message if he wouldn't mind. Of course, they miss her and they love her. They need to talk to her. It's practical begging on their end, pleading to hear her voice. For a moment she thinks about calling them back, to tell them to stop calling Elliot and that they aren't allowed to call him Leo. His name is Elliot. Leave him alone.

She turns the phone over in her hands. 2913. That was the passcode. She could call them.

With her hands trembling, she calls her parents back; she lets them hear her voice that they have so seldom heard over the last 12 years.

They miss her and they love her.

They're sorry, so sorry, they tell her through their tears. Moira bites her lip and listens to their words. She listens about how they parted ways with Charles Kent ten years ago; how they knew something more than *grabbed* happened, how they confronted him but there was nothing they could do. He's gone now, out of their lives forever.

They should've understood.

Moira knows she never gave them a real chance to understand, but even with this knowledge, she cannot find forgiveness. Not now, not yet. In time, she tells them. When she gets back to Wisconsin, she will call them, she promises, however they have to stop calling Elliot. She blushes when they tell her that they like him, that he seems like such a nice young man. He's been nothing but polite to them, such refreshing gentleman behavior, except for his initial joke about kidnapping her. All three can chuckle about Elliot's ill-conceived joke now. They want to meet him, too, if she'll give them the chance. They'd like to thank him.

Her only reply to this is that she'll call them when she gets home. She has to go now.

She ends the call and stares at the home screen with the Brewers background and all the icons arranged in alphabetical order. Amazon and CNN News, eBay, Pandora, Venmo. All the typical apps like the camera, clock, and photos. Her breath is quick in her throat. All the things he uses in his daily life.

"Don't look at his stuff." Leo warns, watching her staring down at the screen. She doesn't move. "Don't betray his trust like that. I know you're upset but don't touch his things."

"You're right." She sets the phone down on the table, urging herself not to reach for it. Instead, she turns out the light and slams herself back down into the pillows. She lay, staring at the ceiling, for a time before she can no longer resist and she snatches his phone.

It unlocks with a click when she enters the PIN code.

The first app she clicks is the Photos but she is disappointed to only find two pictures in the camera roll, one of Molitor and a selfie Elliot took with Molitor, perfectly timed as the dog licks his face, Elliot laughing. She closes the photo album and opens the CNN App, but the news of the world is depressing so she looks at his eBay account to see that the only thing he buys off the site is baseball cards and Brewers memorabilia. On his Facebook she searches through the pictures that Leo Fisch Photography posts. She's impressed with the thousands of likes and shares his pictures get, and more impressed with the shots themselves, even a tad jealous at all the places he's been and the things he's seen.

In a personal album, there are pictures of his family, scanned photos dating back to when Elliot was just a baby to the present. There are many photos of him and Lainey when she was a tiny little girl looking up to her adoring big brother to one a couple weeks ago. A candid shot of Elliot trying to get the scowling teenager to eat a cookie. It's a sharp contrast to another photo of the girl as a toddler eating cake with her brother.

It's too intimate.

She blushes and closes the application. How can she look at images of these personal events in his life in an album that has the privacy setting so that only he and those marked family have access to? And his emails. Dozens of messages from clients and potential clients scheduling appointments, asking for pricing. It isn't just wildlife he photographs but weddings and portraits, engagements and senior pictures; businesses needing promotional photos, a magazine that has browsed his portfolio and would like to meet with him.

This is none of her business, she thinks aggressively closing his email.

At the home screen, she stares, desperately trying to get herself to put the phone down. But a thought keeps flickering across her mind. Did he tell anyone he met a girl and she's pretty, that she's crazy and annoying? That he thinks he's in love, that he met The One?

She opens his text messages.

As her finger hits the screen, her heart sinks with guilt. The messages open to a conversation with his mom; the last message she sent was thirty minutes ago telling him to have a good night, she loves him with moon and heart emojis after the words. Moira's amused to scroll through and see that his mom likes to send him conversations in only emojis and GIFs and Elliot must decipher what she's talking about. She's disappointed that he hasn't once mentioned her to his mom but she knows this disappointment is unfair. After all, she told him she regretted being with him.

Elliot has more text messages between him and his stepdad then he does with his own father and even less with his stepmom. There are countless other messages from people. Friends, clients, family. Moira isn't sure she knows as many people.

Then there is his conversation with Lauren. It's been taunting her since she first opened the messages and now that there are no others to distract her.

"You're a bad person." Leo gripes, sliding onto his hammock.

She sighs and clicks the thread. There are dozens of messages from Lauren begging him to forgive her, to please come home. Telling him that they can work it out. His replies go from scathing to single word replies until the very end, the last message in the thread sent before 5 o'clock this morning when they would have still been entwined in the back of the Jeep.

"I've moved on." It reads and there is no reply from Lauren.

Three simple words.

He's moved on.

Chapter 31
The Ducks, The Driving, and The Call from His Sister

Moira wakes far too early in the morning, leaving her head groggy and heavy but the sun is beginning to shine through the windows, which means Elliot will be up soon and pounding on her door to get her up. There's no point going back to sleep now.

She rises and stretches her arms with a yawn when the dam of images of last night breaks and floods her with memories. She shakes the thought of the SUV flipping out of her head, she shakes the memory of Josie resting her bloody head on her chest. Her eyes find the phone on the bedside table and she remembers the text messages she read. The messages she read that were not meant for her eyes and guilt sinks like a stone in her stomach.

Slumping back into the pillows, she is unable to take her eyes from the phone. She groans and rubs her face, wishing she were still asleep, that she could sleep for days but with sleep eluding her, she gets up and shuffles to the bathroom. She brushes her teeth and combs her hair then stumbles back to her bag to get dressed; she pulls on her pair of jeans and her off the shoulder top, hating that she wore this only a couple days ago. Dressed, with her purse slung over her shoulder, she slips outside into the cool summer morning.

From the hotel, she walks the path that two days ago led to the fairgrounds. Now it looks barren. There is no evidence of there ever having been a festival here, no phantom smells of fried foods, no haunting echoes of music playing or laughter. The festival has picked up and disappeared, leaving no trace, no memory.

She wishes she could forget that whole night, especially when she comes to the park where Elliot punched the drunkard called Karl. Does she really want to forget it, though? She finds the lagoon and sits down letting the dewy grass soak into the denim of her jeans, sending a chill up her spine.

While watching a mother duck with her dozen babies crossing the pond, she thinks that Elliot would get a terrific shot of them with perfect lighting and crisp details. She'll just try to remember how happy and peaceful they look with their smiling beaks. When she feels her eyes become heavy and her head drops against the bark of the tree she leans against with a painful stab into her cheek, she yelps and decides to take a walk into the rundown town.

Many of the storefronts are vacant and those that are occupied are closed until later in the morning. The only businesses that are open are the corner bar, a place Moira only glances at from a distance, and a one-pump gas station where she buys a Snapple and a flavor of Monster that is advertised as being new. She decides, heading back to the motel, she will apologize to Elliot for what she said and how she acted. She's going to make Leo proud.

It isn't a long walk back to the motel but she is surprised to see Elliot sitting in the driver's seat of the Jeep, with his legs outside of the car, jiggling. When he sees her, he jumps up and rushes over to her.

"Moira!" He throws his arms around her, breathing a sigh. "I was so worried! I thought…I thought something happened or you left or…I don't know!"

"I'm sorry. I thought I'd be back before you got up." She places her arms gently around his waist and rubs his back, trying to soothe away his worry.

"I was so worried when you wouldn't answer your door." He sighs, bowing his head to hers when he realizes how tight he is holding her, how close their bodies are. He flushes and pulls away, offering an embarrassed apology as he quickly creates space between them.

"I just took a walk. I'm sorry. I couldn't sleep. But look," she takes the teal can of Monster out of her purse, "It's a new flavor! I thought you'd like to try it."

Accepting the can with a smile, he thanks her but, his eyes are all sadness and sleep deprivation. "I'm glad you're okay." He says with a sigh. "We should get going."

Growing tired of crossword puzzles after the first hour, she tosses the book to the floor in utter defeat, deflating in her seat. Not more than a few words have been spoken between her and Elliot but he seems content to sing along with an old country station on the radio. He beats out a partial rhythm with his thumbs on the top of the wheel and joins in a quiet duet with Don Gibson's Sea of Heartbreak, humming when he can't remember the words. She is whisked back to day one when she couldn't physically get herself to speak, she could hardly look at him except for quick glances.

And it was so awkward.

Just like now with seven more hours before Seattle…and the ride back.

Another hour goes by with her drifting in and out of sleep while trying to focus on the passing landscape. A dip in the road knocks her head against the window with a painful thud but does successfully bring her to full awareness. She looks over to her driver who has both hands on tight on the wheel, eyes focused on the highway winding before them. His eyes are dark and fatigued but concentrated through the high elevation and walls of pines.

She looks around at the traffic and the trees, the rolling mountains, with the sole desire to gaze at all the beauty, all the life, around her. For the next 15 minutes, she absorbs every sight into her skin, into her memory. She's determined now more than ever to not fall back to sleep as she doesn't want to miss another moment of the most beautiful scenery. Her will is broken, however, quite soon after she makes the determination to remain wide eyed and observant, the next time she opens her eyes, she swears she was only blinking.

Elliot nudges her shoulder, "We're in Idaho." His posture has relaxed again in his seat with his left hand draped lazily over the wheel, his right hand resting on his thigh.

"Really?" she perks up and looks outside at the eternity of rolling green hills and mountains.

"I thought you'd like to know you made it to one more state."

"Ah! That's," she counts on her fingers and smacks his shoulder, "five states!" He smiles at her and her grin grows as she turns to Leo. "Did you hear that, Leo? We made it to five different states! Can you believe it?" She strokes him through the plastic and he pushes against her finger, wiggling. "Me either." She whispers, leaning against his bag and smiling.

Soon thereafter, they pull off on a waypoint for a late breakfast and an opportunity to stretch their legs and maybe get a photo or two. From the back of the Jeep, they grab a couple of sandwiches,

Elliot grabs his second can of Monster, the first being the new flavor Moira bought him this morning, and Moira takes her water bottle, then they make their way to the overlook where the view of the pine covered mountains stops Moira from eating.

There's a lake in the distance, nestled snugly within the trees and high above wisps of clouds are painted across the purest blue sky.

When they finish eating and Elliot has chugged his drink, he retrieves his camera because, he explains, you never know when that next big money opportunity is going to strike. Moira didn't realize at the time that this meant for the next half hour she would be waiting on the single bench. She guards Elliot's wallet, keys, and cellphone while Elliot moves around from spot to spot. After each relocation, there are moments of adjusting settings and lenses that Moira can't understand. How hard is it to take a picture?

Still, she can't stop watching him work. She is sitting amongst the greenest of all the world's trees, the bluest sky surrounded by bird song, even an owl in the distance, and she watches him, working up her courage to talk to him. To say what she wants to say but it isn't long before her wistful gaze is broken when his phone starts ringing beside her.

"Who is it?" he asks from across the platform.

"Pam?" she answers, raising her eyes to meet his.

"Can you answer it? Put it on speaker." Moira does as is requested and puts the phone on speakers. "Pam!" Elliot calls, "Dearest illegitimate sister, apple of my eye! What the fuck do you want?"

Laughter comes from the speaker, "Leo, prick face bastard brother of mine! Where are you and please, please tell me you are in Seattle!" Her voice is pleasant and light, with a sing song quality, almost airy.

"Ha! I'm about six hours out yet."

"You were supposed to be here yesterday, I thought. You were supposed to be here *two* days ago, I thought. You said you were getting here ASAP!" The disappointment is thick in her voice. "I thought you were eager to come to Seattle!" Elliot tries to interject but she continues her scolding, making Elliot look over to Moira with a smile and a shrug, accepting his lumps like a good brother.

As the two chatter, mainly Pam berating Elliot for his tardiness, Moira thinks about what Elliot told her about his sister. How Pam is the product of an affair his father had before Elliot was born, how he was barely eight months old when Pam was born and barely a year when Pam came to live with them permanently.

His father's affair had never been a secret and he grew up knowing the details which only strengthened his admiration for his mother's capacity for forgiveness. This respect never faded even after she finally divorced his dad when he was five. 30 years later, he still can't comprehend how his mother managed to stay with his dad after what he did, even taking in Pam as her own. His mother's love of Pam, even now, couldn't be stronger if she had carried the child herself. She is his mother's daughter, never having known her own mother and, like Elliot, never growing close to their stepmom.

"Are you finished, Pam?" Elliot exclaims, drawing Moira's attention back to the conversation happening beside her through the phone.

"We thought you might be dead!" Pam laments, her scathing tone diminishing with woe.

"Well, I'm not."

"Yes, I know. I called mom because I was so worried." Pam tells him and he rolls his eyes; Moira takes note of Pam's use of the term mom and it makes her smile. "She said she was worried, too, but she said you read her message last night so we figured you must have been too tired to talk."

Pam's sentence isn't finished before Elliot's brow knit together, a thousand thoughts racing over his face. His eyes then snap over to Moira.

Moira keeps her gaze unfocused off in the distance pretending to look bored and inattentive but his calculating eyes make her face burn.

"I'll call you later, okay, Pam? I'm busy right now."

"You're busy?" Pam gasps and Moira can imagine Pam bringing her hands to her heart in feigned hurt. "We're still going to dinner tonight, right? We're going to make reservations! Please don't bail!"

"Yea, yea!" he steps over, leaving his camera to hang off his neck, and snatches his phone. He turns off the speaker and brings the phone to his ear. "I'll call you later when I'm in town. I've got to get going, though." He pauses and listens, "Yep. Okay. I love you, too. Bye." He ends the call and drops his hands, one hand still holding the phone, to his side. He doesn't speak and his silence makes her fidget nervously but he goes over to carefully pack away his camera without looking at her.

When he finally does speak, it's when he turns on a heel to face her, eyes focused on her face with decided irritation. "You read my texts?" He asks, point blank, his eyes cutting like daggers into her jugular, bleeding shame from her veins. She doesn't answer, she can't. "You know what. Never mind. I don't want to give you an opportunity to lie to me. Why do women always have to lie?"

Elliot starts up the path towards the Jeep with Moira close behind, having to jog to keep up. Once in the Jeep, she waits for him to slide behind the wheel with her shoulders slumped with the weight of her guilt. When she thinks back to her actions last night, she can't even recall her reasoning.

When Elliot returns behind the wheel, he doesn't speak or look at her. He grips the wheel and pulls away from the waypoint, directing them to the interstate once again.

"Listen," she squares her shoulders, and raises her chin defiantly, "I was bored, okay? I thought you'd have cool pictures. I should have thought about it, though. Why would you use your phone for pictures when you have a real camera?" She flips her hair to the side with a casual flick of her wrist, acting as though this half-truth is the only truth. He gives her a sidelong glance, skeptical and annoyed.

"It's fine." He sighs. "It's fine." Any irritation he was feeling has dissipated into the thick air that settles between them having been replaced by exhaustion and, to Moira's devastation, disappointment. She looks at his sharp profile and taut mouth; she knows she should apologize. Just apologize.

Tell him.

Tell him she wanted to know if he told his mom or sister—or anyone! —about her.

"I think I've told you everything I possibly could about myself. What else could you possibly want to know?" He asks before she can speak.

"Nothing."

"You want to know what's in my bank. I'll log in for you. You want to see what I pay for car insurance or my credit score. I can log you into anything you want to see. He grabs his phone from the center compartment and unlocks it with his finger then tosses it into her lap. "

"No. It's…I was just bored." She sighs, setting his phone back where he usually keeps it.

Scowling, he shakes his head, clicking his tongue. "You want to see what my porn habits are? Is that it?" He looks at her, no embarrassment on his face, just irritation. "Well, that's why the universe invented Incognito Mode, Sweetheart." Her face lights up and she quickly snaps her head around to look out the window.

"Why would you do that? Assuming you aren't really interested in my bank and car insurance and porn? It's disrespectful. Especially, *especially* since I have been so open already about everything."

With her gaze still set outside, she takes a deep, shaking breath, "I wanted to see if you told anyone about me. I wanted to see if you thought I was annoying." Her words go the window, her eyes close to hold back her shamed tears.

"Annoying? I'm annoyed *now*. I was annoyed yesterday morning. Why do you care though, if I told anyone about you, and why would I? You've rejected me so many times now that I don't think my pride will allow me to tell my mom I've met a girl. That she's pretty and I like her. My mom wants grandkids so I'd hate to get her hopes up like that."

His tone is light but Moira's disgrace only stings more, her cheeks burning with the tears that finally spill over. "I'm sorry." She murmurs, keeping her eyes closed and face turned away.

"It's fine." He replies, seeing her tears and letting his own guilt sink in. "Please don't cry."

"I'm just…"

"It's ok. You were bored. I get it." His words hold no conviction but he attempts to smile at her, attempts to erase her sadness while hiding his own.

"It's more than that, Elliot. I spoke to my parents last night and…I don't know. I wanted a distraction from that conversation. I *needed* a distraction." She wipes her tears and clenches her jaw, sniffling aggressively. "It's no excuse."

"Moira…"

Chapter 32
The Sixth State, The Elite, and The Cute Cashier

When they reach Washington state, Elliot gently wakes Moira with a nudge on her shoulder to tell her she has reached the sixth state. Her excitement is muted as she tries with desperation to rub the tracks of her tears from her face and still gaze outside. The sympathy in Elliot's eyes make her cheeks go rosy and hot with embarrassment.

If she could go back to Ylobbí park, she would greet him differently when she woke.

They reach Spokane in a little over an hour with Elliot's speed and easy traffic flow. Once in the city, however, the traffic thickens and suddenly even the speed limit is hard to reach. As they creep along, they learn the delay is for a three-car accident in the left lane but once they pass this obstacle, traffic begins to flow once more and Elliot can cruise along in the fast lane, 10 or 15 miles faster than he should be.

The scenery here is dusty and unimpressive compared to the rugged green beauty of northern Idaho and the city, like all cities, is oppressive and the grey desert rocks surprise her. She always heard that Washington state was supposed to boast unreal natural beauty. She's been duped!

Glaring, she turns from the passenger window to the windshield which hosts an even duller view of a semi-truck's back end.

"It gets better." Elliot tells her as though reading her disgruntled thoughts. "Other side of the mountains. It gets better, I promise."

And so it does but only after a couple more hours of driving through the arid terrain does it give way to the greenery of the majestic Columbia River. Soon they are climbing Snoqualmie Mountain Pass and the views hold Moira's gaze hostage.

"See, I told you it gets better."

Moira smiles. "You weren't kidding." The view is bliss and it brings tears to her eyes. All she wants to do is hug him, to hug Elliot as tight as she can and never let him go. To thank him, for bringing her here, sharing his world with her, and delaying his visit with his sister.

Her eyes are wide and alert as they descend the mountain pass in thickening traffic. She almost forgot the tension between them, but given Elliot's easy manners now, he seems to have let it rest on the other side of the Cascade Mountains, maybe somewhere near Spokane or perhaps in Idaho.

When the Space Needle comes into view, she grabs his thigh, a motion that sends a jolt of electricity through her arm and into her heart so she quickly retreats but not before a squeal of excitement slips through her lips.

He laughs at her, "Welcome to Seattle in rush hour traffic, my dear. My favorite." She beams at him then looks around at the thick Tuesday evening traffic knowing how much he hates driving in this, how tetchy he can get when going through a city. "I'm meeting my sister and her husband for dinner tonight. You want to come with?" He asks, but his eyes remain on the road. "I'm not asking out of any romantic ideas, either, before you jump to that conclusion. I just thought you'd like to go out for a fancy meal."

Moira takes a deep breath, wounded by his words but knowing she deserves them. She casts a glance to Leo, accepting that she didn't make him proud like she said she was going to. She choked.

"I guess," she starts, keeping her eyes lowered to her twisting palms, "it would depend on how fancy. I didn't bring anything to wear that would qualify as fancy. I only brought one dress and that's...uh..."

"I remember it." His words make her blush. "Knowing Tory, that's Pam's husband, it'll be fancy. Like ten types of forks bullshit. I'd put money on it. We can stop somewhere and get you something to wear. Only if you want to. I said it before, I'll say it again. I'm not trick you onto a date with me."

"I don't think you're capable of deception." She smiles, lifting her gaze to the windshield, to the traffic. "I hate the thought of dragging you dress shopping."

"I have seven younger siblings all of whom have dragged me to the mall since I could drive and they couldn't. I don't mind but it's up to you."

"All right. Let's go shopping then."

Elliot nods and presses the phone icon on the computer screen in the dashboard then hits Pam's name from the recent contact. The phone rings through the Jeeps speakers and when Pam answers, Moira listens as Elliot asks if the reservation can be switched to four people instead of three, as he has a guest with him.

"Oh no! Not Lauren!" Pam sighs.

"You're on speaker, stupid." Elliot tells her, grinning at Moira.

"Oh my god!" They can hear Pam's hand smack over her mouth and they both laugh.

"It's not Lauren. You think I'm that pathetic? You think I'd go crawling back? No, I got a friend with me. Just a friend."

"Oh! Thank God. Okay, I'll call Le Nouvión and change the reservation. You have a suit, right? You won't get in without a suit coat."

"Yea, yea."

"Well, listen Tory has made reservations at a hotel for you. The details have been emailed to you. It's a surprise."

"A surprise? I can get a motel, Pam."

"We insist that if you stay in our city, you stay somewhere nice. It's our present to you."

"It'll be too fancy!"

"Why are you so anti anything fancy?" Pam laughs. "You're going to hate Le Nouvión."

"I already do." Elliot rolls his eyes and smirks at Moira who listens to their banter with a smile of her own.

Shopping at the Pacific Place mall reminds Moira of being with her mom on Saturday afternoons browsing for the latest fashions. It was her mother's rule that Moira never returned to school on the following Monday without a new outfit. She relished the attention her mother showered her in, the laughs they shared and how she loved getting a Cinnabon at the food court. She would go home and model for her dad all her new clothes and he would kiss her head and tell her how pretty she is. While this mall, Pacific Place, is far more extravagant than the Grand Avenue was back in its hay day, it makes her smile at her happy teenaged memories.

With Leo around her neck and Elliot a few steps in her wake, she pushes down those memories, though pleasant, and focuses on finding a dress. They stop outside of a store she has never heard of and decides that it seems to be a good choice to look. She leaves Leo in Elliot's capable hands and proceeds inside alone. She didn't ask him if he wanted to wait outside but from his glazed expression, she figured he was better off. Her dad, she remembers fondly, used to get the same far off look in his eyes, an expression of doom, when he would come to a store like this.

Fifteen minutes later and with the assistance of an immaculately dressed saleswoman, Moira finds a red lace dress that hangs above her knee higher than she is used to but it glitters fiercely in the light. The back is open, clinging perfectly around her shoulder blades coming together at the very bottom of her back with a tiny, hidden zipper.

In the mirror, she spins this way and stares at the shimmering fabric then spins that way and examines the shimmering fabric, her smile growing with each turn.

"Is it too fancy to wear to Le Nouvión?" she asks of the saleswoman who enthusiastically admires Moira's figure and hair.

"Le Nouvión?" she cries, hands on her heart. "You must be dining with *somebody*!"

Moira looks at the woman in the mirror and tilts her head, "Yea, I'm going with someone. I'm not going by myself."

The woman tosses her head back with laughter and wraps her manicured hands around Moira's shoulders. "You're not from around here, are you?"

"Wisconsin."

"Well, Le Nouvión is for Seattle's elite. I think this dress will be perfect."

"The elite, huh?" she looks herself up and down in the mirror, her anxiety creeping to her face, making her frown deeply and allowing her self-consciousness to crash against her like storm driven waves.

The woman, sensing Moira's discomfort, rubs her bare arms with motherly care and a gentle smile. She helps her get undressed and then they go to the shoe departments where Moira picks up a sparkling pair of gold high-heels adorned with a shiny satin bow, and a clutch to match. Moira passes on jewelry claiming with stubborn fierceness that Leah's earrings will suffice. The saleswoman is politely aghast at Moira's insistence but when Moira wears them, she thinks of Leah and she smiles. She is determined to never not wear these earrings even if they don't match her fancy new red dress.

Moira's feet stop moving for a moment, as the saleswoman leads her to the registers, when she sees Elliot in the front chatting up the cashier with his charming, crooked smile. The cashier writes her phone number on a piece of receipt paper and slides it to Elliot who accepts it with playful eyes and a debonair smile that enrages her. She swallows this rage and approaches; when he sees Moira, he stands up straight and tells the cashier that she's not his girlfriend.

"I was sitting outside with Leo but people kept giving me money so I came inside." He explains to Moira when she stops beside him. "Do I look like a bum or something?"

"You look like a man who's been driving for 10 hours but I wouldn't say a bum." She glances at the cashier's blond curly hair, cut in a bouncy A-frame, and sky-blue eyes.

"Well, I got 30 bucks!" he waves a crinkled pile of singles and fives in the air and drops a handful of change on the counter. "This fish draws sympathy."

"No wonder you let me in the car, then." As they speak, the cashier rings up Moira's total, something she didn't want Elliot to see knowing from her past life experience that stores like this, while not Louis Vuitton, carry with them a hefty price tag.

The total rings up to $300 and Elliot gawks, "Dinner with my sister is not worth that!" tapping the card reader, he looks at the screen with a horrified expression over his gentle features. "Here!" he hands the haphazard pile of cash to the cashier, then slides the change in her surprised direction. "Take it. I only got this hobo money because of your fish. You take it. Honestly. This is crazy talk. Did you buy a diamond ring or something? A new car?"

The clerk deducts the cash from the total leaving Mora to swiper her debit card, which Elliot watches with disapproval. She laughs at him and tells him it's fine but he simply shakes his head, his brows knitted together with concern.

She takes her receipt and thanks the cashier, Elliot also smiles, wide, at the cashier who smiles back, blushing. Before leaving the store, Moira turns to Elliot who returns Leo to her; she bows her head to accept the fish as though she were accepting an Olympic medal. Elliot takes her bags and they leave, Elliot still shaking his head.

"It's okay." She reassures him.

"You shouldn't have spent that much on dinner with my stupid sister."

"Honestly, Elliot, it's fine. Did you know Le Nouvión is for Seattle's elite patronage?"

Elliot groans, throwing his head back with exasperation. "Can't we just go somewhere regular?"

Moira offers a compassionate smile, overtly familiar with a zealous family eager to show off their status by being part of anything and everything exclusive. It makes her wonder how Elliot would get along with her parents. Would they still find him to be a gentleman knowing he lives out of his car more often than not?

Thinking of her parents as they head back to the Jeep, she's reminded of her despicable actions yesterday by snooping through his phone, telling him he was a mistake. When they close themselves into the vehicle, she turns to him, swallowing hard.

"Elliot, I just want to say…that I'm sorry. I shouldn't have looked through your phone and being bored isn't a very good excuse. But…I'm sorry. I'm sorry for a lot of things."

With his left hand draped over the wheel, his right on his leg, a pose often taken whilst driving, he looks at her, searching her face, gazing into her eyes, glancing at her lips. He finally takes a deep breath, "We just got to move on, right?"

She knows those are her words, that it's what she wanted, a desire born out of fear, but it isn't what she wants, what she ever wanted, and she can't find the words, her voice, to tell him so. Going back to just a girl and her fish and a boy and his camera—strangers—seems so foreign and obscure, so lonely. Her words, to move on, are such lonely words.

And she is so sick of being lonely.

Moira takes a deep breath and turns to him, prepared to say something or do something—kiss him or tell him she loves him—when she sees him look at the number from the cashier still in his fingers and smile, a wry, urbane smile, tinged with self-consciousness. He sets it in the compartment under the radio, swapping the paper for his sunglasses then, shifting the Jeep into gear, they head to the hotel that Tory reserved for him not offering a peek, a glance, even a blink her way.

Moira decides to stay quiet.

Chapter 33
The Nap, The Zipper, and The Ailing Fish

Through the door to their room at the Four Seasons, Moira's eyes drift straight to the view across the room. Her mind doesn't focus on the single king bed in the center of the room but only on the sweeping panorama of the waters outside.

"You know what water that is?" Elliot asks, dropping his bag on a plush chaise armchair in a motion of pure exhaustion. Moira looks at him for the answer. "Elliott Bay." He smiles now leaning on the back of the chair, propped up with an elbow, "With two T's."

Her smile broadens, her eyes flitter back to the window that she dares to open, only slightly, to filter in the sounds of the bay. The gulls outside welcome her and the cool breeze pushes the sheer white curtain against her legs. Behind her, Elliot collapses on the bed with a moan, rolling to his back and covering his eyes with his elbows. She turns her back on the playful gulls and looks at Elliot breathing deeply as though he were sound asleep.

While Elliot lays there, she takes a moment to release Leo into his bowl and feed him, also adding a few drops of Stress Coat to his water. Leo looks tired, almost as much as his human counterpart. As he swims, he begins to tip but he rights himself to move to the front of the bowl to watch Moira.

"Oh, Leo. You don't look well, my little love."

He doesn't reply, his voice has gone silent.

Elliot peeks at Moira from under his bent arm, "Is there time for a nap?" he mumbles, his eyes disappearing under his arms again.

She inhales deeply and goes to the bed where she lies beside him, curling to face him. "You tell me." She smooths her hand over the white quilt underneath them, a slight tremble in her fingertips, when suddenly he thrusts his wristwatch into her face. "It's almost five." She tells him after maneuvering his hand to a position that she could read the time.

He groans and returns his arms to his eyes, "We can sleep for a half hour. That's it though."

Moira, lying beside him, is convinced she will not be able to fall asleep while lying beside him but she does and almost instantly. However, only a moment later, she is being shaken awake.

"We're going to be late." He claims, rubbing the nap from his eyes with one hand, the other hand, resting on Moira's shoulder.

"Huh?"

"It's a quarter after six and dinner is at seven. We gots to go."

"Nuh-uh!" she protests, certain she only just fell asleep. He shoves her again, harder this time, before stumbling away to the bathroom. With a grunt, she sits up and drops her feet, still wearing her shoes, to the floor.

Outside the sun is slowly easing down beyond the horizon turning the sky coral orange and hazy blue; the bay sparkles and reflects the sky's palette and the gulls have gone to roost for the night making way for the songbirds' evening melodies. Listening to the ebb and flow of the tide and the harmony of the birds, she takes off her espadrilles and digs her toes into the plush carpeting.

"I have to run to the Jeep. I left my suit." Elliot startles her but he doesn't wait for her acknowledgement before slipping out of the room. In his absence, Moira grabs her duffel bag and scurries to the bathroom to ready herself for dinner only popping back out to grab her new dress.

Delicately dusted with makeup, her full lips glossed with pale pink, eyes shimming with gold and brown shadow, she slides into her new dress. It's too short, she woes, looking at where it hangs mid-thigh; she doesn't remember it being so short in the store and it has a zipper back. Why—why! —did she get a dress with a zippered back? She tries and fails multiple times to find the hidden zipper within the lace to close the back. With a huff, she leaves it and focuses on her hair, an unruly mass on the best of days.

It isn't too long before she controls her curls and lets them cascade down her back, tucking them behind one ear, letting them fall in front of the other. Leah's earrings make her smile, how cheerful and mismatched they are.

A final look at her face and she is ready to be zipped, a thought that makes her heart plummet. The zipper in the back dips so low on her body that the lace trim of her panties is visible and the thought of

Elliot's fingers on her skin makes her heart flutter, the thought that he'll have to unzip her later.

She shakes her head; there's no point thinking about that now. She emerges from the bathroom to find Elliot facing away looking down at his phone and is reminded of how he looked when she found him in her apartment. The memory of smashing a bottle on his head, busting his lip and how she foolishly thought he was offering her ibuprofen when really, he needed a drink so *he* could take them.

"Can you help me?" she finally asks, bringing his attention up from his phone to her. "I can't get it zippered."

"You look beautiful." He tells her, staring, but he shakes off his awe and grins self-consciously, "Why do women get dresses they can't put on? I once had to drive all the way to West Allis to Pam's apartment to lace up the back of her dress for a party she was going to. I lived in Waukesha at the time so it was quite the haul. But I learned how to lace a dress."

"Funny the things we do when we love someone." Moira comments, averting her gaze to the floor. To see him in his fitted suit with his red striped tie sends a chill over her body. "You look good, too, by the way."

"Women love a man in a suit." He shoves his phone into the pocket of the suit coat.

"I guess we do."

They meet at the foot of the bed where she turns and pulls her hair over her shoulder. His fingers find the hidden zipper, lingering on her skin and making her shiver despite their warmth. His right hand pulls up the zipper as his left-hand trails up her spine leaving a tingling path of fire on her back. Even when the zipper is closed, they stand, unmoving, each breathing deeply. She feels him lean down, his breath on her bare neck, his fingers still on her skin until he jerks away leaving her burning skin cold.

"There you go." He steps over to the bedside table and, grabbing his can of Monster that he brought in from the Jeep, takes a large mouthful. "Come on, buddy." He says to the can, "Kick in."

She goes and gets her new purse organized, smiling at him talking to the can, and to put on her new shoes. The stiletto heels remind her of being in high school, going to parties wearing short skirts and crop tops, they remind her of how Jonathan refused to go anywhere with her if she wore heels but she loves heels, especially sparkly ones that make her feet look small.

Like these.

Elliot waits for her with his keys in hand, patting his pockets to make sure he has his wallet, double checking his breast pocket for his phone and taking another swig from his can. When her purse is readied, she starts to walk towards Elliot going through an internal checklist to make sure she isn't forgetting anything.

"Oh!" she hurries over to Leo to say goodbye. She strokes his pale head softly. "I hope you're okay, my little love."

The fish bumps up against her finger before falling to the rocky bottom.

Chapter 34
The Food, The Fine, and The Fancy Family

They are shown to the table by the maître d' and met with open arms by Pam and her husband Tory. Pam and Elliot throw their arms around one another in a swaying, laughing, delightful embrace. Pam exclaims, horrified by the wounds on her brother's face, touching his bruised eye and scarred brow with a thousand questions flying from her lips. Her husband, Tory, also expresses his concern but Elliot brushes it off as nothing then introduces Moira.

"Oh! Look how beautiful you are!" Pam exclaims, taking a step back, smacking Elliot's arm. The affection pours from her lips, oozes out of her every pore. Her face is soft and gentile, shining kindness; her hair is fairer than her brother's but Elliot's seems to be highlighted by a stylist where Pam's seems to be her natural color. They have the same sharp nose and wide smile, easily shown off. Pam, however, did not inherit the gene of height, as a petite woman standing more than a foot shorter than Elliot. "You're lovely. Leo, she's just lovely. I love her."

Moira tries to thank her for the compliment but her nervousness makes her stutter and Elliot puts paid to any words that may have escaped her nerves.

"I just want to clarify this immediately, here and now, before there are any misunderstandings." His voice is firm and, as he speaks, the waiter seats the ladies, Pam across from himself and Moira beside him, "Moira is not my girlfriend in any way, shape, or form. She's my downstairs neighbor who needed somewhere to go." There is no playfulness in his tone and Moira feels ashamed for his ferocity and the conviction in which he speaks.

The two across the table are surprised by the announcement but they don't argue, though they exchange skeptical glances as the tuxedoed waiter hands each of them a leather-bound menu and informs them of tonight's specials, followed by immaculate pronunciations of Le Nouvión's finest wines, which Tory expertly orders only to be teased by Elliot for his pretentious tone.

"Living in Seattle is turning you into a pretentious snob, Tor. I remember when Ramen and Jack Daniels for dinner it was." The men laugh and reminisce about their days as roommates at UW-Madison. The conversation moves with the power and energy of a freight train moving from college days to high school days, last Christmas to Christmas '98. Moira is left to quietly observe, enjoying every comment, which is exactly what she wants.

"It's always like this when we get together." Pam says to Moira when there's a break in the conversation, reaching over and patting Moira's folded hands. "So, tell me, how did you two meet?"

"Before we start all that," Elliot scolds, "why don't we open our menus *then* we can harass her."

The table falls quiet except for Tory's recommendations, as he and Pam are regulars at Le Nouvión. By Elliot's shifting in his chair, Moira can sense his discomfort and she thinks that, perhaps, she has found an environment that puts him out of his depth, that chafes against his normally relaxed demeanor. His unease is noticed by Tory who lectures Elliot for not expanding his world to include the higher class, art and fine wine, rich foods, and the symphony.

"You can't beat eating a peanut butter and jelly sandwich from mountain peak or cooking pancakes over a fire on a sand dune in the middle of the Wisconsin River." He protests and Moira silently agrees, although it is nice to get all glitzed up and fancy with civilization, too.

The waiter returns, interrupting any further discussion on the topic, and takes their orders and their menus. The wine is poured and the conversation between brother and sister commences, thrilling Moira with their antics, their uncontrollable laughter.

The uppity patrons around them turn to look, clicking their tongues and shaking their heads making Moira think of her parents, as they would be amongst the judgmental crowd. Perhaps, if she had spent her adulthood with them, she too would be one with the snobbish. She'd have her family but would she have the same joy that emanates from Elliot and his?

She listens as Pam explains how Elliot introduced her to Tory with the sole purpose of them getting married just so he wouldn't have to choose between his two best friends. Pam insists this is the sweetest thing while Elliot uses it as an example of his own selfishness.

"It's not selfish!" Pam laments, smacking her hands on the table. "It shows how much you care. Look how happy we still are!" She smiles at Moira, raising one eyebrow, "So far, anyway."

"Look what good it did me, though!" Elliot laughs, "You guys moved across the country and left me! My plan backfired." The table laughs and still the chatter flows, meandering wildly with a jovial chaos.

"Oh, you poor thing." Tory says, turning his icy blue eyes to Moira's face. "You must think we're crazy and after being stuck in the car with him for three days. You have my deepest sympathies."

Her eyes snap up to Tory's then move swiftly to Pam, "No. It's okay." She finally looks at Elliot who gazes at her with unmistaken affection but he shakes himself, frowning.

"We're an obnoxious family." He takes a sip of his wine then replaces it in his hand with his glass of water.

"See, Leo and I are kind of the black sheep because we each have different moms than the other six." Pam begins, smiling at Moira. She continues on a tangent filled explanation of their family tree; she explains how she doesn't know her biological mom so when she says mom, she means Elliot's mom, she names the other six and their ages. The details had already been mentioned to her by Elliot during one of his monologues of desperation in the car but Moira nods along as though it is all new to her. Elliot tells Pam several times that Moira already heard about their dysfunctional family but Pam waves him off, declaring he probably left out too many details.

Moira doesn't mind, though, hearing about Elliot's siblings and how they are too much like his stepmom even if she has heard it already. It makes her feel, and the thought makes her shift in her seat and turn to her wine, that she is part of a family, his family. She's thankful when the food arrives, plated so fancy that it may have been designed by an artist, as it gives her somewhere to look, something to distract her from her desire to touch Elliot's leg or grasp his hand. To hide the desperate need to go back to Montana, back to that night and that morning, and choose new and honest words guided by her heart instead of fear.

Over dinner they talk about their plans for tomorrow with Pam begging Elliot, and Moira, to have lunch with her while Tory is at work. Moira is delighted to hear that they won't be heading home tomorrow; she isn't ready to go back. Not yet.

Elliot agrees to lunch and Pam squeals with joy, clapping her hands. "Oh Moira, I have a place in mind that you will just love! You guys can just walk down from your hotel."

"I just assumed you two would have lunch alone so you could catch up." Moira replies, her eyes flickering between Pam's taken aback expression and Elliot's unreadable one. "I shouldn't keep intruding."

Pam shakes her head, "You're not intruding!" She then smacks Elliot's arm, making him drop his fork. "Tell her."

"You're not." Elliot says, "Honestly."

Hesitant to agree, Moira nods, watching Elliot, searching his face for deception or disappointment. She sees nothing more than a man deprived of sleep.

When they've exhausted all their topics, for a time, the questions take aim at Moira. Elliot warns the table that she is not a storyteller, she is a one-word kind of conversationalist but Pam waves her hand, dismissing Elliot's cautions, turning a motherly smile to Moira. Her eyes, the same as Elliot's, crinkle at the corners and shimmer much like the Bay outside the hotel window. Pam asks, to Moira's dismay, what she does for a living. The answer is nothing. Moira does nothing.

She would love to say that, to say the one word: nothing. For that to end the conversation but society dictates, so she thinks it does, that she must say more. To be polite and honest and impress Elliot with her ability to communicate. She can converse. "Uhm, currently…I am unemployed. But before that, I was employed." She can converse!

In her own way.

"Ok…" Pam raises encouraging eyes but is met with shyness, silence.

"She got fired on her 30th birthday!" Elliot explains, "And she won't tell me why."

Moira sighs and dabs her mouth with her napkin. "I got fired," she turns her eyes to Elliot, "because I got more presents on my birthday than my boss did on his." Her tone is petulant but comedic, a smirk on her face that she learned from observing Elliot's stories.

The table guffaws to the chagrin of the other patrons; they quickly lower their voices but not one can stop laughing and it pleases Moira to have entertained, to have said something to make Elliot laugh for a change.

To converse.

Chapter 35
The Plans, The Bathroom, and The Knowing Sister

When dinner is cleared away and Tory commandeers the check, demanding not to be challenged by this action, the conversation moves into making plans for tomorrow. Plans for lunch and the baseball game. She had almost forgotten about the game...how many days ago was it that he asked her to come with him. Two days ago, three? She told him it wasn't a date, so violently she rejected his offer, and how hurt he looked and how she wishes now, again, to go back in time. To Montana, to that point in North Dakota when he stood at her door and told her about the game, to her apartment when he asked her to dinner. To go back and change her words.

Elliot, leaning back in his chair with his hands hanging in his lap, looks up from his transfixed vision on the candle. "I'll buy the tickets because *this* is on me."

Pam stands and smooths out her royal satin dress, "Don't spend too much." She comments with a smile; Elliot waves his hand dismissively, "No amount is too much when it comes to the Brewers, I guess. Now then, we girls will go freshen up and then we can go because you look like you might fall asleep right here, Leo." Picking up her bag, she smiles at Moira indicating with this one look that Moira should do the same.

"I don't understand why you have to freshen up." Tory rolls his eyes, "We're going home."

Pam grins, "Don't you want me to be fresh when we get home?"

"Shut up." Elliot moans, "I don't want to hear my little sister's sex talk." His hands are laced behind his head, he leans back in his chair with his legs stretched out, crossed at the ankles.

Pam laughs, "Ya-ya. It's also how we ladies can get to know each other a little better."

Moira can feel the heat creeping into her cheeks when she looks at Elliot who slumps forward, resting his chin in his palm, his fingers covering his mouth. She can't read his expression and she can't look at him long enough to decipher his eyes. She is led to the washrooms by Pam.

In the bathroom, there are two stalls at the far end of the open space, the corners of the room each dressed in vases of exotic flowers on glass tables. The diamond inlaid vanity stretches across a mirrored wall and lit by crystalline chandeliers hanging above each of the porcelain sinks. Near the door, a matron quietly stands, waiting to be needed.

"Did you have a nice night?" Pam asks through the stall where she comfortably relieves herself. Moira's shy bladder would never allow herself to go right now so she is forced to remain at the vanity, avoiding her own eye contact.

"Uh, yes." Moira answers, reminded of why she hates public restrooms. The toilet flushes and Pam returns to the sink to wash her hands. Moira runs her hand gently over the sparkling granite countertop, unsure where to look or what to say.

"I'm so glad Leo found you." Pam says, accepting a towel from the matron. "Lauren never made him happy. She always treated him like dirt, absolute dirt. I hated her and I would tell Leo so but he would just ignore me."

"That's sad." Moira mumbles, wishing she could change the subject.

"It's funny because I was kind of happy that it happened. Not, like, happy-happy, but I was happy she was gone. I was worried that he would just settle for her. They would get married and I'd have to pretend to be happy for him. They'd have a baby and I'd have to pretend to be happy for him again. Let me tell you, Lauren is the last human being on this earth that should reproduce!"

"If he knew you hated her, wouldn't he know you were pretending to be happy for him?"

Pam laughs and turns a broad smile to Moira who flushes and looks down at her purse. "I don't have to worry about that now that he has you."

"Honestly, it's not—"

"Pish." Pam waves her hand. "I don't care what either of you say. I can see the way he looks at you. I know when my brother's in love. I don't think he ever looked at Lauren the way he looked at you all night."

"I'm just the neighbor." She mutters, keeping her red face down at the clasp on her clutch. "Besides, we've only known each other six days."

Pam gives Moira a knowing smile, "Let me tell you, when Leo introduced me to Tory, it took me six seconds to fall in love with that man. You can fall in love in six days." Taking Moira's hand, Pam gives it a squeeze, beaming. "Aren't you going to use the bathroom?"

"Uh, I have a shy bladder…"

"Oh my god, you're just the cutest thing."

The two gentlemen are leaning in towards each other in serious conversation when, as they approach, Tory shakes his head with a furrowed brow and slump backwards in his seat.

"I'm sorry, brother." He says and it makes Moira's heart sink. The two men turn their attention to the women as they seat themselves. "You ladies have fun?" Tory asks, turning contemplative, excruciatingly knowing eyes, to Moira.

Elliot turns his tired eyes over to Moira, who nods, then he shifts his attention to his sister.

"I like her, Elliot. She's *much* better than Lauren." Pam shrugs her slender shoulders, a haughty smirk on her face.

Elliot slumps back in his chair and lets out a long, aggravated groan; he rocks back on his chair, balancing it on two legs, and casts his defeated eyes to the painted ceiling. "I told you, Pam."

"Oh blah, blah! You two aren't fooling—" Pam begins but Tory places a hand on her leg interrupting her, shaking his head.

"Leave it." He whispers.

She knits her brow at her husband, puckering her lips in confusion, but she silences herself on the subject, only flickering her confused gaze on Moira then back, alarmed, to her brother. Moira's shame burns on her cheeks, unrelenting embarrassment.

Dropping his chair back on all fours with a thud, he sighs, "We got to go."

Pam reaches over and grabs Elliot's hands, her eyes moving over to Tory and Moira, "You guys can go. I need to talk to Leo for a minute."

Tory and Moira wait in silence, Tory under an umbrella and Moira under the awning, each watching the rain as it drizzles across the city. After several minutes, the other two join them in the cold. Pam moves over to her husband, taking shelter under his umbrella, Elliot stands with his hands in his pockets beside Moira.

The family exchanges their final goodbyes and parting stories before Tory and Pam's cab arrives. Pam is determined to spend as much time with Elliot, and Moira, as possible before he leaves again, whenever that may be but no doubt it will be too soon. It's always too soon in Pam's eyes but Elliot only smiles and says that he didn't tell them to move across the country.

When the cab does pull up to the curb, the final hugs are offered, Pam embracing her brother while Tory turns to Moira and takes her hands with his one free hand, the other still holding the umbrella.

"It was nice meeting you. I hope that you and Leo can work it out." Tory's smile, brotherly and warm, silences her, making her cheeks flare and her mind race with what Elliot may have told him, what he will then tell his wife. How will they look at her tomorrow? Whatever negative thoughts they may conjure, she knows she deserves them but she quickly hides the gloom creeping onto her face when Pam steps over and offers her a hug, loving and constricting.

"Oh, Leo!" Pam releases Moira and whales around to Elliot who leans against the awning pole, stifling a yawn, Tory stands at the cab with the door open waiting for his wife. "Give this girl your coat; she's freezing!"

"She's fine." He mutters, yawning again and turning his attention to the street at nothing in particular. Pam grunts her disapproval, smacking his arm as she walks over to the cab.

With the final goodbyes said, Tory and Pam disappear into the back of the cab, which then pulls away. Once they are out of sight, Elliot leads Moira down the two blocks to where they parked. He wipes the rain from his eyes then slips off his suit coat, toggling the umbrella from one hand to the other to get out of the sleeves.

"Pretty cliché, huh?" He rolls his eyes as he throws it over her shoulders without ceremony or care but she doesn't argue, relishing the residual warmth of his body.

"Do you always do what your little sister says?"

He smiles, saying nothing, an oddity for him, so they walk on in silence, Moira wrapping the coat tight around her as she hugs herself. She's thankful, and she's sure Elliot is, too, when they get to the Jeep and can be out of the misting rain.

When he opens the door for her, she blushes and looks up at him. His sagging face hangs with fatigue, his eyes are glazed over and unfocused, staring beyond her. Moira thinks of Tory's words and wonders what exactly Elliot told him, how was she painted—was it with bitter strokes or wistful ones? —and can she make it right?

Before getting in, she places her hand covered in the sleeve of his jacket on his shoulder drawing his attention. She pulls him towards her and kisses his cheek. "Thank you." She says, lowering her eyes to avoid his startled gaze. Quickly, she gets into the car so he can close the door and get himself out of the rain.

As they drive, Moira is dazzled by all the passing lights of the skyrise buildings and streetlights blinking reds and yellows and greens. All the headlights and taillights, and peoples' blinkers. All different lives moving to and from their destinations, just like they are. Two people deep in a large city, each in their own thoughts.

It's only when they get nearer to the hotel that Elliot turns to her to speak, hesitantly, his voice is hushed and dark like the night around them. He apologizes if she was uncomfortable or if he was obnoxious but she only laughs at him, casting a pensive gaze upon his features.

"It was nice. I felt like I was part of a family so thank you. For taking me with."

"You're welcome."

"You've been nothing but nice to me since I met you." She murmurs, then scoffs, turning her eyes to the passing lights outside.

"Nice is the right thing to be."

She looks at him, "Not after all the stupid things I've done to you. I don't deserve your kindness." Her voice is barely a whisper, her eyes lowered, unable to focus on his profile.

"I like you, Moira." He says without looking at her. "I've not stopped liking you since the moment I saw you carrying that...I think it was a record player, which is weird and cool at the same time. You were trying so hard to be polite to John but he just wouldn't shut up. You were so fucking cute and covered in..." She'll never know the butterflies that this memory gives him.

"Paint, flour, and water. I was such a mess! And you were…you were talking about laundry." She smiles towards the window.

"That's right. Larceny. I'll tell you how pathetic I am. I didn't take my laundry to my mom's house like I planned because I was hoping…" he shakes his head and she looks at him, at his bright cheeks. "I was hoping I'd run into you down in the laundry room. Never did run into you. You're like a phantom."

"Oh…I always time my laundry when no one is down there. If I saw the lights were on, I'd wait."

He scoffs, "Of course you did." He runs his left hand through his hair, keeping his right on the wheel. "It's alright though. I'll get over you." Grabbing the receipt paper from where he tossed it earlier, he holds it up and smiles, "I can't remember her name, Catherine or Christine or something, but I got that cashier's number. Maybe I'll take her to the game tomorrow." He cannot react before Moira snatches the paper and throws it from the window after crinkling it in her palm.

She gives him a sidelong look through lowered lashes, her cheeks rosy; he smiles letting the sound of his indicator signifying his impending left turn into the hotel parking lot be the only reply between them.

No words are needed.

The only light they turn on in their room is the one over the kitchenette allowing the pale glow to envelope the quiet they have settled upon. Elliot crumples onto the armchair, stretching his legs out with a groan, his arms are left to dangle down the side, flat like a rag doll.

Moira sits on the edge of the bed determining how to say what she wants to say, to find those magic words that will erase her past behavior and hurt she caused. To tell him how she's falling in love with him. Can she say that?

Love?

She stares at her gold shoes and thinks of Jonathan and Charles Kent; she thinks of her own loneliness and Elliot's. Could it be forever or only until Wisconsin and does it matter? She's been independent, she's been successful, and she's been alone for 12 years (can Jonathan be counted since her sincere happiness was in question?).

To just enjoy life for the thrills and the sorrows, for the brightness and the darkness and to allow herself to heal; to believe that she doesn't need but she wants this man before her to be in her life, to find happiness with her and guide her to trust.

Elliot's breathing is deep where he lay on the chaise but when her lips touch his, his eyes flutter open, hand instinctively reaching for her cheek as she pulls away.

"I must be dreaming." He murmurs, his eyes drifting closed again.

She brushes his face, each wound she inflicted, with featherlight fingertips, following each one with a gentle kiss before backing away from his peaceful face. "You're not." Her voice is a low whisper, nearly inaudible. He looks up at her, unable to hide his fatigue, but he smiles, he blushes; she'll never know the tremble in his chest, the nerves slipping into his fingers.

All they do is smile at each other, both too scared to make another move towards each other.

Moira finally turns her burning cheeks, her awe-struck gaze, from Elliot's own; wringing her hands in front of her she moves around the bed to Leo's bowl. He lay on his hammock with only his mouth moving, slow and rhythmic. When he sees her, he slides off his hammock, falling as he swims, tipping again from a failing swim bladder. Kneeling, she pets him where he struggles to hover before her in the bowl.

"My little love…" Behind her, she can hear Elliot move from the chaise so she turns her teary eyes to him, all at once thankful for his presence and guilty for his exhaustion. His tie hangs loose down the front of his chest, his eyes dark and his posture sagging, but still, he looks at her with sympathy. "I don't think he's going to make it much longer." She says to Elliot, looking back to Leo, who sinks to the bottom of the bowl, his aging fins unable to keep him upright any longer.

Moira pulls the bowl down to the floor and wraps her arms around it, around Leo, her tears breaking through the floodgates. Elliot lays beside her, enveloping her in his warm embrace, murmuring how sorry he is.

"He's all I have."

"You still have me." His voice is laced with sleep as he forces himself awake, to be there for her; he nuzzles his face into her hair, pressing closer to her body to hold her tighter, to include Leo in his arms.

All alone with their thoughts, deep breathing the only sound in the room, the only light the warm, orange glow of the kitchenette. Moira wants to speak; she wants to speak to Leo, wants to speak to Elliot; she wants to be held like this forever and doesn't want her voice to make him pull away.

She doesn't want Leo to go.

Tightening her grip around the bowl, she finally speaks, in a shaking voice. "Leo told me…and you'll think it's crazy…but he told me you were the best thing that ever happened to me."

He shifts against her, raising his head to look down upon her tear steaked face, "He's a smart fish."

For a time, there is silence except for Moira's quiet sobs, her shoulders shaking with every gasp. Each time, Elliot nuzzles into her and squeezes just a little tighter, trying to offer her comfort, to let her know that he's there.

"Moira…" he whispers, rubbing her arms still draped in his suit coat, "Oh, Moira, please, it's going to be ok."

"I love you." She whispers in a hasty, breathless voice with her face pressed against the glass of Leo's bowl.

"Are you talking to me or Leo the Fish?"

She pauses, a small, incredulous laugh escaping her parted, panting lips. "Both."

Chapter 36
The Goodbye, The Many Truths, and The Seeing Eye Fish

The sun hasn't risen yet, though it would be hidden from the thick cast of grey clouds if it had begun its ascension, when Moira wakes Elliot when she sits up from the floor. Her voice can barely be heard.

He's gone.

Leo's gone.

Elliot apologizes and holds her from behind as she silently sobs over Leo's bowl, her tears cascading down her cheeks in blackened streaks of mascara and eyeliner leaving trails through her rouge.

Outside, it's cold and the sky is dropping a steady stream of fat droplets onto the city, onto the bay, and onto Moira and Elliot as they walk side-by-side with the shell of what was once a lively Leo to the waterfront not a five-minute walk from their hotel.

Neither know how long they were asleep or when Leo passed but now, they go to release him somewhere wild, somewhere he would have loved. Even if Elliot doesn't understand this sentiment, he smiles with kindness and sympathy, obliging Moira's every wish.

At the water's edge, she whispers to Leo how she loves him, how she will be strong. She can and will make him proud of her yet; she whispers how she hopes he doesn't get eaten by a big, ugly fish but that he makes it out to the Pacific Ocean.

"I'm still going to make you proud, Leo. You taught me to see…and now…" she lets out a sob, takes a shaky breath that shudders her entire body, "…go feed the Earth, my little love." In a brisk motion, she throws the water into the air, Leo's little body flickering for a moment in the dim park lights behind her then disappearing into the darkness only to be heard by the tiny splash that may or may not have been a raindrop.

After a moment of staring out into the black water, Moira steadies herself and turns to gaze into Elliot's drooping eyes, to set her eyes upon his loose tie and untucked shirt, his matted hair.

"I'm sorry I didn't hold the door for you, Elliot. And I'm sorry I ate all the brownies that I baked for you."

He cocks a brow, "Brownies?"

She explains, nearly gasping at her words, how she thought he was cute and that he might be different from all the men of her past; she wanted to thank him for being nice to her, for not yelling at her when she was so impolite. To say sorry. She wanted to talk to him so she baked him brownies then she ate them all while she sobbed on her sofa.

And she never thanked him for saving Leo and she was so mean when he asked her out and she looked through his phone! She beat him up—scarred him, his beautiful face! —and never thanked him for helping her clean up the water.

Her apologies come out in quiet sobs, uncontrollable and desperate to escape. For so long she kept her feelings locked away but now they have been freed and they will not be stopped until they are fully expressed. She confesses how she snuck to his apartment that night, she knocked on his door.

She told herself she didn't know why she did that, what she wanted but she did. "I just wanted you. I wanted to feel safe and warm and you made me feel safe. But..." she groans, her fists clenching tightly, her jaw, too.

"I knew I heard something." He chuckles. "I went to the door and no one was there but I thought I smelled your perfume. I thought I was being obsessive."

"I wanted to hate you so bad. But I don't, Elliot. I don't hate you. I love you!" She gasps at her own words, her hand coming to her lips, she drops her eyes down to her feet.

He puts an arm around her, bringing his head to rest on hers while still holding the umbrella. "While you were busy trying to hate me, I was busy falling in love with you." Time freezes for a moment, a tender few seconds as man and woman settle their own nerves, to find their voices once again.

It's Elliot who speaks first, "When we get back to Wisconsin, would you like to go to dinner with me?"

She laughs and nods, "Yes, I'd like that."

Dropping the umbrella, he kisses her and this time, when their lips meet, there is no apprehension, no fear. It's soft and sweet, his hands cupping her cheeks, hers slipping upwards tenderly to rest on his chest. They'll go back to their room, hand-in-hand, heart-to-heart with the rain cooling their hot cheeks.

Once in the safety of their room, shy eyes find each other with unmasked desire and slow movements, timid lips, shaking hands. When he holds her, pulling her close to his body, removing his suit coat from her soft, unsteady shoulders, she can feel him trembling; when he kisses her, it's at first with hesitancy that quickly ignites into passion.

What was raw in Montana is slow and sweet in Seattle and there is no regret in the glow of dawn to find herself entangled in his embrace and soft, white linens, his body, his glistening skin, pressed against her own. There's no pause, no fear, to rouse him with a kiss and to claim him as her own until the sun hangs well above the horizon.

In the darkness of their room, Elliot whispers in her ear how he can and will make her happy; that he'll spend the rest of their lives making sure of it. He'll show her everything she's ever wanted to see, take her anywhere she wants to go; he'll hold her hand and make her laugh, cook her dinner and send her flowers if he is away on a shoot.

He'll spend the rest of his life teaching her how to properly swear at an umpire for calling a strike out of the zone and she can teach him the art of silently solving a crossword puzzle.

Every sweet nothing he whispers is something.

Most importantly, it's happiness and when Leo said happiness wasn't overrated, he was right.

She sees that now.

FIN

That's fin…like a fish.
See what I did there?

A Bit about Beans

R.B. Beans, a simple office worker by day, wannabe superstar novelist by night, lives in Wisconsin with her husband and their two guinea pigs. An avid Milwaukee Brewers fan, she writes in between innings, when they're losing too badly, and during the off-season. A terrible cook, crooked quilter, and all-around klutz, R.B. Beans takes inspiration from her life, be it her unsuspecting family and friends, or the quirks of life's little moments, in the hopes of bringing a smile to the world.